NEVER FORGET, NEVER FORGIVE

Denise Smith

Copyright © Denise Smith 2021

ISBN: 978-1-8381173-6-8 (paperback)
978-1-8381173-7-5 (e-book)

Cover Design by Meg Saunders, using an original photograph by D N Smith

Patience and planning. That's what's important. Mother taught me that. If you have patience, she said, and wait until the timing is perfect, and if you plan carefully, you can get away with anything. Even murder.

Chapter 1

The dark, pig-like eyes stared unblinking out of his fleshy face. Her hand shaking, Beatrice reached over and tentatively checked his thick neck for a pulse. Nothing. Reluctantly she pressed harder. She could only feel her own blood pumping hard and fast through her body. The man's skin was pale, mouth open slightly, with his tongue lolling to one side. She bent over more closely and placed her ear next to his mouth, pulling her long hair out of the way. There was no sound, and no gust of air being expelled. He was dead.

As her eyes settled on a pill bottle by the side of the body, Beatrice became aware of a buzzing in her ears, rising in pitch to a high whine. A trickle of sweat rolled down her back. The room became a haze and she felt she was going to topple over. She sat down heavily on the cabin's wooden floor, back against the wall, bending her head between her legs. She closed her eyes and took slow, measured breaths, in through her nose and out through her mouth, repeating until the dizziness receded.

'Come on, Beatrice,' she muttered. 'You need to call for help.'

With care, in case she became light-headed again, she stood up and backed away from the body, avoiding looking at its face. At the cabin entrance she ducked under the lintel and closed the door behind her. She stood for a moment in the clearing, surrounded by the deep green of trees and took in the cool air and scent of pine. The ringing in her ears was subsiding and her heartbeat returning to its normal rhythm.

Beatrice pulled her phone from her bag and checked the screen: no reception. Not even emergency access to another network. She paused, then slipped back inside the cabin. Glancing around the wooden hut she saw it was set up as an office: desk, chair, computer, telephone. She considered using the landline but decided to leave the scene undisturbed. The man's body took up a significant portion of the floor. He was large: tall and obese. She used her phone to take pictures of the room and the corpse before she hurried out again. Beatrice's long legs made quick work of the stone path back to her car in the blazing sunlight. Her call to emergency services was made with trembling hands.

The ambulance arrived, lights flashing but no siren. The medics were soon followed by two young constables in a police car. Both vehicles parked outside the imposing house. Beatrice directed them around the back to the trees, where the cabin was hidden from view, then waited by her car, what she'd seen preying on her mind.

The sun was beating down and Beatrice could feel sweat pooling at her armpits. Rummaging in her bag for a scrunchie, she tied her dark brown hair up in a messy bun, then eased her tall frame into the car and switched on the engine for the relief of the air conditioning. Moments later the paramedics left empty-handed. Beatrice watched them pass and drive away, wondering why they weren't taking the body. Had the police told them to leave it? Were there questions over the nature of his death? The shock of finding him was fading and Beatrice tried to fight the prickle of excitement she could feel at the idea of being involved in an investigation, even if it was only as a witness. She shook her head. A man is dead, she told herself.

Her thoughts were interrupted by a second police car parking in the space vacated by the ambulance. A sergeant in uniform climbed slowly out of the passenger side: the dead man would wait. At least twenty years older than her, in his mid fifties, he walked with the ease of someone who had seen it all before. She switched off the engine and got out to meet him and his driver.

'Good afternoon, Miss. Are you the lady who made the emergency call?'

'Yes, that's right, Beatrice Styles.'

'I'm Sergeant Jones, this is Constable Taylor. I need to ask you a few questions, if you don't mind.'

'Of course. Then can I go?'

'I'm afraid I need you to come back with me to the body first. Perhaps you could show me the way?'

Beatrice glanced quickly in the direction of the cabin. 'Is it really necessary?'

'I'm afraid so. I wouldn't ask otherwise. You're looking a bit pale, if you don't mind me saying so.'

'I'm ok, it's just...' her voice tailed off.

'We'll be there with you. Nothing to worry about. Best to get it over with.'

'I know. I'm being an idiot. You're right, the less time there is for me to think about it the better.'

'That's the ticket. Lead on.'

Beatrice made herself look at the body. The Sergeant nodded at one of the constables, who scrambled to get a notebook from his pocket.

'Do you know who the man is?' asked Sergeant Jones.

'No. It may be Simon Bayfield. I don't know. He lives here, but I've never met him.'

'Why were you here, Miss Styles?'

'I had an appointment with Mr Bayfield. We were to meet at his house,' she pointed back towards the main building, 'at twelve o'clock.'

'Why were you seeing him, if you didn't know him?'

'He telephoned and asked me to come here. He was thinking about employing me.'

'And he wanted to interview you here, at his home?' The Sergeant frowned. 'Isn't that rather unusual? What sort of work is it that you do, Miss Styles?'

Beatrice couldn't bring herself to lie, but didn't want to reveal the complete truth. 'I used to be a tax Inspector at HMRC, but I'm doing private work now.'

'Really?'

She noticed he looked up at her for several seconds. Could he sense something in her tone or was she reading too much into it?

'And he called you, you say?'

'Yes,' said Beatrice.

'Did he say why he wanted to hire you? Trouble with his tax was it?' The Sergeant glanced down at the pill bottle, still on the floor where Beatrice had seen it earlier.

'I don't know. He didn't want to talk on the phone. He said he'd explain in person.'

'You've never been here before?'

'No.'

'And he wanted to meet at the house?'

'Yes.' Beatrice crossed her arms.

'How did you happen to find him tucked away here then? Did you know this office was in the woods?'

'No, I didn't. When there was no one answering at the house I checked the stables and the cottages, but I couldn't find anyone. I phoned and left a message on Mr Bayfield's mobile saying I was here, that I'd stay for another ten minutes. I had nothing better to do so I had a look around. I just followed the path through the trees to this clearing. That's when I found him.'

'I see,' said Sergeant Jones. 'Right, can you explain to me please exactly what you did from when you arrived outside the office?'

'I looked in and saw he was on the floor. I opened the door…'

'It was closed then?'

'Yes, but not locked,' said Beatrice. 'I went in and knelt down, on his right side,' she pointed. 'I checked for a pulse. I had no signal on my mobile so I walked back to the house and dialled 999.' Beatrice was ashamed of her impulsive decision to take the photographs and knew she wouldn't be able to explain to the police why it seemed a good idea. It felt like a foolish thing to have done and she hoped it didn't show in her expression.

'Can you look around please and tell me if there is anything different to how he is now from when you found him.'

She allowed her eyes to move across the room systematically, taking in the changes. 'He's on his back,' she said. 'He was sort of lying on his right side but more with the front of his body near the floor and his face was looking towards the door. His tie is pulled loose now. Do you think it is Mr Bayfield?'

'We won't know until we have someone to identify the body. Best not to jump to conclusions. Right, thank you, Miss. That will be all for now. You're looking a bit unwell still. I'm going to have Constable Taylor take you home now.' He spoke firmly and the PC jumped to attention.

'It's fine. I'm ok to drive,' said Beatrice. She was certain she'd feel better once she was away from the body.

'Well, best not take any chances though, eh?' The Sergeant turned away before she could protest. 'Taylor?'

'Yes, Sir?'

'Please drive Miss Styles home in her own car and make sure she's alright. Where is home exactly?'

'Fifteen Cecil Street, Lincoln.'

'Good. Off you go then, Taylor,' he said checking the other constable had made a note of the address. 'You'll be relieved later.'

'Yes, Sir.'

There was no point arguing further, so Beatrice trudged along behind. Perhaps it was for the best, she thought. She took a last look back towards the body: was it Simon Bayfield? The man who would have been her client. She considered the empty pill bottle. Had he killed himself? Had he planned for her to find his body? If it was her client then her first and only job had just vanished.

Chapter 2

Beatrice barely noticed the journey home, feeling tired and unable to focus. The fields of rape seemed to whip by in a blur of bright yellow until the car reached the edge of the city. She soon found herself outside her own front door. She fumbled in her bag for the key. PC Taylor took it from Beatrice's hand - she was having some trouble getting it to fit the keyhole - he unlocked the door and stood aside to let her in first, guiding her with a light touch on the small of her back. The front door of her terraced house opened straight into the living room; Taylor steered Beatrice to the sofa, down into its soft cushions and said something she didn't quite catch. Then he disappeared. The next thing she knew he was pressing a cup into her hands.

'Here you go,' he said. 'Sweet tea. Mum always said it's good for a shock. Sip it slowly, it's hot.'

Beatrice's mind didn't seem to be working well so, in the absence of anything else to focus on, she sipped at the burning liquid. It felt like such a normal thing to be doing and it began to revive her.

'Not much furniture in here, is there?' Taylor said.

'What? Oh, no. I've just moved here, a few of weeks ago.'

'Nice pictures though. Monet are they?'

Beatrice nodded. 'I'll be ok now,' she said. 'I'm sure you've got better things to do than sit with me.' She wanted to be alone, with time to think about what had happened and what it meant for her fledgling business.

'Sorry, I've got to wait until someone else comes.'

They sat in companionable silence until it was interrupted by intrusive banging at the front door. The sound echoed in the sparsely furnished room. Taylor sprang to his feet and opened the door.

'Right, where is she?' called a loud, booming voice. It came from a heavily built man, in his fifties, with a big round face and a grubby looking moustache. He wore a crumpled shirt with sweat patches at the armpits, and a discontented look on his face. Behind him was a short, slightly plump woman with light brown, curly hair. She smiled at Beatrice.

'This is Beatrice Styles, Sir,' said PC Taylor. 'Who found the body,' he explained.

'I know that, Constable.' The man bellowed. Taylor winced. 'Why do you think I'm here?' The man narrowed his eyes as he studied Beatrice whilst Taylor's face flushed red. 'Why don't you put that fine brain of yours to some use and run along and make me a cup of tea? I expect the girls will want a cup too.'

Everything about the man repelled Beatrice: his expression of superiority, his noise, his dominating attitude. Calling her a girl didn't help create a good impression either. The anger she felt rising at his aggressive invasion cleared any residual feelings of shock. She stood up to her full, impressive height, stepped up close to the outspoken man and looked down at him scowling. Her mouth twitched in satisfaction as he stumbled back and blinked in surprise.

She looked him straight in the eyes. 'I think you'll find,' she said in a stern, clear voice, 'that I decide what goes on in my own home. We're not in a police state yet: I assume you are from the police?' She put her hands on her hips and looked him up and down with as much disdain as she could muster.

He cleared his throat. 'That's not very hospitable is it?' he said. 'Don't you offer your guests refreshments?'

'Funny,' she replied. 'I don't remember inviting you in.'

His mouth opened and closed a couple of times.

Beatrice knew she had to talk to the police, and although it was a shame they'd sent this lout, the other two couldn't be held responsible for him. Especially as she had a sneaking suspicion he was supposed to be the 'superior' officer.

'Perhaps you could tell me who you are?' she said.

'I am Detective Sergeant Fisher, CID.' He said with pride, as if he thought she should swoon. Fortunately, she wasn't the swooning type. When he got no response he carried on. 'This is Detective Constable Wilde.'

'Do you have any ID?'

Grunting a complaint, but unable to refuse, he rummaged around in his scruffy coat and pulled out a warrant card. Beatrice took it off him and spent longer than was necessary examining it. The picture wasn't flattering, but the real-life version wasn't exactly pretty. She noted his first name was Derek. For the purpose of annoying him, she sighed and shook her head before returning his card. Constable Wilde handed Beatrice her ID without prompting. Beatrice gave it a quick glance – the DC was a Susan – and handed it back to her with a smile. Happily, the difference in treatment wasn't lost on Fisher and he frowned.

'Please won't you all sit down?' Now she'd reminded him whose home he was in, Beatrice planned to cooperate and be courteous – if he remained polite. 'Would anyone like a drink? Tea, Sergeant?'

'Yes.' he grunted. 'Please,' came the after-thought.

'Constable Wilde? Tea?' she asked.

'Yes, please.' DC Wilde had a pleasant, gentle voice.

'Constable Taylor, since you already know your way around the kitchen would you mind making us all a drink? If it's ok with Sergeant Fisher, of course?'

Taylor looked at Fisher, who gave him a brief nod, and then went through to the kitchen at the back of the house.

'Now, I'm sure you have lots of questions, so, please go ahead.'

Sergeant Fisher grunted. 'Let me see if I've got this right. A man, who you say you'd never met and didn't know, phones you up out of the blue, and offers you a job, and he won't tell you what it's about?'

'That's right.' Beatrice was running out of patience. She'd already explained what had happened several times. They were going over the same ground again and again. At least she had learnt from the detective that the body had definitely been Simon Bayfield. 'Look,' she said, 'you can check his phone records, can't you? You'll see he was on the phone with me for hardly any time at all: just long enough to arrange a meeting.'

'Oh, come on. Do you seriously expect me to believe that?'

'I don't care what you believe.' And she didn't. 'It was what happened and your belief in it or otherwise doesn't change it, does it? Besides I don't see what it's got to do with his death.'

'Why would he need you? A businessman like that will have an accountant to sort out his tax.'

Beatrice paused. There was never going to be a good time. 'It may not have been about tax.'

'You told Sergeant Jones you worked for the Revenue.'

'I used to, yes. But now I'm a private investigator.' She spoke firmly, telling herself as much as Fisher. DC Wilde looked up from her notebook and Beatrice could feel the younger woman's eyes on her.

'For tax and the like?' Fisher narrowed his eyes and glared at her.

Beatrice took a deep breath. 'Not just financial investigations. Anything people need help with, they want investigating.'

'What do you think the police are for?' demanded Fisher.

'It seems that Mr Bayfield at least had something he didn't want to talk to the police about,' said Beatrice.

'So you think because you've dug around in a few tax investigations you know all about police work? Well, you're not a real detective, are you? I am.' Fisher pointed his stumpy finger at her, prodding the air for emphasis. 'You're some interfering woman who likes putting her nose into other people's business.'

'Well, putting aside the fact that you don't know anything about me, you like to spend your time looking for missing pets, serving papers and conducting insurance investigations do you? I didn't realise the police in Lincolnshire had so much time on their hands. Shall I refer those cases to you then?' Beatrice hoped she sounded like she knew what she was talking about.

'Never mind that.' He waved his hand. 'What with me being an actual detective, Miss Styles, I know what we have here is a sudden, and as yet, unexplained death. It seems reasonable to me that the person who found the body is someone I should pay close attention to.'

Beatrice had had enough. The vile man couldn't seriously think Mr Bayfield had died from anything other than natural causes or possibly suicide. He was doing this because she hadn't let him bully her. Or possibly because he hated private investigators. Or women. Or both. More likely he hated everyone.

'Do you have any proper questions left to ask? If all you've got are insinuations, you can leave.' Beatrice stood up and both junior officers followed suit, with DC Wilde snapping her notebook closed. Fisher, realising it was all he was getting, pulled himself slowly to his feet.

'Well, thank you for your time Miss Styles,' he sneered. 'If we have any further questions I'll let you know. In the meantime, the Constable here will type up the interview notes into a statement. You'd better come to the station tomorrow afternoon to read through and sign it.'

Standing behind Fisher, Wilde frowned and Taylor looked surprised. Clearly Fisher expected his junior to work on getting the statement done in far too quick a time.

'I'm happy to sign a statement,' said Beatrice. 'But I won't be able to make it to the station until Wednesday at the earliest. I have other commitments, I'm afraid.' She didn't, of course, but she wasn't going to allow him to use her as a reason to take his annoyance out on the DC.

'I suppose that will have to do then, won't it,' he said, walking over to the front door.

Taylor rushed across and opened it for him. Without another word Fisher left, Taylor close on his heels. Constable Wilde grinned at Beatrice, gave her a wink and a thumbs-up sign before closing the door gently behind her.

Beatrice had taken the dirty mugs to the kitchen and was standing by the sink, pondering on the bizarre nature of Detective Fisher, and whether it was possible she'd overreacted a bit, when the doorbell rang. Surely he's not back already, she thought. Opening the door she steeled herself for another confrontation. However, a much more pleasant sight met her eyes in the form of James Marland: a tall, well-muscled man, with short black curly hair and vivid blue eyes. He had a large bag dangling from each arm. Beatrice stared at him for a few seconds before springing into action.

'I am so sorry,' she said. 'Please come in.'

'Is everything alright? You did say this afternoon didn't you?' said James, frowning.

Beatrice almost dragged him into the house, not wanting her handsome guest to make an escape. 'Yes, I did. It's fine. I've had a busy day. It slipped my mind for a moment what with the police and everything.'

'The police? Taken up the other side of the law now, have you?' He grinned at her, then his face became serious. 'You do look a bit frazzled. Are you ok? Can I get you anything? Tea?'

'I think I've had enough tea for now. I'll make you a drink though and tell you all about it. Then we can move your stuff into your room. Pop your bags there for now.' She pointed to the bottom of the stairs.

'I really appreciate you letting me stay. I couldn't stand that place any longer, what with all the noise and the mess.'

'It's doing me a favour actually. I'm glad Adam mentioned you needed somewhere. It's forced me to sort out some of the unpacking. Your room will be fine, but watch out for boxes around the rest of the house, won't you? I don't want you having an accident.'

'Fair enough, I'll keep an eye out for any packing boxes that are trying to take me out.' James smiled. 'So what has made your day so hectic? Got some work, have you?'

'Well, I thought I had, but things are not looking good on the work front given I found my first ever client dead this afternoon.'

Chapter 3

At the detached house in Sudbrooke, a quiet village a few miles north of Lincoln, Beatrice parked in Adam's space, next to Rosie's tiny VW Fox. As she approached the front door it opened. Rosie had been watching for her.

'What time do you call this? I expected you an hour ago. Did you come via Skegness?' As Rosie talked, she gave Beatrice a quick kiss on the cheek. It amused Beatrice that even from her sister's vantage point on the raised doorstep, she still had to stand on her tiptoes to reach her marginally younger twin.

'Good morning to you too. How are you? I'm fine thank you. It's so nice to see you,' parroted Beatrice.

Rosie narrowed her eyes. 'There's no need for sarcasm. We've already spoken today.'

'Oh, yes, I remember. When I received my orders to attend.' She saluted.

'Stop messing about. Come in. I'll put the kettle on.' Rosie stomped off to the kitchen, her golden curls bouncing as she left to follow.

'I bought you a present,' said Rosie, filling the kettle. 'It's over there on the side.'

Beatrice looked across to where Rosie had indicated. All she could see was a pink plastic bowl with black paw prints printed on it. Surely it wasn't that? Beatrice looked across at Rosie, who grinned.

'Oh no!' said Beatrice.

'You're welcome,' returned Rosie. 'I think you meant to say 'thank you' anyway. And you imply I don't have any manners.' She tilted her head to one side and raised her eyebrows.

'I'm sorry, Rosie, but I don't need this.'

'It's just a bowl. What's the problem?'

'The problem is she's not my cat,' said Beatrice. 'I don't have a cat and I don't want a cat.'

'She may as well be yours given how much of the last couple of weeks she's spent at your place. You can't keep feeding her off your plates. It's disgusting.' Rosie wrinkled her nose.

'I suppose so.' Beatrice sighed. 'Thanks. It feels too much like giving in, getting her a bowl.'

'Well, if you don't want her, stop letting her in and stop feeding her. She'll go back to her proper family in their new house.'

'I tried ignoring her, but she sits there and meows until I let her in,' said Beatrice.

'She seems to be training you rather successfully, doesn't she? You'd better take the bowl and accept that she's living with you for as long as she wants.' Rosie handed Beatrice a full mug. 'Besides, I think you like her really, you just don't want to admit it.'

'I'm having tea then?' said Beatrice looking into the mug.

'You like tea!' exclaimed Rosie.

'I like to choose though,' said Beatrice.

'Do you want me to make you a coffee instead?'

'No. I'll drink this.'

'You're in a right mood this morning, aren't you?' said Rosie.

'I suppose so, shall we call a truce?'

'Fine by me. Let's go into the living room. It's more relaxing in there. When I'm in the kitchen I always feel as though I should be cooking or cleaning.'

They made themselves comfortable, side by side on the sofa, but angled so they could look at each other. It was a large suite which Beatrice could easily sit in and stretch out her long legs. Rosie on the other hand looked lost in her corner.

'You said there were three things,' said Beatrice.

'Pardon?'

'When you phoned,' Beatrice reminded her. 'You said I needed to come over this morning; you had three things to talk to me about. I can't say I think the first one was worth it. I hope the others are an improvement. They can't get much worse than a pink cat bowl can they? Did it have to be pink?'

'Never mind that.' Rosie dismissed the question with a wave of her hand. 'Why didn't you tell me Simon Bayfield was dead and you found his body?'

'I thought you believed in a mystical twin connection. Is yours broken?' Beatrice laughed.

'There's not need to be facetious, Bea. I'm serious. You found a dead body. That's something most people would want to tell their closest relative about.'

'Perhaps,' Beatrice admitted. 'Anyway, the police asked me not to discuss it.'

'I found out when Adam came home from work yesterday. Even if you wanted to be all secretive, didn't it occur to you that it might affect us? That perhaps you ought to let us know?'

'What on earth do you mean, might affect you?' Beatrice could see her sister was upset and not just winding her up. But she didn't understand why.

'Bayfield Renewables is one of Adam's biggest customers,' said Rosie.

'Oh, well I can see why you'd be interested, but Rosie, why do you look so worried? What's the matter?'

Rosie raised her chin and shook her head. 'Nothing's the matter. He's an important customer and you should have told me. I *am* your sister.'

Beatrice studied her. There was something more going on, she was sure. 'You can talk to me, you know.'

'It's nothing,' said Rosie. 'There was another thing I wanted to tell you. The main reason I asked you to come.'

'Well, I've had a cat bowl and a telling off so far, so this should be good. Out with it then.'

'It is good news. Well, in one way. In another way, it's not good at all.'

'Rosalind! Get on with it.' Beatrice put her cup down on the side table and folded her arms.

'I've found you some work,' said Rosie.

'Not another dead client, I hope?' said Beatrice. 'One of those is more than enough.'

'Do you want work or not?'

'Sorry. Carry on.'

'Do you remember Natalie and David Saunders?' asked Rosie.

'I'm not sure.'

'You've met them here at a party. They're the older couple with a teenage daughter, Cassie.'

'Oh, yes,' said Beatrice, nodding. 'I do remember. They're friendly, homely sort of people.'

'That's them. Well, it's Cassie. She's gone missing.'

Beatrice felt the blood drain from her face and she quickly looked away from Rosie's penetrating gaze, certain they were thinking of the same thing. 'How long?' she croaked.

'She was due home last Saturday, just over a week ago.'

'That's terrible,' said Beatrice, her mind already racing about what could have happened to Cassie. 'They've been to the police though, haven't they? She's fifteen, isn't she?'

'Yes. Sixteen later this year,' Rosie said. 'The trouble is the police have done everything they can, but they've got nowhere. It's like she's vanished into thin air. Everyone's expecting the worst. I told Natalie and David you could help.'

'Have the police used the press and internet?'

'It was all over this week's paper.' Rosie reached to the table beside the sofa and handed Beatrice a copy of the county paper. 'Haven't you sorted out getting the Lincolnshire Weekly delivered yet?'

'I've been busy moving house,' said Beatrice, glancing at the front page showing a picture of a young girl in school uniform.

'There's no unpacked boxes left then? It's all sorted?' asked Rosie, clearly knowing the answer.

'Never mind that now,' said Beatrice.

'You need to get yourself organised if you want to know what's going on locally and what kind of place this is. Anyway, I told Natalie and David you'd go around and see them.'

'When?'

'Now, of course, Bea. They're going out of their minds with worry. It's not like you've got anything else to do, is it? Unless those boxes are more urgent than I realised.'

'Oh, alright, I'll go now. Not because you told me to, but because I would like to help them if I can.'

'Great, I'll give them a ring and let them know you'll be there in a few minutes. They're a couple of streets away. You can leave your car here, if you like.' She stood up and walked into the hall, wrote an address on a piece of paper and handed it to Beatrice, who had joined her.

'So you can find out all the details when I come back to get it?' said Beatrice. 'No chance. Besides, I may need to go from there, if there's something I can get working on straight away.' Beatrice thought it unlikely. She'd have to familiarise herself with the details of the case first, but she was determined that a move nearer to her sister started as she meant it to go on – two separate lives which overlapped sometimes. Rosie was too apt to get bossy, and given half a chance would want to know everything about her life.

'Be like that then,' said Rosie, clearly not believing her. 'Oh, Bea?'

'Yes?' said Beatrice opening the front door and stepping out.

'I just thought you should know - James is gay.' Rosie smiled and closed the door on Beatrice's surprised face.

Chapter 4

The Saunders' home was in an older part of the village. A single garage was integrated into the plain, rectangular façade making it look like a box with large windows cut out. It was as well looked after as the surrounding properties, except for the lawn, which was, Beatrice thought, probably longer than it was usually allowed to grow. The Saunders had other things on their minds.

Just like at Rosie's, Beatrice didn't have to knock before the door opened, but this time a more anxious face greeted her. In her mid-fifties, Natalie was older than the mothers of most teenagers. She looked small and hunched up, vulnerable.

'Oh, Beatrice, I'm so glad you're here. Please come in.' Natalie stood back to let her into the small hallway. 'Go on through, to the lounge.' She indicated the door on the right.

It was much as Beatrice expected it – a large room, tidy and with furniture that was a bit dated and worn.

'Sit down, I'll fetch David.' Natalie had followed her in. 'Would you like a drink?'

'No, thanks.'

'Make yourself comfortable. I'll just be a minute.'

Beatrice took the opportunity to look around the room. Her attention was immediately drawn to the photos on the shelf over the fireplace. There were ten silver frames, all different designs, each one containing a photograph of Cassie. Taken together they showed her life, arranged so that she was a sleeping baby on the left, through to a serious looking young woman on the right. She looked happy in all the pictures, every face smiling at the photographer, except the last. Beatrice picked it up. It was the same as the one the police had used in their newspaper appeal, showing a young girl, with a pleasant, round face. Her long, blonde hair was tied in two thick plaits. She wore a school tie and blazer. She looked young to Beatrice, innocent.

More so than the girls she'd seen around town, all dressed up to look older. Where could she be? Would she ever be coming home?

'Beatrice, thanks for coming.' David walked ahead of Natalie, arm outstretched. They shook hands. He was a few years older than his wife, but he looked in good shape physically, apart from the tiredness etched into his face.

Beatrice put the photo back down where she had found it.

'That's the photo we gave to the police,' said David. 'It's the most recent picture we have you see?'

'She's self-conscious about her looks these days,' added Natalie. 'I suppose all girls are. She doesn't like having her picture taken anymore. She used to love it when she was small.'

David carefully adjusted the position of the photo so it was exactly in line with the others before he spoke again. 'Sit down, please,' he said, indicating an armchair.

Beatrice settled into the comfortable seat, the couple sat opposite on the sofa.

'It's good of you to come and see us,' said Natalie. 'We're so...'

David took his wife's hand. 'We want to be out there, looking for her. Scouring the whole of the country if necessary, but we don't know where to start.'

'And the police said one of us should stay at home,' said Natalie. 'In case she comes back or phones.' Her voice waivered as she spoke.

'They said we should for the first forty-eight hours,' David corrected. 'It's been longer than that now. The police are doing their best. They've talked to her friends and the school. They've put out appeals in the papers and on TV, even the internet. Social networking they called it. I don't think there's much more they can do. There's still no sign of her. Even with everything they've done, we're no closer to knowing if she's alright or where she might be.'

'That's why when Rosie mentioned you, we both agreed it was a good idea,' said Natalie. 'After all, it can't hurt can it, to have an extra person looking for her?'

'I'm sure the police are doing everything they can to find Cassie,' said Beatrice.

'It seems that way, but there was one man, Fisher he's called,' said Natalie, with some bitterness. 'He was horrible. A bully. I don't think he cares about finding where she's is. The way he was talking to us. He thinks we've murdered her. I know he does.' Her voice cracked.

'Natalie, love,' said David. 'He's just trying to do his job.'

Natalie pulled a tissue from up her sleeve and blew her nose. 'We'd like you to talk to Cassie's friends and her teachers,' she said. 'See if you can find out something the police have missed.'

'Is that likely?' Beatrice asked. 'You said they've already spoken to them.'

'They have,' said Natalie. 'But they might know something they don't want to tell the police. They're more likely to be honest with you.'

Beatrice tried to imagine Fisher being pleasant to Cassie's friends, persuading them to tell him about her, but couldn't see it. Maybe she was doing him a disservice. Maybe he could change his manner according to situation and would have been gentle with the girls.

'Perhaps one of them knows something,' said David. 'She may have told her friends about what she was doing that weekend.'

'They wouldn't want to get Cassie in trouble,' Natalie added. 'So they might have kept quiet about what they know.'

'Do you think she was in trouble then? Or might be?' Bearice asked.

'No.' David was emphatic.

'If you'd asked me ten days ago, I would have said no too,' said Natalie. 'But now I'm not so sure.'

'You read all about kids these days, getting involved in drugs and alcohol. Cassie isn't like that at all. She's never showed any interest.' David regarded Beatrice earnestly.

'I expect that's why she and Sunita are such great friends,' agreed Natalie. 'Neither of them is into the usual teenage things.'

'They're good girls.' David nodded.

'They took some things from her room for DNA.' said Natalie, with tears in her eyes. 'That means they think she's dead, doesn't it?'

'Oh, no, not at all, said Beatrice. 'You mustn't think that. I've read a lot about this kind of situation. It's to help identify people when they're found. It's routine for the police. It doesn't mean anything.'

'Really?'

'Yes.'

Natalie looked like she wanted to believe Beatrice's assurances, but her expression showed doubt. 'Did they do that when your mum went missing?'

Beatrice froze. Rosie. She must have told them. She cleared her throat. 'Yes. It's normal procedure, and it's not always needed, but they have it ready if it is. When it's a child, the police take a disappearance even more seriously. You mustn't think the worst.'

'But she doesn't know how to take care of herself,' said David.

'She wouldn't have gone off like that without telling us. Something's happened to her.' Natalie wiped the tears from her eyes.

'It's hard to believe, but the vast majority of people who go missing are eventually found: alive.'

'But you see it on the TV. Children disappear and then they turn up dead,' said Natalie.

'That's because the news doesn't report on all the times when people disappear. Most are ignored by the media. They pick out the stories that make good headlines. How many times have you read a sensational news story in the paper, for it to dominate for a few days and then suddenly go quiet? They can't always be bothered to report the outcome – especially if it doesn't sell a paper or push up viewing figures. Please. Don't lose hope. Not yet. The police are still working on finding Cassie.' Beatrice regarded the couple in front of her. They seemed genuinely upset and concerned, but she was very aware of the statistics on murders and the likelihood of relatives being involved. Could this benign looking couple have had anything to do with their daughter's disappearance? It was clearly something Sergeant Fisher had considered, in his heavy-handed way.

David broke into her thoughts. 'How long has your mum been missing?' he asked.

Beatrice swallowed. 'Almost two years.'

'Oh. I'm sorry. It must be terrible.'

'Let's focus on Cassie. How has she been recently? Has anything in her life changed?'

The couple looked at one another and shook their heads. 'Everything is the same as usual,' said David. 'She's been fine.'

'Do you think she could have left on purpose? Gone somewhere with someone she knows or met?' Beatrice asked.

'She's no reason to.' David sat with a stony expression. 'Cassie knows how important she is to us. How much we love her. We thought we'd never have kids. We wanted to, but it didn't happen. And then, when we'd given up hope, we found out Natalie was pregnant. We were overjoyed. She couldn't have been more wanted or loved.'

'Will you help us? Please?' Natalie's anguished face tore at Beatrice's heart.

'I'll do what I can.'

'You will? Oh, thank you.' Natalie gushed. 'It doesn't matter what it costs, we want her back.'

'I'll talk to her friends and her school for you, but you need to understand the chances are I won't learn anything the police don't already know, and this is going to take some time. I know this is very difficult for you, but you have to try to be patient.'

'At least we can feel as though we're doing something this way,' said David.

'I need you to tell me what happened first,' said Beatrice. 'All I know so far is what Rosie has told me.'

It took a long time, with lots of questions and a pot of tea with biscuits to get the full story out of them. They repeated themselves, talked over each other and Natalie got upset a lot of the time. David remained stoical, but Beatrice could see behind his mask, he was as distressed as his wife. They both clearly adored Cassie and she had to remind herself to remain sceptical about whatever they told her, for Cassie's sake.

The account Beatrice received, and made careful notes of in her small notebook, was limited. Cassie left for school on Friday fourth May as usual. She had her school bag, crammed full, and a plastic carrier bag with some clothes in. She was wearing school uniform. It was normal for her to take two bags into school on a Friday, because she worked in the restaurant at the Copper Kettle pub in Nettleham village, on Friday evenings. The carrier bag would have had her work clothes in it.

The usual arrangement was that Cassie would catch a bus from her school in Welton straight to Nettleham, and help to get the restaurant ready for the early evening service. That was how all the Fridays for the last six months had gone. The only thing different about the ninth was that Cassie had asked to stay overnight in Nettleham with her best friend, Sunita Banerjee. The girls were going to have a sleepover and catch a bus into town on Saturday to do some shopping. When they said goodbye to Cassie on Friday morning, Natalie and David didn't expect to see her again until late in the afternoon on Saturday, when she would come home and change, ready for working at the restaurant again that evening.

When Cassie wasn't home by five pm her parents thought she must have been running late and gone straight to the restaurant. But when Paul Haynes, the owner of the Copper Kettle, called at seven o'clock that evening, to ask where Cassie was, they started to worry. She didn't have a mobile for them to call. 'She's too young,' was David's comment. David had phoned the Banerjee home, but there was no reply. He left a message on their voicemail. The Saunders kept trying to contact the Banerjee's all through the evening, but couldn't get to speak to anyone. David drove to Nettleham and pushed a note through the letterbox of the Banerjee's empty house, asking them to call as soon as they got home, no matter what time it was.

Dr Banerjee called the Saunders on the family's return home from visiting relatives. They hadn't seen Cassie. She hadn't stayed at their house on Friday night and Sunita had been with them all day, at a long-planned family visit, so the girls couldn't have gone to town together. Once they were able to understand all of this, Natalie and David became frantic. So much so, that they phoned the police. Here they were, ten days later, with no news of their daughter and with their lives falling apart.

Chapter 5

Beatrice had obtained as much information as she could from Natalie and David, who both looked exhausted from the experience. David had also emailed her a copy of the picture he'd given to the police. There was nothing else she could find out from them for now.

'May I look at Cassie's room please?' asked Beatrice.

'Yes, of course.' David stood.

'Can you put it back as you find it?' said Natalie. 'She won't like it if she finds out anyone has been through her things. She complains when I go in to change the sheets and put her clothes away.'

'I'll be careful, I promise.'

Beatrice followed David up the stairs. She stepped through the door he opened for her. He stood on the landing peering in at her.

'I'll come down to the living room when I've finished, shall I?' said Beatrice.

'What? Oh. Yes. We'll wait for you there. Take your time.' With a couple of glances back at Beatrice, he made his way down the stairs.

Beatrice shut the bedroom door and leant back against it. She closed her eyes and tried to calm her feelings. She'd wanted David to leave her alone so she could search unobserved, but, when she'd closed the door, she also felt relief she was away from them. Their anxiety and grief was contagious. Their feelings were raw and it was difficult to be around them. Her own loss weighed heavily on her mind. Her heart ached for her mum: to see her again, to hold her, to be told everything was going to be alright.

When Rosie had told her Cassie was missing, her thoughts had leapt to their mum; she was sure Rosie's had too. But she had hoped to be able to put her personal feelings aside. She hadn't anticipated the Saunders asking her about it and it had thrown her off balance.

She took three slow, deep breaths, emptying her mind of distractions, ready to focus on the task in hand.

She opened her eyes and surveyed the room. The bedroom was at the back of the house and, like the rest of the building, a simple rectangle. The door was set at the end of one of the longer walls. The wall parallel contained a large window in the middle of it, with a narrow sill. Beatrice glanced out at a lawn edged with shrubs. Underneath the window a radiator was partially obscured by the single bed pushed against it. At the foot of the bed was a desk and chair. The surface was empty except for a pot containing pencils and pens. The rest of the furniture consisted of a bookcase and a built-in wardrobe.

Although the layout and furniture were unremarkable, the atmosphere wasn't what she'd expected. Cassie was a fifteen-year-old girl, but Beatrice wouldn't have guessed by looking at her bedroom. The walls were painted a pale cream colour. The duvet cover and pillowcase were a matching set in dull beige. There were no pictures on the wall. No posters of good-looking popstars, of either sex, or pictures of friends. Beatrice compared it to the room Abbie and Katie, her twin nieces, shared. There's was a room full of bright colours, photos, posters, and their own artwork. Although much younger than Cassie, they had stamped their characters on their space. Beatrice had no doubt that their tastes would change as they got older, but she couldn't imagine them sleeping in a room like this. Cassie's bedroom was nondescript. There was no personality. Nothing to indicate that a young woman lived there, what her interests were, what she liked and who her friends were. She would need to know more about what kind of girl Cassie was and hoped a thorough search would help.

Half an hour later Beatrice had picked through the entire room. She'd been methodical and diligent in her search of the contents of the bookcase, the drawers and the wardrobe. Everything was scrupulously tidy and the lack of Cassie's personality continued throughout. The books on the bookcase were all either school textbooks or the kind of 'classics' that conservative parents might think appropriate for their child. Where were the novels of teenage angst, the adventure stories or even the Harry Potter books? The clothes were similar in their blandness. Items of school uniform hung in the wardrobe, carefully ironed. The casual clothes seemed limited to a few pairs of jeans, a couple of skirts, some plain t-shirts and jumpers. Beatrice had looked under the bed, pulling out the storage boxes, crammed full of soft toys, to make sure there was nothing hidden behind or beneath them.

Beatrice looked around the room. Who were you Cassie, she wondered? How did you cope with living like this? Why didn't you feel you could express yourself?

Every teenager had things they needed to keep from their parents. It was a normal part of growing up, as far as Beatrice could tell. She and Rosie had spent hours whispering secretly together. Their parents never pried, leaving them to have part of themselves separate. They were probably reassured by their being two of them to keep each other safe. But what about Cassie? When did she get the chance to be herself – to not be controlled by her parents and their expectations? To be the young woman she was becoming? Beatrice didn't believe it was possible the fifteen-year-old was the girl her parents presented her as being. Cassie must have found a way to express her opinions and self, away from the confinement of the house.

They said she didn't have a phone, but what teenager would be without one? She had money from her job and a cheap pay-as-you-go phone wouldn't require any bills or be difficult to get. The tricky part would be hiding it from her parents. Even if she kept the phone on her all the time, wouldn't she have needed somewhere for the charger? She couldn't have charged the phone at school, so she'd have to do it at home.

Her parents didn't seem to think Cassie needed much privacy and her mother came into her room whenever she felt the need, so it would have to be somewhere well hidden. Natalie had talked about changing the bedding and putting away Cassie's clothes, so the usual teenage hiding places like under the mattress and at the back of the wardrobe wouldn't have been much use, and she'd already searched them. But what were the alternatives?

Despondent, Beatrice sat heavily on the bed, staring at the floor. Then she frowned. What was that noise the bed had made? She stood up quickly. There it was again, a metallic clonk. She bounced lightly on the edge and heard the noise again. Yes. There was something. She stood up and shook the headboard. No noise. She knelt on the floor and pulled the boxes from underneath the bed and saw nothing new. Leaving them out, she sat back down and heard the noise again. The only thing that was left was the radiator, which the bed was pushed up against. Perhaps it wasn't fitted properly. She reached over and pulled on the cold radiator. It shifted and the noise was louder this time. Beatrice kneeled on the bed, positioning herself so she could peer down the back of it. There was something behind it. She selected the torch function on her phone and shone it into the space. Reaching down, Beatrice had to force her fingers into the narrow gap to grab the object. She slowly and carefully pulled it up. Once it was out she looked at it in surprise; a cross-head screwdriver.

Beatrice sat on the bed tapping the screwdriver in her palm. The tool was the only thing out of place in the room, the only thing which didn't fit with the meek daughter image. Had one of her parents been fixing something and, having dropped it, forgotten and absently left it behind, or was it something Cassie herself had brought into the room? If the former, then it was a blind alley. But what if Cassie had kept it there, out of sight.

Beatrice tried to imagine what she would do if she had been in the same circumstances as Cassie. If she had things to hide, she'd want to put them in a place which took a bit of effort to find; you couldn't just stumble across it. If Cassie had hidden the screwdriver for a reason, it meant she needed to be looking for something fixed with cross-head screws, which was either out of sight or so typical in a bedroom it wouldn't be noticed.

Beatrice worked systematically. She began with the wall the door was in and quickly passed over the light switch with its flat-head screws. The door itself was normal. The frame was solid wood. She moved onto the bookcase, pulling it out to look behind and checking each shelf carefully. Nothing. The second wall was filled with the built-in wardrobe, which she'd already searched. She then checked all around the desk and the bed.

She got down on her hands and knees and crawled around the edge of the room. At intervals she tested the carpet to see if it would raise. It was fixed firmly down on to the grippers and showed no signs of having been lifted. Beatrice sat back on her haunches. She was convinced there was nothing in the room. But why the screwdriver? She jumped up, inspiration had struck. She'd searched the wardrobe, but didn't the carpet extend into the floor space of it? She opened the doors. She was right, the carpet in the bedroom had been cut to cover the whole of the wardrobe floor too.

Beatrice pulled out the storage boxes she'd already been through, clearing the floor space. She lifted the carpet, starting in the left-back corner. She was lucky first time. As she pulled the carpet back she uncovered a chipboard floor. But although it was what she expected, the jagged cuts which had been made to form a rough, square panel, wouldn't have been put there by builders. It must have been Cassie: presumably using her parents' tools when they were out. It was an effective hiding place.

Beatrice undid the screws holding the panel in place and prised it up. In a space between the joists, Beatrice found a diary and a small packet. The diary was A5 size, with each week spread across two pages, an academic year diary of the cheap sort which could be found in bargain shops. Beatrice sat on the edge of the bed, checking every page to ensure she missed nothing. The first few months were blank except for a regular appearance of stars spaced roughly every four weeks. Presumably the reason Cassie bought the diary in the first place. In December Cassie had started adding extra notes. She must have been concerned about the diary being found, despite her precautions, because she used abbreviations. Some of the notes were crossed out, others with ticks next to them. Were they dates, parties, or some other social event? 'CF' began to show up regularly. Next to the more recent entries Cassie had doodled: 'M + C' with love heart symbols. So there was someone Cassie was interested in.

Beatrice put the diary to one side and examined the packet. It was small, made of brown paper with an elastic band wrapped tightly around it. Beatrice pulled off the band and unrolled what turned out to be a paper bag. She reached in and pulled out a small plastic bag.

'Oh, no.' She stared at the three yellow pills. What the hell had Cassie got herself into?

What should she do? If she told the Saunders, their idea of their daughter would be shattered. What if Cassie never came home and she had been responsible for destroying their memory of her? She could take them to the police. But if they found Cassie, would they charge her with drugs offenses? That would be no way to get the girl smoothly back into her life. Beatrice tucked the pills and the diary into her large handbag. She'd have to think. For now, she'd keep what she found to herself.

Beatrice checked under the rest of the carpet in the wardrobe, but found no more hidden secrets. She spent a few minutes putting the room back to how it was when she arrived, including dropping the screwdriver behind the radiator.

Beatrice paused outside the living room to take a breath. She knocked with a light tap and walked in. Natalie was sitting on the sofa and David stood, staring out of the window. Both looked over as she entered the room.

'I've got a couple of questions, if that's ok. Then I'll be off.'

'Of course.' David returned to the sofa by Natalie.

Beatrice sat back down. 'Did the police take anything away from Cassie's room?'

'Her hair and toothbrush,' said Natalie.

'Does Cassie have a laptop?'

'She doesn't need one,' said David. 'There's a computer in my office upstairs. She uses it for school work.'

'We converted the small bedroom into an office,' Natalie explained. 'The police took the computer away for a few days to have a look, but they brought it back. Do you want to see it?'

'No, thank you. You said Cassie used the family address book.'

Natalie led the way to the hall where there was a narrow table with a telephone and address book. Beatrice looked through each page. The only entry in Cassie's handwriting was for Sunita. 'Are any of the other numbers for Cassie's friends?' Beatrice asked.

'No. I guess she sees her friends at school so she doesn't need to phone them.'

'Do you know the names of any of her other friends?'

'No. She only ever talks about Sunita to us. I'm sure the school will know.'

Beatrice smiled at Natalie, who led her back to the living room, where David had moved back to the window, keeping a lookout.

After talking through fees and expenses, and getting a signed contract and deposit, Beatrice left the Saunders with a promise of letting them know of anything that she found out during her investigation. She had a letter to the school's Head teacher giving her permission to talk to Beatrice about Cassie and her life at school. She also had an appointment to see the Banerjees and their daughter, Sunita. She hoped Cassie's best friend would have insight into what her plans had been the evening she disappeared.

It was Mother who showed me the way to control and use my anger. I can still remember feeling so angry I thought it would burst out of me. I wanted to scream and shout.

I was eight years old, at school, and I'd spent all morning working on a painting. Choosing the colours carefully and taking the time to clean my brushes thoroughly. Each arc of the rainbow was in bright, fresh colours, all separated by a thin line of the paper. I was going to take it home to Mother, trying to please her, hoping to put her in a good mood.

A careless boy - I can't remember his name – knocked over the jar of water for brush-cleaning. Of all the paintings on the table only mine lay in the path of the grubby, discoloured water. I watched as the thin paper was soaked; the colours of my once-bright rainbow mixing and mingling, turning muddy and dull.

'I didn't mean it,' he wailed, drawing the sympathy of the adults in the room.

Where was the sympathy for me? For my ruined painting?

It was an accident, I know that, and I think I knew even then, but I'd spent so much time on it, pinned my hopes of a quiet spell with Mother on it, so that when I saw what he'd done I was devastated. That feeling quickly turned to anger and I felt the heat and rage take over me. I stood shaking, fists clenched. Why my painting? Why no one else's? How could he be so stupid and clumsy? Why were they comforting him? Telling him it didn't matter!

He tried to help clean up, but the paper turned to pulp and my beautiful painting, which I'd been so proud of, had disappeared forever.

'I'm sorry,' he said. 'I'll help you make a new one.'

I wouldn't listen to him and ran to hide in the toilets.

Later, when I went home, I told Mother. I couldn't keep it from her. She could tell straight away something was wrong by my face, even though I really did try my best to look happy: how she liked me to be. My trousers were spotted with dirty water which had seeped through the apron.

'What's that muck on your trousers?' she demanded. 'What have you been doing? If you think I'm washing them tonight you've got another thing coming.'

I felt things change that day. As I told her about the painting she looked at me like she never had before. She was thoughtful and silent as I talked, listening to what I said. Once I finished explaining I stood quietly, waiting. My fingers twisted anxiously behind me as I tried to keep the rest of my body still. She hated it when I fidgeted.

'So, he messed up my present did he? What did you do about it?'

I shook my head.

'Huh. Nothing I suppose.' Her eyes narrowed as she looked at me. 'You're not going to let him get away with it are you?'

I shrugged. Mother looked at me, like she could see me without being annoyed. Right then I existed as something other than an irritation.

'I bet he did it on purpose,' she said.

I frowned in confusion.

'He was jealous I expect. Of your painting. It was too good. Better than he could do.'

I thought about what she said. It was good. My best picture ever. Maybe he was jealous. Maybe he did do it on purpose.

'We can't let him get away with it, can we? Oh no, he needs to be taught a lesson.' She smiled at me. She actually smiled at me. But, I didn't know what she meant. What could I do? How could I teach him a lesson?

'You can't just leave it,' she said. 'You have to wait though: be patient so no one connects it with your painting. Revenge is best served cold.'

I didn't know what she meant by that, only she'd make me do something.

'You'll have to watch carefully,' she continued. 'Look out for an opportunity to get him back for what he's done. When you see the chance, you have to take it. No hesitating. Just do it.'

I was happy she was talking to me, treating me like a real person, but I didn't want to get in trouble at school. Some of the teachers were nice to me.

'I won't forget you know,' she said, reading my mind. 'I'm already looking forward to hearing what you do. And it had better not be something pathetic like ruining a silly painting.'

Chapter 6

Beatrice watched the day gradually arriving as the sun rose. It filtered through the deep red curtains, making the light more diffuse, creating a comforting red glow. She'd managed some sleep, but not much. The last two days had given her too much to think about. She'd been awake for a long while, thinking over what to do about Cassie, and in the last half-hour had been trying to resist an urgent need to visit the bathroom so she wouldn't disturb James. It was no good though. Nature was calling and she had to go.

She threw back the duvet and swung her legs out of bed, sitting upright on its edge. She switched off the alarm: it wasn't due to go off for another hour. She stretched her arms up, trying to loosen her back a little and then checked herself over. She was wearing her usual bedtime outfit - knickers and a T-shirt. Not quite decent enough, she decided, and pulled on a pair of jogging bottoms. Just in time, because there was a gentle tapping on the bedroom door.

'Hello?' She could tell from the hesitant voice and light tap James was trying to be heard, but also trying not to wake her if she was still asleep.

Beatrice opened the door.

'Sorry, I've really got to go to the bathroom,' she said, as she hopped from one foot to the other.

'I thought I heard you were up. I've made coffee. I'll be in the kitchen.' He leaned back against the wall as she darted past him, across the small landing.

After she finished taking care of business, she looked in horror at herself in the bathroom mirror. She couldn't believe she'd let James see her like this. Generally she didn't worry about her appearance, but this was a new low. I look like some sort of wild freak, she thought. Her hair was a badly built bird's nest, she was pale – ghostly almost – and her eyes showed how little sleep she'd managed with their contrasting dark circles. She brushed her hair, tied it into a pony tail and splashed water over her face. She looked again at her reflection. Better, she concluded, deciding she merely looked dreadful now, instead of freakish.

James was sitting at the solid oak dining table with two steaming mugs of black coffee.

'I wasn't sure how you had yours, so I left it black,' he said, smiling at her.

She walked over to the fridge. 'Milk, no sugar. The same as I like my tea,' she said.

Beatrice pulled out the chair opposite him and sat down. It was strange seeing him sitting at her dining table so early in the morning. On their short acquaintance she'd decided she liked him, but it would take a while to get used to sharing her space with someone. The only other times she'd had men over for breakfast was when they'd stayed the night - and they'd already seen her at what she considered to be her worst by that point: naked. He looked much better than any of the men she'd been involved with though. It appeared early mornings didn't make any dent in his attractiveness. He looked athletic in his shorts and T-shirt: fit and strong.

'Did you sleep ok?' she asked.

'Yes thanks. It was much quieter than I'm used to, what with all those students and my housemates at the last place. How about you?' James asked. 'How did you sleep?'

Beatrice tilted her head and raised her eyebrows. 'You mean you can't tell by the way I look this morning?'

'A gentleman would never presume to comment on such a thing,' he said, holding his hands in the air.

She laughed. 'I should hope not. I did have some sleep, but not enough. I've been awake for ages.'

'More coffee?' he stood up.

'Yes, please.' She handed him her empty mug. The first drink had gone down well.

Beatrice was surprised she wasn't finding it more intrusive, the way he'd made himself so comfortable in her home, but he was fitting in easily.

James put the kettle on and started rinsing out the cafetière. 'You must have been quite disturbed by finding Bayfield's body,' he said. 'It's no wonder it's messed up your sleep.'

'I've never seen anyone dead before. When dad died we didn't get to see him afterwards. Rosie and I that is. Mum saw him, of course: she had to identify him.' She pushed the worrying thought of her mother away. 'But mainly I've been thinking about Cassie. I'll feel better when I've made a start on looking for her.'

She accepted a fresh mug of coffee from James, with milk this time. 'Did you know him? Simon Bayfield?'

'Not to speak to,' said James. 'I've seen him a couple of times over the last few months, when I've been working at Adam's garage. When he came to visit, everyone kept busy and out of his way. I followed suit. I got the impression he wasn't well liked. Adam didn't look forward to his arrival.' James sipped at his coffee. 'Do you mind if I use the shower whilst you finish your drink? I could do with a clean up after my run and I'll only be a few minutes.'

Beatrice looked at the clock on the wall. It was six-twenty. 'You've been for a run already?'

'Yeah. I like to get up early and get on with it.'

'Do you have any plans for where you'll go to?' she asked. 'After here, I mean.'

'Not yet,' his mug paused halfway to his mouth. 'But don't worry, I'll find something.'

She nodded decisively. 'I'm sure you could. But would you like to stay here? As a lodger, I mean. Adam said you were after somewhere longer term.'

'I am. But I thought you weren't looking to share. Adam said it was only for a few days, which I do appreciate.'

'That's what I told him. But the only work I've got isn't going to bring in much, and the savings I have will disappear if I don't get my business up and running soon. It hasn't been a promising start.'

'I suppose not.'

'If you'd like to rent the attic bedroom, perhaps we can come to some sort of arrangement.' Beatrice paused. 'Sorry, I'm not sure that came out right. For the avoidance of doubt, I am not propositioning you.'

He smiled. 'I didn't think you were. Well, it could work. I like living in town, and this is a nice part of it.'

'You forgot my charming personality.'

'Of course, there's that too.' He waggled his eyebrows. 'It goes without saying that's the main benefit.'

'How do you feel about cats?'

'I'm not fond of them, but they don't bother me.'

'I supposed I'd better let her in.' Beatrice placed her mug on the table, walked to the back door, turned the key then pulled it open. A small tabby walked in, meowing a complaint.

James bent down to stroke the animal who was rubbing herself against his leg.

'Look, how about we give it a trial,' said Beatrice, filling a soup bowl with water before placing it on the floor; Rosie's pink bowl was hidden in the back of a cupboard. 'Say a month, and then we can see how it's going, for both of us? If we're happy we can carry on, if not, you pack up and no hard feelings?' Beatrice added a small plate of cat biscuits next to the bowl.

'Sounds good. How much rent were you thinking of charging?'

Beatrice sat back down. 'I don't know, what with being new to this landlady business. I'll have to find out what the going rate is. Do you mind if I do some research and then we discuss it?'

'Sure,' said James. 'One other thing though?'

'Yes?'

'Does that door lead to a cellar?'

'Yes, why?' asked Beatrice.

'Well, I do a bit of weight training,' said James.

'Oh, really?' said Beatrice, as if she wasn't acutely aware of the rather impressive muscles under his T-shirt.

He grinned back at her, as if he knew what she was thinking. Beatrice felt her face flush.

'So, as well as renting the bedroom, if I can make it work, can I rent the cellar too and put my weights in there?'

'Sure, feel free. I don't have any use for it. I'm not sure how suitable it will be.'

'Great. I'll take a look later. What are your plans for today?' he asked.

'This morning I'm going to retrace Cassie's last known movements and I'm seeing Sunita – that's her best friend – and her parents at five o'clock. This evening I'm going to meet Marina Bayfield.'

'Bayfield?' He raised an eyebrow. 'I thought you didn't know him or his family.'

'I don't, but Adam and Rosie do. Did. She called yesterday afternoon and asked me to see her. She must have got my number from Rosie. She wants to talk about Simon's death because I found his body.'

'And you're going?' James asked.

'Yes. Why wouldn't I?'

'For one thing, didn't you say Sergeant Fisher thought you could have had something to do with her husband's death?'

'Well, he implied that, but I don't think he really believes it.'

'But maybe he mentioned it to the wife, who now wants to exact revenge.'

'Rosie said she's a nice woman. Nicer than her husband was at least. Besides, she sounded fine on the phone. Not mad at all.'

'Bea, people can sound perfectly sane and sensible and still be as nutty as a fruit cake. Especially if they've lost someone close to them. She's not going to be feeling her best right now, is she?'

'No. I suppose you're right. I've said I'll go now, she's expecting me. I don't think she's crazy.'

'Take care, won't you,' said James. 'Any signs of lunacy and you get out of there – ok?'

'Yes, Mum.'

He grinned. 'I'm off for that shower. I'll catch up with you later this evening.'

Beatrice watched him leave the room. He had an outstanding pair of legs. Strong and shapely. Looking at them was a great way to start the day. It was just as well he was gay. At least it meant there wouldn't be any temptation to get involved with him. It was much better for them both if he stayed simply as a tenant. He was right though, thought Beatrice; Marina Bayfield could be so distraught she was looking for someone to blame for her husband's death. Beatrice didn't think so though. When they spoke, she was upset, but didn't seem irrational and Beatrice didn't sense any animosity. It was kind of James to consider her safety, but she'd had to get on with her life for long enough by herself. She had to trust her own judgement.

Chapter 7

Beatrice planned to spend the morning in town. She had a couple of things to pick up, but more importantly she wanted to see for herself the last place Cassie had been seen. It was a warm day but with the cool relief of cloud cover, so she picked up her raincoat and headed off down what seemed to be the only hill in Lincoln. It took her through the city, which changed from the old to the new as she descended the hill. Leaving the magnificent cathedral and the ancient castle behind, the cobbled road of the unimaginatively named Steep Hill gave way to the flagstones of the modern High Street, with its mixture of contemporary shops in aged buildings. In just a few minutes she reached the lower part of the city. It wasn't just the small size of Lincoln that made it so different to London, it was the atmosphere. People here were living life at a less frenetic pace. As she walked, Beatrice felt more relaxed and at ease than she had done for a long time. She could imagine making a home here and, now she had a lodger and some work to get her teeth into, it felt like things were falling into place.

According to the Saunders, Cassie had last been seen getting off the bus from Nettleham heading towards the market. The bus station was small. It was noisy and dirty: neglected. The office for travel information was a cabin, possibly a temporary arrangement organised a long time ago. It was early in the day so there were several buses at their stands, passengers rushing off, heading to work. Beatrice noticed an older woman pulling a tartan shopping trolley.

'Excuse me.'

'Eh?' The old woman looked up at Beatrice.

'I'm sorry to bother you, but I wonder if you could point me in the direction of the market, please?'

'Oh,' said the woman. 'Yes dear. You see that alleyway?' She pointed. 'Head off down there and you come out with the market right in front of you.'

'Thank you.' Beatrice smiled.

It was a squeeze with people pushing through the narrow passage in both directions, but it was short and Beatrice soon found herself facing two large fruit and vegetable stalls. After browsing the selection on offer she explored the rest of the market. There were two main indoor areas, one larger than the other, but neither spacious. She walked back to the way she had entered, to buy some oranges.

'What time do you close in the week?' she asked the woman who served her.

'Oh, we're usually done and packed up by four o'clock.'

The market would have been closed by the time Cassie had arrived in town so it was unlikely the stall holders would have seen her. It was important to be thorough though. She fished out her phone and found the picture of Cassie.

'Have you seen this girl?'

'Are you with the police?'

'No. Why do you ask?'

'They were here with one of those last week.'

'I'm a friend of the family,' said Beatrice, slipping the phone back into her bag.

'She's still not come back then?'

'No.'

The woman shook her head in sympathy. 'Well, I'll tell you what I told them: I didn't see her. School kids don't go in much for the stuff we sell. Not enough sugar, I reckon.'

'Thanks anyway.'

'That's alright, love. Look, it might save you some time, but none of us on the market saw her. We'd all closed up and most had left by then. I spoke to the constable who was doing the asking. He told me it was as if she'd disappeared, "like magic", he said.'

At a small cafe in the market Beatrice ordered a cup of tea and sat down to think. She could carry on going through the same motions as the police, almost certainly coming up with the same answers. Or do something else. Contrary to the impression given by TV shows, the police weren't incompetent. Sure, they could make mistakes like everyone else, but it would be a poor use of her time to repeat what they'd done. They had the resources and authority to question members of the public. They'd have done an organised job of it. They would have checked CCTV footage too. She should think of it from Cassie's point of view instead, though that was difficult. From what her parents had said, and from looking at her bedroom, Beatrice didn't have a real sense of what sort of girl Cassie was.

She was in a prime age for rebellion, and must have had her own ideas, thoughts and feelings. The little yellow pills, whatever they were, proved that. She must also have felt under scrutiny at home. There was no space for privacy. No doubt the Saunders' thought they were protecting Cassie from unsavoury aspects of the world, but Beatrice couldn't imagine anyone living under such tight control. Had she been unable to contain herself any longer? Reached breaking point? One thing was clear: Cassie had lied about her plans for Friday night and shopping with Sunita.

What must it have been like being so wanted by your parents? Did she feel pressure to be the ideal daughter for them? Had she tried hard to be the kind of person they wanted her to be and then finally cracked under the stress of it all? Did it drive her to drugs? And where had she got them from? They were now hidden at the back of Beatrice's wardrobe and soon she'd have to decide what to do with them. She didn't want to get Cassie into trouble, but would their source help the police track her down? There was the diary too. What did CF mean? Was it where she got the pills? And who was the mysterious M Cassie seemed keen to be linked to?

She had access to a bit of money from her job so she could have bought a bus or train ticket. Had the police checked it out? If so, what had they found? Her school uniform would stand out so she'd likely change clothes: perhaps what was in her second bag, instead of her work clothes. But where would she change? It must have been after she'd got off the bus. Toilets were the obvious place.

Beatrice pulled out her notepad and scribbled down the questions she'd thought of and who might have the answers. Once she'd spoken to Cassie's friends and the school she'd know what was still unanswered and could go back to the Saunders if necessary. The questions only the police knew the answers to were another matter. Beatrice wondered about DC Wilde, the smiling woman who had said little during Fisher's interview, but had made an impression. Her departing thumbs up suggested she might have some sympathy with Beatrice. Would she be willing to share the results of the police enquires? Or be allowed to? It could be worth asking.

She finished her tea and took the cup to the counter, asking for directions to any public toilets. She came out of the café and headed to the first set. The ladies were attached to the market building. They were old with three cubicles but they were clean enough. The sign outside listed closing time as 5 p.m. Cassie could have made it to them before they closed. A quick change no one would notice, then off to wherever she'd decided to go. If she planned to leave the city, the train to Nottingham would have connected her with train lines to anywhere else in the country. But wouldn't the police have seen her on the station CCTV?

The other set of toilets were in a small shopping centre. They were much cleaner but busier, with the cleaners popping in and out frequently. It wasn't a good place to spend a lot of time if you didn't want to be noticed. There were security cameras in the centre too. If Cassie had thought much about it and didn't want to be found it, was another reason for using the older facilities.

At the public library a helpful librarian found her copies of all the local papers from the previous week. Beatrice sat with her notebook and went through each one. The police had done a good job of getting coverage. Cassie's picture featured somewhere in all of them. The story was most prominent in the county-wide paper the Lincolnshire Weekly. A reporter had managed to pull together a long article from the little information available. The only thing new to Beatrice was the reporter's claim to have spoken to some of Cassie's friends, who'd said she was a popular girl and well liked. Beatrice made a note of the reporter's name - Peter Evans - and the address of the newspaper offices.

Having checked online that the offices of the Weekly were open, Beatrice returned to the High Street and walked along it until she reached the High Bridge Café. It was a Tudor structure, built upon the bridge crossing the water, which flowed from the Brayford Pool area of the city. Passing the far side of the café, Beatrice ducked as she skipped lightly down the stone steps of a passageway. She followed the watercourse, covered with a blanket of swans, and through an underpass to where the water opened out into a large pool. Beatrice could see the Lincoln University campus across the water, but she turned away from it to the busy road instead. According to its website the offices were in the bottom of a building towards the railway level-crossing. Beatrice walked along keeping a careful look-out, but the large sign outside made it easy to find.

'Do you have an appointment?' The young man at reception smiled politely at her request.

'No, but I was hoping Mr Evans could spare me ten minutes. It's about a story he wrote.'

'Which one? He writes a lot.'

'The one about Cassie Saunders; the girl from Sudbrooke who's missing?'

'I'll see if he's around. What's your name?'

'Beatrice Styles.'

'Please take a seat.' He pointed to a pair of sofas across the room.

Beatrice stepped away from the desk and made herself comfortable on a sofa whilst the receptionist telephoned through and held a quiet conversation, all the time watching Beatrice. She waved at him and he looked away. After a few moments, he called out to her.

'I'm sorry but Mr Evans is very busy this morning. He said if you have any information to take it straight to the police.'

Beatrice knew she was being fobbed off. She'd need to give him a reason to speak to her. She handed over a business card. 'Can you do me and Mr Evans a favour please and show him this? Tell him it could be the start of a beautiful friendship.'

Jake peered at the card and raised his eyebrows. 'This is you?'

'Yes.'

'Ok. I'll be back in a minute.' He disappeared through a door into the main office through which Beatrice caught a glimpse of desks piled high with papers.

Barely five minutes later a man appeared and poked his head around the door. When he saw Beatrice he paused for several seconds, assessing her, before walking over. He looked around forty. He had dark, curly, thinning hair: the lack of which he was trying to make up for with a large, unkempt beard. His beige suit looked crumpled, as if he'd been sleeping in his car, and his eyes were red.

'You must be Beatrice.' He held out his hand.

Beatrice shook it. 'And you must be Peter.'

'Urgh,' he said as he tilted his head up to look at her. 'Only my mother calls me that. Pete will do fine.'

'It's nice to meet you, Pete. I'll try not to take up too much of your time. Is there somewhere private we can talk?'

'Come on through.' He took her into the office. The reporters and other team members worked in a chaotic, open-plan office environment, but there were a couple of rooms set aside for meetings and Pete led her to one.

'What can I do for you?' he asked as they both sat. 'It's about the Saunders kid, right?'

'Yes. Cassie. Look I want to talk to you, but I don't want anything we discuss to appear in the paper unless I've agreed to it.'

'Why would you worry about what I write?'

'Because this is the county paper and I've got investigations to conduct without them getting messed up by information getting into the wrong hands.'

Pete looked at Beatrice thoughtfully. 'You know, there's not many PIs in this area.'

'I know.'

'You mentioned something about a friendship. How'd you see that going then?'

'We're both in the business of obtaining information, right?'

He nodded.

'Well, I think there will be times we could help each other out. If you give me a bit of information, which will only be a few minutes of your time, maybe in the future I could reciprocate.'

Pete appeared to be thinking it over as he stroked his beard, dislodging crumbs onto his shirt.

'We are talking about a missing kid,' said Beatrice. 'I'd have thought you'd be happy to help, if you could.'

'What the hell?' said Pete. 'Wait here. I'll get my file. But this goes two ways remember.'

He was back quickly with a thin sheaf of papers. 'What do you want to know?'

'I'm sure you're aware that there's been no sighting of Cassie since Friday the fourth. Her parents are extremely worried. Despite everything the police have done and all the publicity, including yours, there hasn't been a hint of where she could be.'

'Is that who you are working for? The parents?'

'Yes.'

'What makes you think I can help? It's no use getting another article in the paper. Until there's anything new, my editor won't want to know.'

'As far as I can see the police have followed all the obvious things up. I noticed though you spoke to some girls who said they were friends of Cassie.'

'Oh yeah, them.'

'Who were they?'

'They were from the restaurant where she worked. Said they were friends of hers. Didn't seem to know much about her though.'

'What did you make of them?'

'My main impression was that they were both orange with hair straightened to within an inch of its life.'

'Orange?'

'Yeah. What is it with these kids and fake tans? Don't they know what they look like?' Pete shook his head. 'Anyway, they liked the attention alright. Wouldn't talk to me to start with, looked at me like

I was dirt, until I showed them my Press ID. Then they became very friendly.'

'Did they tell you anything that you didn't put in the article?'

'Hang on.' Pete pulled a scuffed notebook out of his jacket pocket and leafed through. 'Here we are. Yeah, I remember. They said that she was secretive. The taller one said Cassie wasn't the sweet innocent people thought she was.'

'What did she mean?'

'I don't know. I asked, but she clammed up then. I don't know if she made it up to sound interesting or if she knew anything. Probably the former, I thought. How's the search going?'

'I'm just starting.' Beatrice stood up. 'Thanks for your time, I appreciate it.'

'Not so fast,' said Pete.

Reluctantly Beatrice returned to her seat.

'So,' he said. 'Now I've given you what you want, perhaps you could tell me about Simon Bayfield.'

'Pardon?'

'Let's not have any funny business. I know you found his body.'

'How?'

Pete waved away the question. 'I have my sources. I am a reporter.'

'I can't tell you anything, the police told me to keep my mouth shut. Not that there's much to tell.'

'I can get all the details about his death elsewhere. What I want to know from you is why you were there. I was told your name, but not that you were a detective. I recognised it when I got your card.'

'So that's why you agreed to talk to me?' Beatrice shook her head. She should have known.

'Did you know him?'

'No.'

'So why were you at his house? You were working for him? I won't publish anything without your approval. You can trust me.'

Beatrice wasn't so sure. 'I don't know why I was there.'

'Come on.'

'Seriously. He phoned me the week before and we made an appointment. He wanted me to do something for him, but he wouldn't say what it was over the telephone.'

'Could be a good story there.' Pete scratched his beard. 'Look if you do find out why he called will you let me know? His Sunrise development was big, contentious news around here. If it's to do with that I could do at least one article.'

'I don't see how that's going to happen. He is dead.' She wondered about Sunrise, but didn't want to ask Pete and be in greater debt to him.

'Just don't forget about me. Here's my mobile number.' Pete handed her a business card. 'Try to come with something for me next time you want information from me.'

Chapter 8

Sunita sat on the sofa between her parents, still wearing her school uniform. She was a short, slim girl, with long, black hair and a warm complexion. She held her hands clasped in front of her, knuckles pale, as she stared at the floor. Her hair hung like a curtain across part of her face. Beatrice had arrived at exactly six o'clock, as agreed. She'd been ignored by Sunita when shown into the room by Mr Banerjee and asked to sit. He was a short, slight man, in his late-forties. His almost smooth head showed a few wisps of black hair. He looked nervous, shifting in his seat and kept grinning at Beatrice, throwing her small fleeting smiles whenever she happened to glance his way. He looked across at his wife every now and then as if waiting for some signal from her.

In contrast, Dr Banerjee, as she insisted she was called, looked at ease. Taller than both her husband and daughter, she sat back in her seat, a glass of wine in one hand and her legs straight out in front of her, crossed at the ankles. She wore a black skirt-suit and a white blouse. Her face was relaxed as she stared across at Beatrice, sipping her drink. Allowing the silence to continue Beatrice looked around the room. It was similar in taste and layout to the Saunders'. The only point of difference she could see was a table in one corner which appeared to have a small metal bell, some ornaments and a framed picture of what Beatrice thought may have been Krishna.

Beatrice could see that neither Sunita nor her father was going to talk without permission. She was used to dealing with lots of different people in her old work investigations, but Dr Banerjee was one of the few people she'd taken an instant dislike to. There was an arrogance and sense of superiority in her looks. The way her family responded to her didn't encourage Beatrice to think any better of her either.

Reminding herself of why she was there and thinking of Cassie and her parents, Beatrice resolved to get on with the interview and to do her best to focus. She had to remember she was there for information and that was all.

Beatrice addressed Dr Banerjee. 'I believe that Natalie explained who I am and why I'm here?'

'Yes,' said the woman, continuing to sip her drink with studied unconcern. She waited.

Beatrice ploughed on. 'So, I've come to ask Sunita about Cassie.' She looked across at the girl - who still had her head bowed - and then back to the dominating woman. 'Natalie and David are worried about her, as I'm sure you can appreciate. I understand the girls are close friends.'

'They were. But Sunita will not be associating with her when she finally decides to come home in disgrace.'

In her peripheral vision Beatrice detected Sunita's head drop further and Mr Banerjee's hand slipped down to fleetingly touch his daughter's leg. 'You said 'in disgrace' Dr Banerjee. Do you think you know where she is then, what she's doing?'

'No, of course not. But it appears she is the kind of girl who lies to her parents and is allowed to run around uncontrolled. Not the sort of girl Sunita is going to have as a friend.' Dr Banerjee pulled herself forward to sit on the front of her seat. 'The police have been here already, asking their questions.' She wagged a finger at Beatrice. 'It makes no sense for you to come as well. I don't know what they think it will achieve. We don't know where that girl has gone. It is nothing to do with us.'

'Natalie and David feel the need to do something, anything, to try to find their daughter. Can you understand that?' Beatrice looked intently at the woman. 'If Sunita was missing, wouldn't you do whatever you could to find her?'

Dr Banerjee placed her glass on the side table and folded her arms. 'I know where Sunita is all the time. The Saunders should never have let Cassie take on the job at the restaurant.' She spoke with absolute certainty.

It was clear she felt that Cassie's parents were responsible, even if indirectly, for her disappearance. Beatrice, despite her dislike, hoped this inflexible woman wouldn't have to learn the hard way, like she herself had, how unforeseen and random events could turn a person's life upside-down. Beatrice was surprised though at the lack of empathy or sympathy from the doctor. In her profession she was meant to be able to show compassion for others. Did she think her patients deserved their illnesses? Or was she a good doctor with a blind spot when it came to parenting?

'Dr Banerjee, do you think that Mr and Mrs Saunders are responsible for their daughter going missing?'

'Of course not.'

'Then what did you mean?'

The woman looked a little uncomfortable. She was probably not used to being challenged. 'Nothing at all.' She picked her wine glass up. 'I thought you were here to talk to Sunita.'

'I am. Perhaps I can speak to her alone?'

Mr Banerjee moved as if to get out of his seat, but his wife glared at him and he settled back down.

'That won't be necessary. We don't have secrets in this house.'

Beatrice held her gaze for a few seconds, before turning her attention to the girl who was still intent on examining the floor. 'Sunita?' she said, waiting until the girl looked at her. Beatrice smiled. 'Did Cassie tell you anything about that Friday? About what her plans were?'

Sunita shook her head.

'Did she say where she was going?'

'No,' muttered Sunita.

'Was she meeting anyone?'

'No.'

Beatrice bit her top lip in frustration. 'Did she have a boyfriend?'

'No.'

Dr Banerjee stood up. 'That's enough. We've told the police everything we know, which is nothing. Sunita didn't know what Cassie was up to.'

Sunita glanced up at her mother, her cheeks reddened, then looked across to Beatrice and realised that she was being watched. She took a keen interest in the carpet again.

'Our evening meal is almost ready, so I'd like you to leave now. My husband will show you out.'

Beatrice knew she was not going to get anything useful whilst Dr Banerjee was present. She'd have to find a way to speak to the girl alone and discover what she was hiding. Beatrice stood up, closed the empty page in her notebook and glared at the other woman.

'Thank you for your time,' she said doing her best, but failing to keep the anger out of her voice. 'I'm sure Natalie and David will be pleased to know they have such a caring friend. That in their time of need you've jumped at the chance to help them.' Beatrice saw the words register in the shocked expression on the woman's face? 'It's good to know who you can rely on in a crisis.' Before Dr Banerjee could reply Beatrice headed for the exit. 'I can show myself out.'

Angry and frustrated Beatrice walked back to her car, which she'd left in a car park behind the main street of the village. Her feelings gave her speed and it felt like no time at all before she was back with her keys in hand. Pausing she realised she hadn't any idea of what she was going to do next. She also needed to think more sensibly, which meant calming down. A walk always helped her to get her thoughts straight. She could check out the village and think about what to do next.

Nettleham was a village to the North of Lincoln. It was around one mile west of Rosie's home in Sudbrooke. Beatrice wandered in a random way around the streets, sometimes covering the same ground again, but she was building up a better understanding of the layout and facilities on offer. It was much better served than many villages: there were a good number of shops, including a Coop, hairdressers and fish & chip shop. There was even a small library, though an angry Rosie had told her that most of the libraries in the county were now run by volunteers after the council slashed their funding. Several pubs and takeaways complimented, or at least competed with, the Copper Kettle where Cassie worked. At some point she'd go inside the restaurant to talk to Cassie's boss, but it was clear from the signs outside service was due to start and they'd be too busy to speak to her.

It was a warm, pleasant evening. The atmosphere in the picturesque village was calming and as she walked Beatrice thought more about her encounter with the Banerjees. They were only one source of information. The visit to Cassie's school the next day would give her more people to talk to about where Cassie had been going in town that Friday night.

Beatrice remembered that the police headquarters were somewhere in the village. She looked at her watch. It was getting late but maybe she'd be able to get her statement signed. She stopped a middle-aged couple walking their friendly, podgy Labrador to ask for directions.

As instructed she followed the stream which cut across the village. A narrow path ran next to it behind some of the houses and the shallow water gurgled away next to her. She soon found herself outside the police headquarters. It was a large, ugly building; designed with function in mind and little attention given to its appearance.

At the reception desk sat a woman who wasn't hopeful about anyone being left in CID, let alone DC Wilde. 'It is rather late,' she said, picking up the phone and dialling.

'I was nearby anyway so thought I'd call in. I can always come back another time.'

The receptionist held up her finger to silence Beatrice as someone answered the phone. 'Good evening. There is a Ms Styles here to see DC Wilde. She has a statement to sign. Ok, thank you.' She replaced the receiver and smiled at Beatrice. 'It's your lucky day, she's still here. Take a seat and she'll be down soon.'

Ten minutes later DC Wilde bustled into the reception area. 'I'm so sorry to keep you waiting. I was on my way down when I got dragged into something else. How are you?'

Beatrice stood up and shook hands with her. 'I'm fine thank you.'

'No lasting effects then?' DC Wilde studied Beatrice's face from below as if she were trying to detect signs of distress.

'Well, I haven't forgotten the experience, but I'll be alright.'

'I'm glad to hear it. If you'd like to follow me, we can get this done.' She waved the file in her hand. 'There's an interview room through here we can use.'

Beatrice was disappointed. She had looked forward to seeing what a real CID office looked like. Her only experiences had been from watching TV. She followed DC Wilde into a small office, furnished with a desk, four chairs and a telephone. A window looked out over the car park. Clearly not a room they used to interrogate suspects.

Susan laid the file on the desk and placed a pen on top. 'You need to have a careful read through before signing in the spaces provided. And I'll need you to initial each page. Make sure you're happy that everything it says is correct. We can change any mistakes or add anything extra to it.'

Beatrice sat down in front of the file and pulled out several sheets of paper. She was surprised at its length. She didn't remember saying anything much at the time. It felt odd being on the other side of interview notes for a change.

'Would you like a drink?' asked DC Wilde. 'I'm having one so it's no problem.'

'Oh, yes please. Tea would be great. Milk no sugar.'

'You sound like someone's offered you manna from heaven. The tea here isn't that great.'

'I've had a stressful meeting this evening. Anything warm and wet would be good.'

'I'll get us both a drink. You start reading.'

It didn't take long for Beatrice to read through the statement. DC Wilde had written a clear account and there was nothing Beatrice wanted to alter or add. Though it was purely factual, it caused Beatrice to recall some of the shock she had felt at coming across the body. She signed and dated each page of the statement, wrote her name clearly in block capitals and passed it back to the DC who had returned with two mugs.

'Thanks.'

'You're welcome.' Beatrice sipped her tea. It was worse than she'd expected and she soon put it aside.

The younger woman grinned at her. 'It is terrible, isn't it?'

'I think it might be the worst I've ever tasted,' said Beatrice smiling back. She sat back in her seat sensing the other woman wanted to chat.

'It's better than nothing though, which is the alternative. No one has been able to work out how it can taste so bad. It's teabags and water. How can it go wrong?'

'It is quite an achievement, when you think about it.'

'I suppose so,' said the DC, placing her cup on the desk. 'How long have you been a PI then?'

'Why do you want to know?'

'I'm interested. This isn't an interrogation. I'm not taking notes. We're just talking.'

'Well, if you must know Simon Bayfield was going to be my first client.'

'He was?'

'Yes.' Beatrice sighed. 'I wasn't expecting to find him dead.'

'That's bad luck.'

'More for him, though it's not the start I was hoping for.'

'You said you'd had a meeting this afternoon though. You've got another client?'

'Yes.'

'Look, Ms Styles...,'

'Beatrice. Call me Beatrice.'

'And you can call me Susan, but not when the boss is around please. Don't want him thinking we're too friendly.'

'Sure.'

'What I was going to say is, you should be careful. Fisher is annoyed with you right now. You showed him up. It doesn't matter that he deserved it, he'll be looking for a way to get back at you.'

Beatrice folded her arms. 'I only reacted to Fisher because I was still upset at finding the body. He was being a bully.'

'I know. But you need to think about the future. If any of your investigations overlap with ours you'll have to decide what to tell us and what to keep to yourself. Fisher could make life difficult for you, particularly if you withhold information. You'll be held responsible for any fallout.'

'It's all got rather serious.'

'I'm sorry. I didn't mean to come down hard on you.' Susan sipped at her tea, grimaced and put it back down. 'I don't want to see you get into trouble, that's all. Tell me about this investigation you've got.'

'You already know about it.'

'Oh bugger.' said Susan whose attention had been caught by something outside.

'What is it?'

'Fisher's back.'

'I'd better go.'

'Give him time to get in the building and up to the office. Then you can nip out quick before someone in CID tells him I'm down here with you.' Susan regarded Beatrice for a few moments. 'Go on. You were telling me about your investigation.'

'You know Cassie Saunders?'

'Of course.'

'Her parents have asked me to search for her.'

Susan put her elbows on the desk and put her chin in her hands. Beatrice met her steady gaze. 'I see,' said Susan. 'They're unhappy with what we've done?'

'They feel it's out of their control. They wanted to be doing something to find her.' Beatrice hesitated. 'They seemed a bit worried that you thought they're involved in her disappearance. That maybe you won't look hard enough at other possibilities.'

'I see,' Susan repeated.

'It can't hurt if I'm looking for her too, can it? I might even be able to do something useful.' Beatrice lay her hands flat on the desk and tilted her head to one side. 'Look, is there anything you can tell me about what you've found?'

Susan sighed. 'I suppose I can tell you what's in the public domain. When anyone sixteen and under goes missing we have a set of procedures to follow. You can look up the details online, but broadly we assess the level of risk and take action accordingly. It makes sure none of the standard stuff gets missed. For example, we get the name and a picture out in the papers and on social media as soon as we can. We tell the neighbouring police authorities and notify social services in case they've already had contact with the family, or need to get involved at some point. That sort of thing. You can take it from me, we've done everything we could.'

'But the trail went dead after the bus station?'

Susan nodded.

'Thanks.'

'You'd better go. Fisher should be safely tucked away in the office now.'

'Is there a back way out?'

'No. You'll be fine, but Beatrice?'

'Yes?'

'Take this.' Susan handed her a business card. 'You find out anything about Cassie you have to tell us.'

Beatrice swallowed and nodded. 'Of course,' she said, then left in a hurry. If Fisher really was out to get her, admitting removing the pills and diary from Cassie's bedroom wasn't a good idea. If she didn't get anywhere she could always go back to the house and pretend she'd only just found them. It's not like anyone else would know. On the other hand if she was caught with the drugs and charged with possession, her new career would be over before she'd solved her first case.

Chapter 9

Beatrice forced herself out of the car and knocked on the door. The familiarity of the route she'd taken on the day she found Simon's body filled her with a sense of foreboding. She half expected no answer to her knocking, but in a short time she heard the quick tapping of high-heeled shoes on a tiled floor and the door opened. The woman who answered was around forty-five years old. She was a good six inches shorter than Beatrice, of slim build with short, highlighted hair, in a style which must have needed regular attention to maintain. Her bare arms had well defined muscles.

'Mrs Bayfield?'

'Yes.'

'I'm Beatrice Styles. You asked me to call.'

The woman looked at her watch. 'Good grief is it that time already? Please come in.'

Beatrice entered an impressive hallway. A wide staircase rose in the centre of the hall and swept around to the left as it reached the first floor.

'Come through to the kitchen. I'll put the kettle on. Is tea ok?'

'Yes. That would be great, thanks.'

Beatrice followed her and stood in silence, admiring the expensive looking units and island as Mrs Bayfield prepared a tray. When the drinks were ready they sat at a small table, set in a large bay window, overlooking the back garden. Her host had selected a seat with her back to the view, which obliged Beatrice to sit opposite and she could see the path that led to the office, to where she'd found the body. She forced herself to look at the woman instead.

Whilst Mrs Bayfield poured the tea, still without speaking, Beatrice took a closer look at her. She was carefully made up, no doubt using a well-practiced routine, but there were dark circles under her eyes that even a layer of expensive foundation couldn't conceal.

'Mrs Bayfield. I didn't know your husband, but I'm very sorry for your loss.' It was an American-sounding phrase, which Beatrice disliked, but she couldn't think of anything more appropriate to say. She didn't know either of them, so more of a personal offer of condolences would seem false.

'Thank you. Please call me Marina, everyone does. Mrs Bayfield is Simon's mother.' She sniffed. 'Wait here. I want to show you something.' She stood up and left the room.

It was difficult to relate the pile of flesh Beatrice had seen on the office floor in the woods to the photograph in the album. The cold staring eyes she remembered were nothing like the expression on Simon's face in the picture. In it Simon and Marina were standing close together, his arm around her shoulders. He towered over her with a large round face that showed no interest in the photographer. Instead he was looking down at Marina, a tender smile on his face. He looked like a man who knew his good fortune in having such an attractive wife. She was staring out of the picture, looking relaxed and happy. So different to the woman who had opened the door to her a few minutes ago.

'That picture was taken at John and Fiona's wedding two years ago. John works, I mean worked, for Simon. They'd been together for years but resisted getting married for ages. I think their kids just wanted a party.'

'It looks like it was a good day.'

'It was.' She took the book from Beatrice and peered at it, brushing the picture with the tips of her fingers. 'It's hard to believe he's gone, that there's nothing left of him.'

'You don't have children?' Beatrice asked gently.

Marina shook her head. 'We wanted to, but we couldn't.'

'I'm sorry.'

She snapped the book closed and placed it on the table. She pulled a tissue from her sleeve and blew her nose. 'Thank you for coming to see me.'

'You're welcome, though I'm not sure why you asked me to come.'

'To start with I'd like to know why you were here on Monday.'

'I explained to the police.'

'I know you did. I want to hear it from you.'

Beatrice hesitated. Simon wasn't her client. He hadn't got around to hiring her. And there was little to tell anyway, so did it matter if she told Marina the small amount she did know? She made up her mind. She always did prefer being straight with people.

'I had an appointment to see your husband.'

'And you're a private detective?'

'Yes, that's right.'

'Why did he want to see you?'

'I don't know.'

'You must have some idea.'

'I'm afraid not. In my line of work people can be reluctant to talk over the telephone about whatever is concerning them.' Beatrice didn't bother to add it was even more likely when it involved a situation of possible adultery. 'They'll make appointments without telling me what it's about, preferring to do it face to face.' She was stretching the truth a little but she didn't want to sound a complete novice. 'With missing animals, people will open up easily. Anything more complex tends to be done in person. I promise you, I don't know what he wanted to see me about. Didn't he talk to you about it?'

'No. He never mentioned you were coming. He's had something on his mind for the last week or so, but he wouldn't tell me what. I assumed it was to do with the business.'

'He called on Thursday and asked me to come around on Monday morning. He said he'd heard of me through my sister.'

'Your sister?'

'Rosie McNee. She's married to Adam who runs the garage your husband takes – took – his fleet of business vehicles to.'

'I know Rosie. I thought she had a twin?'

'Yes, that's me.'

'You don't look -, Sorry, I'm sure you get that a lot.'

'I spoke to Adam and it seems he'd mentioned to Mr Bayfield I was moving here. He called Adam on Thursday to get my number, right before he phoned me.'

'I see.'

'I did ask Adam, but your husband never told him what he wanted me for.'

'He didn't ask?'

'Well, I understand that Mr Bayfield didn't encourage questions.'

'No that's true. He was used to getting what he wanted without having to explain himself to anyone. When he got focused on something there was no stopping him.' Her lips formed into a small smile. 'I know how Simon could seem, Miss Styles, but he wasn't a bad person. I know he has a reputation, but you'll have to take my word for it.'

'Call me Beatrice.' She paused. 'Why did you show me this?' she asked tapping lightly on the photo album.

'I wanted you to see him as he was. I wanted you to understand he was a real living person.'

'Why?'

'I'll come on to that.' Marina poured them more tea. 'He built himself up from nothing you know. It was just him and his mum growing up. They were quite poor, I think, he didn't like to talk about it much. He wanted to be successful in life, make a lot of money so he could take care of her.'

'What happened to his father?'

'I don't know.'

'Really?'

'Like I said, he didn't like to talk about it. The one time I pursued it he was angry. He said he didn't have a father and it was clear I wasn't supposed to mention it again.'

'But you're his wife.'

'When Simon made his mind up about something, that was it. He decided I didn't need to know so he didn't tell me. I imagine there's only his mother who knows the truth now.'

'Didn't she tell you anything about it?'

Marina laughed. 'Oh no, definitely not.'

'Why?'

'Well, for one thing, if Simon told her not to she wouldn't disobey, not for anything. For another she enjoyed knowing something I didn't. She didn't like me, or the fact that Simon married me. She thought I was after his money.'

'How long were you together?'

'We've been married fifteen years. But it wasn't long enough to convince her there was more to it than me being a 'gold-digger'.'

'Maybe she didn't want to be replaced?'

'I don't know. Look, you're a detective and I want your help.'

'What kind of help?'

'Nothing bad, I assure you. It's just that I don't understand why Simon died.'

'It can be hard losing someone close. I know it can be difficult to accept they're gone.' Beatrice felt her eyes moisten at the memory of her father. She cleared her throat.

'Sorry, I'm not explaining myself very well. I know he's dead and never coming back.' Marina cleared her throat. 'The police said he must have had an angina attack and had run out of pills. But it's not possible. Simon was careful about his medicine. He always had spares. He wouldn't have been without them. You could have called him paranoid: after all his life depended on them.'

'I don't understand.'

'Well, the police told me his medicine bottle was empty.'

Beatrice thought back to Simon lying on the floor; his arm outstretched and further across the office floor was a pill bottle – empty. She'd seen it and briefly thought he could have committed suicide.

'I remember,' said Beatrice. 'Is it possible -' she tried again. 'Do you think he took too many? Maybe by accident?' she hurriedly added.

'Oh, no. They're not that kind of drug. They were for his angina. He knew exactly how to take them, he'd been taking them for years. And there's no need to be coy: the police asked about suicide. Simon wasn't the type. There's no way he would have killed himself. I don't think it's even possible with the pills he took. Besides he'd lost a bit of weight these last few weeks and he was feeling good. I know he was a big man, but he'd started thinking more about the future; what we could do if he retired. He never mentioned it to anyone else, not even his mother, but he was watching what he ate more. We even began walking for a bit for exercise. He was healthier than he'd been in years. He had everything to look forward to.' With shaking hands, Marina lit a cigarette. She offered the pack to Beatrice, who declined. 'Hang on. Did you think he'd killed himself and arranged for you to find his body?'

'I did wonder. Maybe so you wouldn't find him.'

'Well you can get that idea out of your mind.' Marina shook her head and took a long hard drag of her cigarette, blowing the smoke out with force. 'Simon wasn't like that. It's not possible he would do that to someone. What surprises me is how he could have run out of pills. He'd never get down to the last dose. He had spares in the car, in his jacket, all over the place. I'd keep coming across bottles in his clothes when I was sorting them out. I put them back in the bathroom cabinet, so he always knew where there were more.'

'I'm sure you knew your husband best.'

'Yes, I did and that's why it's bothering me. That and why he asked you to come here.' Marina poured them more tea, which was now dark brown. 'I want you to do some work for me,' she said.

'What exactly?' Beatrice sipped politely at the overly strong drink.

'I want you to find out how Simon could have run out of pills and why he wanted to hire you.'

Beatrice studied the other woman's face. She seemed serious. 'Mrs Bayfield,' she began.

'Marina, please.'

'Marina, I hope you'll be honest with me. Why do you want me to work for you? Your husband was not a well man. You said he had angina. Do you think it could be anything other than a bad attack?' She took a deep breath. 'And does it really matter why he wanted to see me?'

Marina bent her head to stare at the table for a few seconds before looking Beatrice in the eyes. 'I know it was angina that killed him. But I can't understand how he could have had no pills left. I know my husband. I know his habits. He wouldn't ever be without them.' Tears rolled down her face, splashing on the table top.

'What do you think happened?' asked Beatrice.

'I don't know. It doesn't make sense to me and I can't let it rest until it does. Can you understand that? Will you help me, please?'

'How?'

'I want you to ask questions. Find out things. Talk to the people who knew Simon.'

'What is it that you think I'll find out?'

'I told you, I don't know. Talk to people and see where it gets us. Find out what he was worried about, why he wanted to hire you. Ask them if they had seen Simon with his pills. Had he said he was running out of them? Please? If you come up with nothing, I won't blame you. But will you try?'

'Shouldn't the police be looking into his death?'

'They don't want to know. They said the autopsy showed Simon died from a heart attack, brought on by his angina. There's nothing for them to investigate.'

Marina looked worn out. She had the same kind of lost look in her eyes that Beatrice had seen in Natalie yesterday. Would it hurt to do what she wanted? She probably wouldn't find out anything, but if it helped the bereaved woman feel at all better, perhaps it was worth it?

'Please. There's no one else I can ask.' Marina stubbed out her half finished cigarette.

'Ok. I'll do it.'

'Thank you.'

'Here,' Beatrice handed her a business card. 'Contact details are on the front, basic fees on the back. There'll be expenses; I'll keep them to a minimum.'

Marina turned the card over and examined it. 'Do you work exclusively on an investigation?'

'Right now I have another one ongoing.'

'Can you postpone it and concentrate on this?'

'I'm afraid not, I'm already committed. I'll only charge you for the hours I work on your case. I'll need a £200 deposit up front.'

Beatrice took an electronic payment using the portable card reader she kept in her bag. The connection to her phone wasn't strong, though it worked well enough for the payment to be confirmed. Marina signed a contract and Beatrice gave her a copy.

'Here's a list I've prepared of people for you to speak to.' Marina pushed a piece of notepaper across the table. 'I'll talk to Simon's mother and let you know when you can go to meet her. The rest you can contact yourself.'

'I'll give it a go, but no promises.' Beatrice took the list and scanned it. It included key people at the business, Simon's Doctor and his mother. 'Can you tell me anything about those on here?' she asked.

'Well, John Jakes is the best person to speak to at the business. He and Simon go way back. They've been good friends for years. He knows everything about how Simon ran the place.'

'They got on well then?'

'I'd say so. They disagreed sometimes about how things should be done, like with the new development, but there never seemed to be any real problems. It was John's wedding I showed you the photo of.'

'Is there anything useful you can tell me about the others.'

'Barney is Simon's Doctor and his friend. He might be able to help. Kerry was Simon's PA. As for his mother, well, you'll have to watch yourself with her.'

It was weeks later when I finally acted. When everyone had forgotten about my painting. It was simple really. It just took a quick push.

We were at the top of the climbing frame. He'd taken to following me around at break times, wanting to play games. I'd climbed up thinking it was too high for him: he was smaller than the rest of us. But he was determined and followed me to the top. I loved the feeling of being high where no one else could reach me. He was spoiling it by being there.

'Shall we go down now?' he asked, clinging to the metal bars.

I just wanted to be left alone, but then I realised: now was the time. Mother had said to watch for the opportunity. Wasn't this it?

'Why don't you come and sit up here, next to me?' I smiled at him.

He looked down nervously, then nodded. Slowly he reached up to the next rung and began to pull himself up. I looked around the playground and found the two teachers on duty. They were both occupied with other children. I turned back to see him sitting next to me. He didn't have the art of balancing, his body wobbled and his leg reached out to push against another bar to steady him.

'We could go and play football with the others,' he said. His face was pale, his knuckles white as he gripped the frame.

The ground below us was far away: nothing between us but air. Keeping an eye on the teachers I wrapped one leg around a vertical part of the frame and let go with my hands. I held them in front of me.

'Can you do this?'

He raised one arm shakily out in front of him. His body wobbled and he quickly grabbed back on the frame.

'Perhaps you should go down, if you're afraid,' I goaded.

'I can do it.' He was defiant, didn't want to admit he was scared. He wouldn't lose his grip for long, I had to be ready. The teachers were still looking away. His hands came up and he looked at me in triumph.

I smiled and pushed.

I watched him fall slowly away from me. It was almost elegant. He called out in fear. I can still remember the sound of his arm breaking as he landed.

That night, lying in bed, I kept hearing the cracking noise over and over in my mind. I felt terrible and hardly slept: the next morning it showed.

'What's the matter with you?' Mother snapped.

I confessed what I'd done.

'I didn't think you had it in you,' she said giving me a rare smile. 'You should be pleased.'

'I'm scared.'

'What of?'

'He might tell on me.'

'So what?' She shrugged. 'Why would they believe him?'

I was frightened, so Mother made me practice looking upset as she pretended to be a teacher accusing me. By the time she'd finished with me I was convincing. It was the best weekend we'd ever had together, and she seemed happy.

Chapter 10

Most of Bayfield Renewables was hidden from the road by a tall wooden fence. On both sides, trees had been planted to make the buildings less obvious, unless you were looking for them. Beatrice drove through the entrance: the gates were wide open. She passed a small, unoccupied security hut. She slowed down to look at the site. There were two main buildings. One looked like a set of offices, the larger big enough to hold vehicles, equipment and machinery. She pulled up into one of the parking spaces for visitors, next to reserved places for Simon Bayfield and John Jakes. Both were empty. There were two other cars though, a red Fiesta and a purple KA. Beatrice realised how little she knew about the energy business and she needed to learn about it fast. She took out her notebook and scribbled points to research about the Bayfields, the business and angina. When she'd finished writing, she looked up and saw a woman come out of the office building, presumably to find out why she was sitting in their car park.

Beatrice walked over to the smartly dressed woman, who stood a short distance away, her arms folded across her chest. She was around fifty and was frowning.

'Good afternoon,' said Beatrice. 'I was wondering if it's possible to speak to John Jakes, please.'

'Do you have an appointment?'

'Sorry, no I don't. I was in the area and thought I'd call in, on the off-chance.'

'Are you a reporter?' She narrowed her eyes in suspicion.

'No.' Beatrice was surprised by the question. Would reporters be interested in the death of a local businessman? Perhaps the local ones would.

'Would you like to come into the office?'

The woman turned and walked away. Beatrice followed.

The reception area was small, but it was clean with potted plants dotted around the room, making it seem welcoming. A nameplate lay on the desk, bearing the name Sandra. The woman sat back in her chair behind the desk.

'You must be Sandra Davies.'

'Yes, that's right. What of it?'

'Marina Bayfield gave me your name.'

'You've talked to Mrs Bayfield?'

'I was with her yesterday.'

'How is she doing? That poor woman. It was such a shock, Mr Bayfield dying like that and they were so close.'

'She's as well as could be expected.' Beatrice gave Sandra a card. 'Marina's asked me to look into a few things, so I'd like to speak to John Jakes, please.'

'I'm sorry if I seemed rude before, but we had a couple of reporters here earlier in the week. They wouldn't go until I said I was going to call the police.'

'Were they asking about Mr Bayfield?'

'Yes, the vultures. The man's hardly cold and all they want to know about is whether the Sunrise development was still going ahead.' She shook her head. 'You wanted to see John?'

'Yes, please. Is he here?'

'I'm afraid he's out. He's very busy, you'll have to make an appointment.'

'When is he available?'

'Oh, you'll have to make it with his PA, as she's decided to call herself.'

'Who's that?'

'Kerry. Kerry Honeywell. She was Mr Bayfield's PA. Now she's trying to latch onto John. As if she's the only one who's worried about their job.'

'Can I speak to Kerry?'

'I'll see.' Sandra picked up the phone and dialled a short number. 'There's a visitor here in reception who'd like to make an appointment to see John.'

Beatrice noticed the lack of pleasantries and abrupt end to the call.

'I expect she'll be down in a moment.'

'Thanks. Are these your plants?'

'Oh yes. I do like growing things.' Sandra brightened. 'They improve the place don't they? Mr Bayfield always complimented me on them you know.' Sandra sniffed and turned away from Beatrice to wipe her eyes.

'Have you worked for Mr Bayfield for long?'

'Ten years last month. He was a good boss.'

'Sandra, was Mr Bayfield worried about anything recently?'

'I don't think so. He seemed the same as usual to me. He always said hello, stopped for a little chat and asked how I was. Such a nice man.' Sandra reached for a fresh tissue and blew her nose loudly.

Before Beatrice could ask more about their relationship, Kerry appeared in the reception area from a door at the back of the space. She was a very slim woman, in her mid-twenties, Beatrice estimated. Taller than average, the curls of her shoulder-length black hair shone and bounced as she walked. Her light blue eyes sparkled with reflected light. Ignoring Sandra she walked to Beatrice holding out her hand for a quick handshake, with a welcoming smile.

'Hello,' she said brightly. 'I'm Kerry Honeywell, Mr Jakes' PA. If you'd like to come with me, I'll see if I can sort you out.' She led the way out of reception and up some stairs. 'Our offices are just up here,' she called back as they climbed a single flight of stairs, with dull grey decor.

Judging from the door nameplates, the upstairs of the office block had three offices – one each for Simon, John and Kerry – and a toilet. Kerry led her into the first room. She showed Beatrice to a seat in front of the desk and took her place behind it.

'How can I help you?'

'My name is Beatrice Styles.' She handed Kerry a card and watched the young woman's reaction as she read it. There was no change in her expression. 'I'm working for Mrs Bayfield.'

'Which one?'

'Mr Bayfield's wife.'

'I see. And you want an appointment to see Mr Jakes?'

'Yes, please. When is he available?'

'I'll just fetch his diary.' Kerry walked out of the room and returned a short while later. She sat down. 'When were you thinking? Next Friday has a couple of spaces.'

'I need to speak to him as soon as possible, sooner than next Friday certainly.'

'Why?'

'For the same reason I need to speak to you too.'

'Me?' Her eyes widened.

'Yes. Mrs Bayfield has asked me to look into some matters regarding the business.'

'Like what?'

'Almost certainly nothing at all.' Beatrice offered Kerry a reassuring smile. 'But, in the circumstances, I'll need an appointment sooner. And perhaps I can ask you some questions now, whilst I'm here?'

Kerry looked closely at the large diary. 'I can squeeze you in with Mr Jakes tomorrow afternoon at 2 p.m. for half an hour. Is that ok?'

Beatrice nodded.

'I don't think either of us should answer your questions until we've confirmed with Mrs Bayfield you are working for her.' Kerry smiled apologetically. 'I'd like to help, but business information is confidential. I've only your say-so that she's asked you to come here.'

'Why don't you give her a ring now?'

'Sure. If you'll excuse me.' Kerry left the room again and Beatrice heard one of the other doors open and then close.

She wasn't surprised or concerned at the PA's reluctance to talk. She would have been privy to a lot of sensitive information in her role and checking showed she was conscientious.

Kerry returned only a few minutes later. 'I'm sorry, but I couldn't get through to her.'

'I'll get in touch with her and ask her to give you and Mr Jakes a call.'

'Great. I've got your number now.' She waved the business card. 'If there's any issue with you seeing Mr Jakes tomorrow, I'll let you know.'

'I'm sure there won't be, once Mrs Bayfield has spoken to him.'

'Yes, but he may have made another business appointment. He does that sometimes and doesn't always remember to let me know. We're very busy with a lot of work on right now, especially with Mr Bayfield…' Her voice tailed off.

'Perhaps you can spare me some time after I've seen him?'

'Of course, that won't be a problem. Shall I see you out?'

'Actually, is there any chance you could tell me about what you do here and show me around? I'd love to understand what goes on.'

'Well, I suppose that would be alright. Mr Bayfield did like people to see the place and I can show you the engineering building. There's nothing confidential there. I don't get involved much in the technical side of things, but I know enough for the basics.'

The room downstairs in the office block took up all of the remaining space on the ground floor not occupied by the reception. A large conference table with seating for twenty people was positioned with picture boards on the walls around it. Kerry led Beatrice over to the first one showing photos of a variety of buildings with solar panels on their roofs.

'Most of our work is maintenance contracts on solar panels owned by other businesses,' said Kerry. 'More people are getting panels on their houses now, so we also service and repair domestic panels too. In the last few years there have been solar farms. They're very large developments where huge fields of panels are created to generate electricity. They're usually on unused farm land. The business that sets them up often doesn't want to keep responsibility for the repair and maintenance so they use a company like ours to do that for them.'

'That makes sense. So Bayfield Renewables is basically a business which services, maintains and repairs solar panels for a variety of different customers?'

'Yes. Until recently.'

'What's changed?'

'Mr Bayfield decided to branch out by creating his own solar development.' Kerry pointed to the other picture boards. 'These explain the process of making solar panels, right through to putting them in the fields. Mr Bayfield used them to show visitors when telling them about Sunrise.'

'Sunrise?'

'That's the name of the solar farm he was planning to create.'

'Sandra mentioned the press were being a nuisance. Is it because of that?'

'It could be. They probably want to know if it's still going ahead with Mr Bayfield dying. Solar farms are controversial. There are some people who like the idea of cheaper electricity, but they don't like it when it has to happen near them. Personally, I'd rather have solar or wind power than nuclear or fracking on my doorstep.'

'Do you think it will still happen?' asked Beatrice.

'I don't know. I guess it will be up to his wife or Mr Jakes.'

Beatrice walked along the walls and looked at the images in turn. They took her through the details of photovoltaic cells which converted the sunlight to electricity and how they were combined to make panels. There were technical explanations of the angle they needed to be tilted at to maximise the sun. She was surprised to learn that even ambient light could generate some electricity.

She turned back to Kerry who had been watching her. 'You said there was some opposition to the development?'

'Yes, because of the site. Mr Bayfield bought a piece of land on the northwest of Lincoln.' Kerry walked over to the last panel displaying a map and pointed to an outlined field. 'See? Some of the residents in these villages nearby are complaining it isn't a suitable site.' She indicated several villages that ran almost in a line parallel to the proposed development. 'Mr Bayfield was trying to get planning permission and some residents were making it difficult.'

'I see. What sort of things were they unhappy about?'

'Noise. Traffic. The usual stuff. I can show you the storage and workshop area if you like?'

'Thanks.'

As they walked to the remaining building, Beatrice asked about access to the site. 'I noticed the security hut on the way in. It was empty when I arrived.'

Kerry stopped in her tracks and glared towards the hut.

'Is there a problem?' asked Beatrice.

'It's Bill, our day guard. He's probably sloped off home for a long lunch again. He only lives a couple of miles away and he uses any excuse for doing nothing. It's not like he's got a hard job. It's the night watchman, who is most likely to run into trouble. All Bill has to do is sit in his hut drinking tea and occasionally letting visitors in.'

'Did Mr Bayfield know?'

'I'm not sure. I think Sandra covers for him.'

Beatrice remembered Sandra had been quick to come out and see who she was when she'd arrived. Perhaps Kerry was right. 'Is there much chance of a break in? Have you had any trouble before?'

'We don't have the same problem as some places, because we don't have large machinery here, but in a rural place like this we need the night security as a deterrent. Shaun's got a great big German Shepherd. A couple of barks from him would be enough to put most people off.'

They arrived at the largest building on the site, made of a corrugated metal – walls and roof. A normal-sized door stood next to the larger entrance, probably used for vehicles.

'This is where we keep spare parts and a few whole panels for the most popular sort, in case a complete unit has to be replaced.' Kerry opened the door and they entered a large space with a high ceiling. 'That way, if the engineers can't repair on-site, they can use a replacement and repair the broken one back here.'

Beatrice stood next to one of the complete panels which sloped from near her knees up to level with her head. Then they walked from the main area into a walled off workshop. The room consisted of a few work benches covers in bits of wire, of panels and motors.

'Thanks for showing me around,' said Beatrice, as they headed back out.

'No problem.'

'I expect I'll see you tomorrow then.'

'Oh, yes, of course.' Kerry turned away and went back to the office building.

Beatrice wandered back to her car deep in thought. There was plenty of work involved in the solar farm development and plenty to concern Simon. Had he wanted her to investigate the objectors? Did he think they might be planning a protest or sabotage? It was certainly an area for her look further into. Pausing she sent a quick text to Marina asking her to give John Jakes and Kerry permission to speak to her.

Chapter 11

The reception would have been more suited to a company's headquarters instead of a school. Beatrice had seen many businesses looking a lot less professional. The receptionist took her name and asked her to wait whilst Mrs Samson was found. She'd been seated for a couple of minutes, when a short woman with chestnut skin and closely cropped hair stood in front of her.

'Ms Styles?'

Beatrice jumped up, towering over the smiling woman. They shook hands 'Yes. Mrs Samson, I presume?'

'That's right. If you'd like to follow me, we can talk in private.' The teacher paused at the reception desk, 'Louise, would you mind arranging a pot of tea and two cups please?'

'Yes, of course.'

'Thank you.'

Beatrice followed her along a corridor of offices, each with a nameplate. They came to the one marked Head and entered.

'The Head is out this morning: she said we could use her office.'

It wasn't large, but it was functional and well organised, or at least it gave that impression, with its closed filing cabinets and neat bookcases. Mrs Samson indicated a chair to Beatrice and sat in the second visitor's chair, next to her. The receptionist appeared almost immediately with their drinks and a plate of biscuits, placing them on the desk and leaving.

'Biscuits too. Lovely. I wouldn't be getting them without you here.' Mrs Samson leaned forward in her chair. 'Firstly, do you have any identification, please?'

'Yes, of course.' Beatrice gave her a business card and the permission letter from the Saunders.

Mrs Samson read it quickly. 'Thank you. So, you're here about Cassie?'

'That's right. How well do you know her, Mrs Samson?'

'Please, call me Julia.' She poured them both a cup of tea.

Beatrice took out her notebook and pen. 'I understand you were Cassie's form tutor.'

'Yes. I was her English teacher too this year, for her GCSEs.'

'You saw her a lot then?'

'More than any other teacher, I suppose. We have morning and afternoon registration, English lessons four times a week and then there were PSME lessons too – that's personal, social and moral education. Yes, I saw her quite a lot.' Julia sipped at her tea.

'As I'm sure you know, Cassie was last seen on Friday fourth May. I was hoping to find out anything you can tell me about her. What kind of person is she? Was there anything that indicated she was planning to leave home or where she might go?'

'I spoke to the police about her and told them what I could.'

'I know, but they haven't been able to make much progress despite all the media coverage,' said Beatrice. 'Cassie's mum and dad have asked me to go back over some of the same ground and see if there's anything that might have been missed. So please don't worry about repeating yourself.'

Julia reached across for a biscuit and nibbled a small piece before answering. 'She was quiet most of the time, didn't like to draw attention to herself. English is a good subject for getting the students to open up about what they think of things. It gives them a chance to explore different issues and debate with others. But Cassie never joined in much with discussions.'

'Was she shy?'

'I don't know. Maybe. She was difficult to get to know. Reserved. She was never rude or unfriendly, but she didn't volunteer information. She'd answer questions put directly to her, but kept quiet if she thought she could get away with it.' Julia dunked her biscuit in her tea and took a large bite.

'What about in registration?'

'What do you mean?'

'When I was at school, quite a few years ago now,' Beatrice laughed, 'we used to use registration to catch up with friends, especially after the weekend. Did Cassie ever talk about what she'd been doing outside school? Did you ever overhear anything she said?'

'She only talked to Sunita Banerjee. They'd sit whispering to each other and didn't mix with the rest of the group. I never heard her talk about going into town or to parties. I got the impression, from the little bits I did overhear, that neither of them was allowed out much. I think I met Cassie's parents at parents' evening. They're older than most of the others for her year group aren't they?'

Beatrice nodded.

'Perhaps it made them more strict. It would explain why she didn't get much of a social life to talk about. It could be that that's why she and Sunita got on so well. Sunita's parents are...' Julia's voice tailed off and she frowned, trying to find the appropriate word.

'It's ok, I've met Dr Banerjee,' Beatrice interjected.

'You'll have an idea then, of how it was for them both. It must have been difficult to make friends because their lives are so different to the others.'

'I'm not familiar with girls of that age. My nieces are much younger and, as I said, it's been a while since I was a teenager. How were they - and in particular Cassie - different?'

'The other kids would go into town at the weekend, shopping and have parties. They talked about the latest things on social media; music, games, celebrities and the like. Sunita and Cassie didn't join in.'

Beatrice made some notes. 'Do you think Cassie and Sunita could have been bullied because they were different? I remember that teenage girls can be horrible.'

'Bitchy, you mean?'

'Yes.'

'It's true they can be nasty to one another. But I don't think either of them was being bullied. We don't have much of a problem with that here.' Julia paused in topping up their drinks. 'Don't get me wrong, not all of the students get on, but we don't tolerate bullying and always act on any hint of it.'

'How did Cassie find school?'

'She was doing ok in lessons,' said Julia. 'She did her homework on time, her attendance was good. She behaved herself. If she does well enough in her GCSEs, we'd take her back for A-levels. She's one of those kids who might suit college better though.'

'What do you mean?'

'Well, in the sixth form they still have to do homework, be in school every day, call us Miss or Sir. At college they get more freedom to organise themselves. They're different environments. It depends on the personality of the individual which is best.'

'What made you think college was better for Cassie. You said she wasn't trouble.'

'Oh no, she wasn't. I got the impression sometimes that, what with the restrictions at school and at home too, she was chomping at the bit, as it were, to have more freedom. More say in what she did and when. I think college would have been good for her.'

'You sound like you're not expecting her back.'

'I hope she's alright and I'd love to see her back here, but there's been no news. It's hard not to imagine the worst after this amount of time. Do you think you can find her?'

'I'm going to do my best. You said you don't have a bullying problem: how about drugs?'

'Why? Has Cassie been taking drugs?' Julia frowned.

'Not that I know of,' was Beatrice's carefully-worded reply. After all, maybe Cassie hadn't taken any of the yellow pills.

Julia began to look more relaxed. 'Good. To answer your question, we've had the occasional problem with cannabis but nothing harder. The police come around now and then with their sniffer dogs. It's good for their training and the pupils don't know when it's going to happen, so it's a good deterrent.'

'I appreciate I'm here on behalf of Cassie's parents, but I feel I have to ask: did you ever have any concerns about Cassie's home life?'

Julia place her cup on the desk and regarded Beatrice, who held her gaze steadily. 'I've been a teacher a good few years now, so I can't pretend not to know the kind of thing you mean. All I can tell you is I never had any concerns of that kind. She had a sheltered life, but I didn't get the impression she was badly treated or frightened to go home.'

'Thank you. I appreciate your honesty.' Beatrice looked down at her notes. 'Is there anything else you can tell me which might help,' she asked.

'No, really, there's nothing. I wish I did know something to help. She's a young fifteen-year-old, you know? Not as worldly-wise as some of the others her age. I don't know how she'll cope out there by herself. I hope she's got someone looking after her.'

'Would it be possible to speak to Sunita here at school?'

Julia shook her head. 'I'm sorry. We couldn't do that without permission from her parents. It's not like you're the police.'

'I understand.' Beatrice closed her notebook and put it in her handbag. 'Thanks for your help. If you think of anything else at all or hear anything from the other students in her classes, please call me. It doesn't matter how small or unimportant it seems.'

'I did wonder if you'd find this helpful.' Julia reached into her bag and brought out a green exercise book. 'It's Cassie's free-writing book for English. We ask the pupils to write about whatever they want during some lessons. It's good for them to be able to express themselves without being judged, so we don't tend to mark what's in there. They seem to regard it as private, so we get some interesting insights into their characters. There are a couple of pieces that might help you understand Cassie better.'

'Thank you. That does sound like it could be useful. I've been struggling to understand what sort of girl Cassie is'

They both stood and made their way back to reception.

'Good luck,' said Julia. 'If you do find her, tell her not to worry about school. We can sort something out to help her catch up on the work she's missed.' She checked over her shoulder to make sure no one could overhear. 'I would say if she had any plans and if she told anyone about them, it would be Sunita. Thick as thieves those two. But a word of advice – get her away from her parents. She won't say anything about what she knows with them around, especially her mum.'

Chapter 12

Mrs Bayfield's home was a long, two storey, stone-built house on what appeared to be an exclusive part of the village. It was large for one person. Perhaps it had originally been their family home. A pavement passed right in front of it, but there was a front garden of sorts – a narrow strip, about a meter in depth, which ran the full length of the house, separating it from the public path. It was filled with flowers. Beatrice recognised roses but didn't know what the rest of them were. She could smell their scents though, which combined to create a unique and pleasant fragrance. A pink climbing rose grew up around the door, attached to a trellis. It framed the entrance making it look like a chocolate-box ideal of a country cottage.

The much older woman who answered the door to Beatrice's knocking stood in the doorway, examining her. Mrs Bayfield was painfully thin and frail looking, but she stood upright, her arm rigid, pushing up against a walking stick. She was dressed in a crisp white, cotton blouse with a high neck, a cameo brooch pinned to the front below the laced-edged collar. An ankle-length black skirt covered her legs. Her white hair was pulled back into a tight bun on the top of her head.

'Good Morning, Mrs Bayfield.' Beatrice held out her hand. The old woman shifted her stick to her left side, rebalanced her weight and shook Beatrice's hand. Her grip was cool but firm.

'You must be Marina's friend.'

'My name's Beatrice Styles, I'm a private investigator.' The woman looked up at her sharply, her dark eyes bright with interest. 'I'm working for Mrs Bayfield, I mean Marina,' she corrected hurriedly as Simon's mother winced at her addressing Marina by their shared name. 'She sent me a message saying this was a good time to talk to you. May I come in?'

'Do you have any identification?'

Beatrice gave her a business card and showed her driving license. Mrs Bayfield clearly wasn't going to be an easy victim for doorstep fraudsters.

Mrs Bayfield sniffed and turned back to the house. 'You'd better come in then.' She strode down the hall at a surprising speed, using her stick for balance.

Beatrice stepped into the house, closing the door securely behind her.

They entered a low living room. It had dark wood beams crossing the ceiling, making Beatrice feel as if she was going to bang her head at any moment. As she walked, she kept her head bowed in case she misjudged the height. The room was crammed full of furniture, which looked too large for the space. Beatrice didn't think she could stand living in a house which felt so crowded. There was a good-sized window onto the neat back garden, but it was crossed with leading. Everything, including the carpet and furniture, seemed to contribute to making the room feel dark, overcrowded and oppressive.

Simon's mother sat in a wing-backed chair. She pointed her stick at one end of the sofa. 'Sit down then.'

Beatrice sat, thinking about how best to broach what must be a painful subject. She decided the old woman was made of stern stuff and was unlikely to tolerate anything other than a direct approach. 'Mrs Bayfield, first I'd like to say that I'm sorry about your son's death. I don't know what Marina has told you, but as I said at the door, I am a private investigator. She has asked me to work for her.'

'What does she want you to do? And what's it to do with me?'

'She's very upset at the death of her husband. Your son.' Mrs Bayfield sniffed loudly. 'She's also not happy at the circumstances of his death and she has asked me to find out more about it. In particular, Mr Bayfield had wanted to hire me for some work and Marina would like to know what that was.'

'What do you mean not happy? The police were called and said he died of a heart attack. Does the foolish woman think they lied?'

'In all honesty I don't believe she knows what to think. But she has asked me to speak to people who knew Simon to find out anything I can.'

'Miss Styles…'

'Please call me Beatrice.'

'I'd rather not, thank you. Where was I? Oh, yes. Miss Styles, my relationship with my son's wife has not been a close one, for reasons I have no intention of going into with you. However, you should know that I have been told almost nothing about my son's death. I was informed by two young constables who came here to say that he was dead. They implied it was a heart attack but said little else. I have had a brief telephone call from Marina offering her condolences, for what they're worth, and that is it. She didn't even ask me about how I wanted his funeral. As you seem to know more about the situation than I do, perhaps you would be good enough to explain to me what it is you do know. I might then consider answering your questions.'

It was a long, heartfelt speech and clearly cost her some effort. Beatrice felt sympathy for her position. 'I didn't realise no one had spoken to you about your son's death. I'm sorry Mrs Bayfield, of course I'll tell you what I can, but it isn't much yet I'm afraid.'

'Thank you. Would you like a drink whilst we talk? Coffee, tea?'

'No thank you.'

'Well, I am going to have some.'

'Would you like any help?'

'I'm not an invalid yet. I can manage.' She used her stick to help lever her body out of the chair and strode off to the kitchen.

After cursing Marina for dropping her into an awkward situation, Beatrice took the opportunity to look at the room in more detail. There was a large sideboard in dark wood against one wall and it was covered in photograph frames. Beatrice started there, stooping to avoid a concussion.

The pictures were almost all of Simon at different ages. The small number which weren't of him were of his mother in her younger days. The resemblance to the older woman was unmistakeable. The images of Simon showed him as a baby in his pram and as a young boy in school uniform, right through to him as a grown man at the official opening of his energy business. The pictures of Simon showed him to be a happy child. In most of them he was laughing or playing. There were also some of him with friends when he was younger –in a garden, on a beach with another young man and at a party – but there were none of him with Marina. What a strange relationship the two women must have had over the last fifteen years, thought Beatrice. How did they sustain antipathy over such a long period? And what had caused it? Beatrice also noted there were no pictures of Simon's father. Was his mother widowed, or had she taken on the title of Mrs to avoid scandal? It was clear Marina didn't know anything about Simon's father, and Beatrice thought it unlikely that Mrs Bayfield would tell her.

Having examined the photographs, Beatrice walked, crouching, around the rest of the room, as much as she could with the limited floor space. There were lots of ornaments on the window sill and crammed into every available space: mostly holiday souvenirs.

'Simon loved the sea.' Mrs Bayfield pushed a silver, wheeled hostess trolley in front of her, the walking stick hooked over its handle. On it the cup rattled in its saucer and the teapot lid jingled a counterpoint as it rode over the bumpy, carpeted floor. 'He always wanted to go there on holiday, it didn't matter where in the country, as long as it was by the sea. He would always bring a little something back for me whenever he went away.'

'Is that where all these came from?' Beatrice indicated the pottery animals, jugs and other varied shapes.

'Oh yes. I kept them all.'

'Did he grow up by the coast?'

'No. We lived in Derbyshire before here.'

'How did he come to love it so much?'

'He first went to the seaside when he was a boy, on holiday with me. We weren't able to afford to go away much because money was tight, with it being the two of us. But, we managed a couple of short holidays when he was growing up. He was five the first time. You should have seen the look of his face when he saw the sea. He couldn't believe how big it was. "Does it go on forever, Mum?" he'd ask over and over, never happy with my answers.' Mrs Bayfield eased herself back into her chair. 'Then when he was older he got himself a part-time job and saved up every spare bit of money. He was still in school of course, until he finished his A levels. He was a bright lad. Anyway he got on so well with his job that after he'd finished his exams they took him on full time. It made such a difference to us, once he was earning a good wage. He wanted to spend all his money on finding us somewhere better to live, but I insisted that he take a holiday to the seaside first. People never saw that side of him. He was good to me.'

Beatrice sat back down whilst Mrs Bayfield poured herself a drink. The older woman made herself comfortable in the chair again, adjusting her cushions and sipped at her tea. 'You were going to tell me about Simon,' she said.

'Yes. There isn't much to tell, I'm afraid,' said Beatrice, meeting the woman's eyes. 'I was telephoned by your son last week and he said he'd like to talk about some work. We arranged to meet at his home on Monday. When I arrived I couldn't find him.' Beatrice hesitated. 'When I tracked him down to his office, it was too late. He was already dead.'

'You are the one who found him then?'

'Yes. I'm sorry.'

'Sorry? What for?'

'I don't know. This is a difficult situation, not one I've been in before.'

'Never mind that. Carry on. Where was he? Please don't spare any details.'

'He was near the office entrance. He looked like he'd fallen onto his side. I went over to him and checked for a pulse and breathing. He was cool to touch. I thought he'd been dead a while. I left the office to get a signal on my mobile and phoned the ambulance. They came within minutes, but there was nothing they could do for him. Then the police came. They took me home, so I don't know what they did after that.'

'You must have been in a bit of a state if the police bothered to take you home.'

'I didn't feel too good. But I think they wanted me out of the way too.' Beatrice shifted in her seat.

'Did you get the impression they thought it was anything other than a heart attack?'

'Not at all. The ambulance crew and the police seemed to assume it was something like that.'

'Then why has Marina hired you?'

'She wanted to know why Simon asked me to meet with him. She thought he had been worried about something in the last couple of weeks. Whatever was on his mind could be why he'd asked me to visit. But she also said Simon was in the process of improving his health; he was taking care of himself more. And he was careful with his medication, but there was an empty pill bottle by his body.'

'I thought he'd lost weight.' She nodded. 'He looked a bit thinner. He never said though. So she thinks it might not have been a heart attack then? Perhaps hiring you is the first sensible thing that woman has ever done: if you don't count her getting her claws into my son, which I don't. Very well. What do you want to know?'

'It would help if you could tell me about Simon. You must have known him better than anyone.' A little flattery wouldn't hurt, thought Beatrice. 'What was he like?'

'He was an intelligent, capable man. He made his business himself by working hard, knowing what he wanted and doing whatever he needed to achieve it.'

'Was he well liked?'

'He had lots of friends. He was a powerful man.'

Beatrice wondered how many of the people who called themselves Simon's friends knew him well and genuinely cared for him. 'And what about his medicine. How was he with it?'

Mrs Bayfield pulled herself up again and walked to the sideboard, opening one of the drawers. She reached in and produced a container. She walked back to her seat and handed it to Beatrice who examined it. It was a small, white plastic bottle without a label. Both the lid and the and the curved surface of the container had an 'S' marked. Beatrice opened it. It was half full of small, white tablets.

'The S is how I know they're his pills, not mine,' said Mrs Bayfield. 'They're quite similar you know, if you don't look carefully.'

'Can I take these away?'

'They're of no use to me. He always checked them when he came to visit, gave the bottle a little shake to make sure there were some left.'

'Did he ever take any of them whilst he was here?'

'Occasionally. He came over for dinner once a week. I fed him properly. Do you know that woman never gave him a pudding, or cheese and biscuits? Someone like my Simon needs a proper meal not a plate of lettuce.' She paused, her eyes sparkled with tears. 'Needed, I mean.'

'He seemed to have a lot of medication around.'

'Yes. He didn't want to get caught without them. She's right about that, at least.'

'Do you know what other places he kept pills?'

'There was here. And his car, in the glove box. He would have had some at home too, and the office. And in his jacket of course.'

Beatrice made a few notes and slipped the tub of pills into her bag.

'Did you see your son in the last few days?'

'Yes, he often came to visit me. He'd go home late sometimes because he'd stop off here to see me before her. He'd tell her he was held up at work. She didn't like him spending so much time with me.'

'When did you see him last?'

'It was the eleventh. Friday. The one before he died. He called in on the way back from work. We sat and drank coffee together.'

'How was he?'

'Fine. He seemed fine. The same as normal, perhaps a little more quiet than usual.'

'Did he tell you he was worried about anything? Was there something at work perhaps?'

'No, there was nothing like that. He seemed happy. We talked about old times, when he was young and starting out. He stayed until gone eight o'clock. He gave me a kiss and said "See you later, Ma".

Then he left. I never saw him again.' Tears rolled down her cheeks and she dabbed at her eyes with an embroidered hankie, pulled out from her sleeve.

'I think it's time I went, said Beatrice, thinking Mrs Bayfield would want to be alone with her grief.

'One moment. I want to hire you.'

'Pardon?'

'I want you to work for me.' The old woman's spoke forcefully.

'Doing what?'

'What you're already doing. I want you to look into the circumstances of my son's death.'

'I'm already working for Marina.'

'I don't care about that.'

'She might. Besides what would be the benefit? I'm already being paid to investigate.'

'The benefit, as far as I'm concerned, is that I might get to find out what's going on. I presume that if you're working for that woman then any information you find out you'll give to her, but not to anyone else.'

'That's right, unless it's something I have to report to the police.'

'Well then. If I'm paying you too, then you can tell me what you find out.'

'This is irregular, Mrs Bayfield.'

'Will you do it?'

'I'll have to check with Marina. She's already employed me. If she doesn't have a problem with me sharing information with you then that will be alright.'

'I'll be paying you too though. I don't want you two deciding what I can and can't know.'

'I wouldn't do that Mrs Bayfield and, if you think I would, I'm not the right person for you to hire.'

'My apologies.' She sniffed. 'It's her I don't trust. I shouldn't have included you in that. So, you'll ask her and let me know.'

'I'll speak to her, then call you. The card I gave you has my contact details and daily rate on it. You should have a look at the costs before making your mind up. It will be several days' worth of work at least.'

'Tell her I want to know what's going on. I don't want to have another experience like finding strangers turning up on my doorstep to tell me my son is dead.'

Sitting in her car Beatrice reflected on the interview. She understood the anger Mrs Bayfield felt, and the shock at finding out about Simon's death from the police, but suspected that the situation between the two women was at least as much her responsibility as Marina's. The fragile woman had been holding herself together, but she was clearly grieving. The two people who were suffering most from Simon's death and they wouldn't offer each other comfort. They'd rather be alone with their pain and think themselves the most injured, than share some consolation from another person who cared that he was gone.

And what about Simon? Did he encourage them to get on with each other, to make life easier for all of them? Or was he the kind of man who would enjoy being in a mini tug of war between them? Beatrice didn't know enough about him yet, but she noticed his own mother hadn't used any words like kind, caring or compassionate when describing him. The closest thing had been when she told Beatrice that Simon had been good to her. She had called him powerful. Did he enjoy that power and feel he needed the upper hand in all his relationships or were Beatrice's own prejudices getting in the way of a fair assessment of him?

Chapter 13

When there was no reply to her knock at the door of the Bayfield house, she tried phoning Marina. When there was no answer she began to get an uncomfortable feeling of deja vu. Her first visit had started the same way and ended up with finding Simon Bayfield dead. She began to get an irrational fear that something might have happened to Marina. Shaking herself she forced herself to think logically. Marina's car was in its space and there were no horses in the stable. She looked around the site and saw the horse box parked up by the cottages. Beatrice realised it hadn't been there when she'd found Simon. Presumably that was where Marina had been. Now the horse box was here and the stable was empty so Marina must be out on a ride.

She decided to wait. She needed to talk to Marina about Simon's mother, ask her more questions and check she'd given permission to John Jakes and Kerry to give her any information she needed. Rather than sitting in the car, Beatrice decided to stretch her legs. Resolving to lay to rest any lingering apprehensions, she took the route towards Simon's office. If the police had finished with it then she might be able to get a look inside.

Back in the clearing blue and white police tape sealed the office door all around the frame and a notice was taped to the inside: 'POLICE: Do not enter'. She'd have to get Marina to let her know when it would be possible to go inside. Beatrice peered in the window. It was dark under the trees and there were no lights on inside, so it was difficult to make out much, just the shape of the furniture. It was hard to tell, but it didn't look as though it had been altered since she found Simon.

Pulling away, she noticed a worn pathway leading around the back of the office. Ducking under a low branch, she followed it away from the building, through the trees. After about one hundred metres the wood ended abruptly, and Beatrice came into the open. Before her was a large field filled with tall plants, up to Beatrice's waist. The yellow flowers of the rapeseed were an intense colour on the landscape, especially coming from the darkness of the shaded trees. Their scent made her nose tickle.

She could see a gap in the plants which cut through the field to the other side and she felt like walking. If Marina came back, she would see her car and would hopefully phone: it wouldn't take long to get back to the house. It was another sunny day and she enjoyed the warmth on her face as she ambled slowly, pausing for the occasional sneeze.

After ten minutes, she came to the far side of the field and into the next one. Five minutes more brought her to a main road. Beatrice tried to get her bearings. It must be the A15, she concluded: the road heading north from Lincoln. She contemplated the traffic whizzing by: cars and heavy lorries rocked her on her feet as she stood by the roadside. The noise was intense. Across the road, to Beatrice's left, a van with a trailer attached was parked in a layby. The trailer had an open hatch and a badly hand-painted sign which read 'Breakfast! Drinks! Hot + Cold!' Although she was beginning to feel the first stirrings of hunger, she decided it wasn't enough to tempt her to eat at the grubby looking temporary cafe. She turned and retraced her steps, moving more swiftly than she had on the way out. If Marina wasn't there when she got back, she'd have to get on with something else and return later.

Marina was home. The horse, a large black creature with a flash of white on its face, was in its stable munching on a mouthful of food. It stared at Beatrice as she knocked on the door to the house.

'Oh, hello. I thought you must be around somewhere when I saw your car. I couldn't see you and I was in desperate need of a shower: I assumed you'd turn up. Come on in.' Marina stood back to let Beatrice pass, running her fingers through her still-wet hair.

'Would you mind taking your shoes off please? You seem to have picked up some mud. Did you walk across the fields?'

'Yes.' Beatrice looked down in surprise. 'I hadn't noticed the mud.' She slipped her shoes off and left them neatly paired by the front door.

'We haven't had any rain, but the path holds the water from the crop sprinklers.'

'I'm sorry to be back again so soon, but I needed to talk, if that's alright.'

'It's not a problem. I was just going to have a late lunch. Have you eaten yet?'

'No.'

'Is a tuna sandwich any good?'

'That would be great, thanks.'

'Come into the kitchen and make yourself comfortable. I'll put the kettle on.'

Beatrice and Marina ate lunch quickly. They kept off the subject of Simon, instead Beatrice asked about her ride and interest in horses: she'd never been able to understand the fascination people had with animals that looked like hard work, but Marina clearly felt a bond with her horse. Talking about her ride made Marina seem to come alive for a while. It was a stark contrast to how Beatrice had seen her up to now. Once they'd finished eating she broached the subject of the investigation.

'After your text I went to see Simon's mother.'

'That must have been a treat.' Marina reached for the packet of cigarettes on the table. She lit one and sucked on it hard.

'She was very upset by Simon's death.'

'Well, of course she is. For all her bitchiness and attempts to come between us, I know she did love him. Doted on him really. Made him think the world was supposed to revolve around him.' She blew out smoke and looked carefully at Beatrice. 'I can tell you think I should have been to see her, but I've had that woman interfering in my life for fifteen years. She couldn't bring herself to treat me civilly when Simon was alive – why would she expect me to pander to her now he's dead? It might sound callous, but right now I can't face her. It will be bad enough at the funeral.'

'The reason I mentioned my visit to her was because she asked me to work for her.'

'Doing what?'

'Exactly the same as you've asked me to do.'

'Is she crazy? What's the point?'

'She thinks it's the only way she'll know about anything I find out. She wants to know what's happening in the investigation and doesn't think you'll tell her anything.'

'She wants to pay you for work I'm already paying you for?'

'Yes. But you hired me first, so I told her I'd only do it with your approval.'

Marina laughed. 'It's no skin off my nose. Go ahead. Take her money. I want to know anything you find out before she does though. Ok?'

'That's fine with me. I'll charge each of you half the expenses.'

'Good.'

Conscious she was stepping out of her role, Beatrice still felt the need to say something. 'Are you going to talk to her about making funeral arrangements? It's just she mentioned them.'

'No. Don't look at me like that. I'm not being cruel. Simon left very clear instructions about what was to happen to him if he died. He had it written into his will to make certain. Don't let her fool you into thinking she's a helpless old woman. She's tougher than she looks.'

'Since you've brought up the subject, what happens to Simon's property?'

'We each owned half of this house and his share comes to me. The house his mother lives in is – was – owned by Simon. He's left it to me too, on the condition that his mother can live in it as long as she's alive. If she ever needs to go into a nursing home, the house is to be sold to help pay towards her care.'

'Was Simon insured?'

'We both were. We arranged for it to be enough to pay off the mortgage if one of us died.'

'So you'll own the house outright once it's all sorted?'

'Yes.' Marina stubbed her unfinished cigarette out aggressively in the ashtray. 'Don't you think I'd rather have Simon here? What's the point of a big, empty house I probably won't be able to afford to keep?' Marina wiped a tear from her eye.

'And the business?'

'Simon's shares in the company are left 60% to me and 40% to John Jakes.'

'So you'll have control over it. Does John know?' Beatrice wondered how he would respond to having Marina in charge.

'I haven't spoken to him yet, so I'm not sure. Simon may have told him of his intentions, but he may not have. You'll have to ask John. Haven't you seen him yet?'

'I went there this morning, but he was out at a meeting. Kerry made an appointment for me to see him tomorrow. Did you get my text? She said she wouldn't talk to me about Simon or the business without checking with you and John first.'

'Stupid girl.'

'She's just being careful. I understand there's a big development in the pipeline. I imagine information about the business might be helpful to anyone opposed to it. Kerry only had my say so that I was working for you.'

'I suppose so. Though I'm inclined to think she was being difficult just because she could be.'

'Is that what she's like?' It didn't fit with what Beatrice had seen. Other than an understandable caution, Kerry had seemed helpful, if a little reserved.

'With me anyway. She was fine with Simon. He never had any problem with her. Whenever I rang up it was always a big deal for her to let me speak to him. She liked having a bit of power and enjoyed using it.'

'It would be helpful if you could tell John and Kerry to give me whatever information I need, please. I'd like to see the business records and go through Simon's office too, if that's ok. I'm hoping I'll find something to show why he wanted a PI.'

'I'll call John if he can come over this evening so I can tell him about Simon's will too. As for the office here, the police tape is still on it. I don't know why. I'll give them a ring about it.'

'Kerry showed me around the business. She explained about the Sunrise development.'

'That was Simon's idea. He thought he could make a lot of money out of it.'

'I'm surprised he thought you needed it.'

'We don't. We have a very comfortable life, compared to most people. I think it was the challenge that motivated him. He saw others doing it, and not very well: he knew he could do it better. And he did think we ought to be getting into renewable energy more, as a country, I mean.'

'Did he believe they're better for the environment then?'

'Partly, but what really concerned him was how he thought we were too dependent on other countries for oil. I found it best not to start him on the subject, he was perfectly capable of going on for hours.' Marina was smiling as she spoke. Although her words suggested she didn't want to listen to him on his soapbox, she clearly missed him.

'What will you do about the business? Will you sell it?'

'I don't know. I don't know what to do. It never really interested me and I don't want to get involved right now. I suppose I ought to do something.' Marina stared thoughtfully at Beatrice. 'What do you think I should do?' she asked.

'I'm not sure it's something I can give you advice on. Perhaps you should talk to John?'

'He's not exactly impartial and he was more Simon's friend.' Marina ran her fingers through her damp hair. 'I've no one else to ask,' she said. 'You're not close to anyone involved and you've no vested interest.'

'Well, that's not completely true. Rosie's husband Adam services the vehicles if you remember.'

'Oh, yes. I forgot. You did say. What do you think anyway?'

'I would imagine the employees, as well as people like Adam who are dependent on Simon's business, would feel reassured to know if it is carrying on.'

'I can't run it. Besides not wanting to, I wouldn't even know where to start. Maybe I should sell it.'

'The best advice I can give, where something unexpected has happened, is to not rush into anything that can't be changed. Give yourself time to think about what you want. Do you trust John?'

'Yes I do. He was Simon's best friend from when they were kids at school together. I know Simon trusted him. Though they didn't always see eye to eye on how the business should be run, they both wanted the best for it.'

'Why don't you give yourself some time by asking John to keep up the day to day management of the company for the next couple of months say? That way everyone will know what's going on and can get on with their work. But it does mean you'll have to trust John to make decisions. He may do things that neither you, or Simon, would agree with. As far as I can see, the alternatives are you getting heavily involved or going for a quick sale.'

'That sounds sensible. And John owns 40% of the company now, which means he'll want to do what's good for himself too. I'll talk it over with him if he comes tonight. Thanks.'

'You told me before Simon suffered from angina.'

Marina nodded.

'What was he taking for it?'

'Oh, it's a really long name. I'll get you a tub.' Marina disappeared upstairs for a few minutes and returned with two containers. 'This one is for his angina. He was supposed to take it as the need arose. This one is for his blood pressure. He took one every morning.'

'Thanks. Do you want these back?'

'No. Can you take them to a pharmacy when you've done with them so they can dispose of them safely?'

Beatrice looked at her watch. 'No problem, I'd better be off though. I've got an appointment.'

'Is it the other case you're working on?'

'Yes.'

'Do you mind if I ask what it is?'

'A missing person.'

'It's not that girl from last week's paper is it?'

Beatrice didn't see the harm in confirming it. In fact the more people who knew Cassie was missing the better. They might have seen something. 'Yes. Did you know her?'

'No, not at all. I just read about it. It must be awful for her family.'

'Yes.' Beatrice sighed. 'It's a very difficult time for them.' She stepped out of the house. 'Can you let me know when the police have finished with Simon's office? I'll be in touch in a few days though, to let you know how I'm getting on.'

Chapter 14

At five past four a bus pulled up outside the Co-op and a stream of school children, all in the same uniform, poured off. About a third of them went into the shop. A smaller number made for cars parked along the roadside. Beatrice concluded they must live in the more remote villages the buses didn't cover. There was a lot of laughing and joking amongst the shouts of goodbye. At a cafe across the road, she finished the remains of her coffee, tucked her notebook securely into her handbag and set off down the road she thought Sunita would have to take to get home. She kept a close watch on the children but couldn't see her. Then, when the bus had emptied and pulled away, Sunita was left on her own on the pavement. The girl shrugged her bag over her shoulder, put her head down and began to walk home alone. She walked past the open shop door and didn't look at any of the other children. Beatrice allowed her to get clear of the busier area before catching her up in a few easy strides.

'Hello.'

Sunita glanced at her but didn't respond. She carried on walking, staring at the floor.

'I assume you remember me.'

'Yes. So what?'

'You know why I'm here. Cassie is still missing.'

'So?'

'I thought I'd give you another chance to tell me what you know.'

'I don't know anything.'

'In that case you must wonder what has happened to her? If you care about her.'

Sunita looked away so Beatrice couldn't see her face.

'She's your best friend. I would have thought you'd be worried about her.'

'Of course I am.'

'I think you know something about where she's gone.'

Sunita continued to walk in silence.

Beatrice strode ahead of the girl then turned around suddenly and stopped, blocking Sunita's path, forcing the girl to halt. 'If you really cared about Cassie, you'd be doing your best to help me find her.'

'I do care.' Sunita clenched her fists. 'Don't you dare say I don't! She was my only friend at school and now I've got no one. Do you think I'm glad she's gone?'

Beatrice looked into the girl's red, puffy eyes. 'Sunita, please.' She tried to keep her voice gentle. 'I just want to find Cassie to make sure she's ok. I'm worried about what could have happened to her. Is there anything you can tell me?'

Sunita looked away. She didn't answer immediately. 'I don't know where she is.'

'OK, I believe you, but I think you know something. You're her best friend. The one person she'd tell about her plans.'

'What plans?'

'I don't think Cassie was taken by someone. I think she decided to leave: she lied to her parents about where she'd be Friday and Saturday. She had some sort of plan.'

Tears welled in Sunita's eyes and Beatrice understood Cassie had decided to leave her friend too: knowing she had no one else. 'I'm not interested in getting Cassie into trouble. Or you either. But no matter how much she thinks she can look after herself, the world is a lot more dangerous and complex than growing up in a quiet Lincolnshire village would suggest. I just want to find her, Sunita. To know she's ok. If I do, maybe I could persuade her to come back home.'

Sunita looked Beatrice in the eyes and shook her head. 'I have to go now. If I'm late Mum will come looking for me. It's her afternoon off and I don't want her to see I've been talking to you.'

'I'll let you go, but I want you to do something for me.'

'What?'

'Think over what I've said. Here is my number.' Beatrice gave her a card. 'If you change your mind and want to help, give me a call.

Your parents don't have to be involved. But I'm not going to give up on Cassie.'

Sunita tucked the card into her bra – presumably because her mother wouldn't find it there – and stalked off. Beatrice sighed. She was beginning to have a new appreciation for her own childhood. Both Sunita and Cassie must have found it very difficult growing up in such restrictive homes. It's no wonder they had bonded so closely, and Sunita was clearly very lonely without Cassie. Beatrice was even more convinced Sunita knew something. She just had to hope the girl would come to her senses.

Since she was already in the village, Beatrice walked over to the Copper Kettle, where Cassie had worked two evenings a week. The door to the restaurant was closed so Beatrice went into the pub and asked at the bar. She was directed to the kitchens, where she found a short, round man in his forties. He was unloading groceries from a brown cardboard box onto large, gleaming work surfaces. On noticing Beatrice's arrival he stopped.

'If you want to book a table for tonight, ask the girl at the bar. We don't open until six.'

'Mr Haynes, I presume?'

He nodded.

'I'm not here for a meal. I've come to ask you some questions.' Beatrice handed him a card.

'Private detective, eh?' He looked her up and down grinning, in what he clearly thought was a winning manner.

'I'm here about Cassie Saunders.' The man's expression changed suddenly and he became alert.

'Is she home?'

'No. I'm afraid not. Her parents have asked me to look for her.'

'Isn't that a job for the police?'

'They've not had much luck, so here I am. Can you spare me ten minutes?'

'Sure. Come into the restaurant, we can talk in there.' He led Beatrice into a large conservatory, filled with dining tables and chairs.

The tables were bare. 'The girls will be here soon, to set up, so we don't have long.' They sat and Beatrice pulled out her notebook.

'What did Cassie do for you, Mr Haynes?'

'Paul.' He tried his smile again. 'She did the same as the other girls. She was too young for the bar, so she served food, cleared tables and helped out in the kitchen when needed.'

'Mr Haynes – Paul – can you tell me what happened when you last saw Cassie?'

'Well, it was around this time of day, maybe a bit later. The kids usually stop off in the shop to pick up snacks and a drink on their way for. Cassie turned up on Friday to collect her wages.'

'You weren't expecting her to work then?'

'No. She already told me she wouldn't be able to work the weekend, but she'd call in to collect her money.'

'Was it the day you usually paid her?'

'I pay all the casuals at the end of the month. They're youngsters, school kids, so it's not like they have families to feed. They seemed happy with it.'

'I'm not here to criticise, Paul. I just want to know what usually happened and what was different about the last night you saw her.'

'Ok, fair enough. I would normally have given her the month's wages the following week, but she told me she needed the money early.'

'She said this the week before she went missing?'

'Yes.'

'Did she say, or even hint, why she needed it?'

'Not at all.'

'Did you ask?'

'No. It's none of my business, is it? It wasn't a problem, she'd already earned it. The money was hers to do what she like with. It's not like she'd asked for an advance.' He smiled at Beatrice. 'Can I get you a drink? On the house.'

She shifted in her seat. 'No thank you. I won't keep you long and besides, I'm driving.'

'Perhaps we could do it another time? Or dinner?'

Beatrice looked down at her notebook, uncomfortable with his persistence. 'Did Cassie arrive at the same time as usual?'

'Yes. She seemed in a bit of a hurry, but I'd already got the money ready, so I gave it to her, she signed for it in the wages book and off she went. That was the last time I saw her. She must have been here all of five minutes.'

'You told the police she was in school uniform.'

'That's right. They all come straight from school and get changed here.'

'Did she have a bag with her?'

'I'm sorry, I can't remember.' He shook his head. 'She was in such a rush, she was in and out. And I had to get on with prep for opening time.'

'How did she seem to you? Did she look worried, upset or angry?'

'Nah, she was the same as ever. She was a cheerful worker. I think she liked being here.'

'Can you remember who was working for you that Friday?'

'Yes, it would have been my regular girls. I had Cassie, Angela and Kirsty.'

'I don't suppose they're here today, are they?'

He smiled and nodded. 'They should be here soon anyway. I'll go and check in a minute.'

'Thanks. If you think of anything else at all, something you remember from that night or from any other time, please call me. You've got my number. Even if it seems trivial, you never know what might help.'

'Sure. I will. She was a good kid. I hope she's ok.'

Two girls in white blouses and black skirts walked into the restaurant. Paul Haynes followed them.

'Now, girls, this is Ms Styles. She's come to ask some questions about Cassie. You both worked with her, so I want you to make sure you answer her questions. I've assured her you'll be helpful. Ok?' He raised his eyebrows as he made eye contact with them in turn.

'Yes, Mr Haynes.' The girls mumbled in unison.

'Right. Come into the kitchen once you've finished then.' Paul turned to Beatrice and, to her surprise, took her hand. 'Perhaps, when all of this is over, you could come back for a meal.' He squeezed her hand gently.

'Thank you, but I'm very busy right now, with trying to find Cassie.' She carefully pulled her hand back out of his grasp.

'Consider it an open invitation.' He smiled 'I shall look forward to seeing you again soon.' With that he went to the kitchen. The door had barely closed behind him when Beatrice could hear his voice raised, shouting instructions. He seemed nice enough, but she was relieved he'd gone. James was a much more attractive proposition, if he'd been available.

She looked at the two girls. They were typical for their age. The hair on both was severely straightened so it looked like straw, the only difference in them appeared to be their hair colour. They also wore heavy, orange-tinged foundation and thick eyeliner, which Beatrice assumed must be the current teenage trend. Pete Evans' description had sounded cruel, but it was accurate.

'Let's go over here.' Beatrice indicated a table away from the noise of the kitchen. When they were seated Beatrice began to try to break down the barriers they had clearly put up.

'My name is Beatrice. I'm sorry to be taking up your time, but I'm looking into what has happened to Cassie. We don't have a lot of information and I thought you might be able to help.'

There was silence.

'Which of you is Kirsty?'

The girl with bleach-blonde hair spoke. 'I am.'

'You must be Angela.' The auburn-haired girl nodded.

'Are you the police?' Kirsty asked.

'No. I'm a private investigator.'

'Don't be stupid.' Kirsty laughed.

Beatrice took out one of her cards and handed it to her: clearly she was the boss of the pair.

'Who are you working for then?' Kirsty threw the business card down on to the table.

'Cassie's mum and dad. They're very anxious about her. We all are, and we need to find her.'

'Well we don't know anything.' Kirsty looked straight at Beatrice and folded her arms across her chest.

'But you worked with her. You must have known something about her. You must have talked.'

'Only if we had to. She wasn't part of our group.' Kirsty was insistent, her nose wrinkling in disgust.

'What did you talk about?'

'Just work stuff. You know, which tables were ready to order, wanted drinks, or needed to be cleared, that sort of thing.'

'Don't you have breaks though? Didn't you talk then?'

'No. Angela and I usually went outside. Cassie would go into the changing room by herself.'

'Did she ever mention anything about leaving home? About friends she was meeting or any plans she had?'

'No. I told you, she wasn't our friend.' Kristy flicked her hair over her shoulder.

'Are you sure you're telling me everything?'

'Yes. Why wouldn't we be?'

'When you talked to the reporter from the Weekly you gave the impression you knew Cassie well.'

Kirsty began to shift in her seat. 'Yeah, well.'

'What?'

Finally, Angela decided to speak. 'We thought it would be good to get into the papers. You know, a laugh. So we pretended she was our friend.'

'He didn't put our names in though, did he? So that was a waste of time.' Kirsty shrugged.

'Is there really nothing you can tell me. Her parents are in a dreadful state, surely you can understand that.'

'Look, we don't know where she is.' Kirsty stood up. 'We've got work to do, so we need to go.'

Angela remained seated.

'Come on, Angela.'

'You go on. I'll be there in a minute.'

Kirsty strode off.

'Do you know something?' Beatrice's hopes were raised.

'Not really, no.'

'What did you want to say to me? I assume there's something.'

'It's probably nothing. Once I went into the changing room: Kirsty was still outside. It was cold and I didn't want to hang about.'

'You mean you left Kirsty to finish her cigarette?'

'What! How did you know?'

'Don't worry, I just want to know about Cassie.

'You won't tell Mr Haynes about the smoking, then?'

'No. It's a stupid thing to be doing, but not my business right now. You said that you got back to the changing room.'

'Oh, yes. Well Cassie clearly wasn't expecting me. As I opened the door I heard her saying 'I've got to go', then a beep. When I got into the room there was just her there.'

'And you thought it was a phone.'

'What else could it have been?' Angela shrugged.

'But you didn't see one?'

'No, she must have had one though. There was no one else there for her to be talking to. But we're not supposed to have them on at work, so she wouldn't have let me see in case I told on her.'

'When was this?'

'The week before she went missing, I think. Round about then.'

'Did Cassie have any friends? Here or at school?'

'Just Sunita Banerjee. I never saw her hanging out with anyone else. We didn't talk to her away from the restaurant. Like Kirsty said, she wasn't in our group.

'Is there anything else you can think of that might be helpful?'

'No, I'm sorry.'

'Thanks for telling me about the phone. Take my card in case you think of anything else.'

'Can I go now?'

'Yes. Thanks.'

Beatrice headed out of the pub, thankful that she didn't have to fight off the invitations of Paul Haynes again. The bar was much busier on the way back through. She glanced at her watch. It was almost 6 p.m. so the restaurant would be serving food soon. Realising she was hungry, she decided to pop into the Coop shop in the village to grab a sandwich.

The conversation at the restaurant hadn't helped much, but at least she had learnt Cassie had a phone. She must have kept it well hidden for no one to have seen her with it, except for Angela coming upon her unexpectedly. If Cassie had a phone then Sunita would know about it. Everyone said they were close. Which raised the further question of whether Sunita had one too, one that was equally well hidden. If so, it was a piece of knowledge that was a potential lever to use to get her to tell the truth about Cassie. And, if she could get Cassie's number the police might be able to trace it, if the phone was still active anyway. It also meant that if she did still have the phone and she had gone away willingly, then she was deliberately not contacting her parents. Which would mean she didn't understand or just didn't care what she was putting them through.

Her route took her past Mrs Bayfield's house, prompting her to think more about Simon. It was early days, but she had no idea why he wanted to hire her: maybe John Jakes would know something.

The police had said he'd had a heart attack: could it have been brought on by stress, caused by whatever he wanted her to look into? Marina was worried about him running out of pills too. She could ask the people around him about them, but she didn't see how it could help. It would be a good idea to do some research on angina and his medicine so she could reassure his wife.

Chapter 15

Beatrice, arriving at her sister's home, was immediately mobbed by two squealing girls. Katie and Abbie ran down the stairs and threw themselves into her arms with shouts of 'Auntie Bea'. They were a pair of exuberant, nine-year-old twins. Whenever Beatrice came to see them, she was besieged with demands for hugs and attention. She was honest enough to admit she was envious of how much affection the two girls had for each other. People assumed twins had close relationships, and it was true for Katie and Abbie, but it wasn't for Beatrice and Rosie. They got on well enough, but they didn't have the same close bond. They were too different: Beatrice had gravitated towards their father, whilst Rosie was their mother's favourite.

Rosie interrupted her games with the girls to announce their meal was ready. They gathered in the dining room, where the food was on the table. Adam, the last in, sat down without saying anything, merely nodding in Beatrice's direction: a stark contrast to how she'd seen him behave on previous occasions. After a very noisy meal, dominated by the girls, and during which Adam had remained largely silent, he slunk off to the garage, whilst Rosie cleared up and put the girls to bed. Beatrice put the kettle on and made coffee. When she took two mugs through to the living room, Rosie was already there; sitting in her usual spot, looking glum.

Beatrice sipped at her coffee before she spoke. 'Rosie, what's the matter?' She saw her sister raise her chin to rebuff her, but forestalled her. 'And don't say nothing. It won't wash. Not after that performance at dinner.'

Rosie stared into her mug as she spoke. 'I'm sorry I got mad at you the other day, about not telling us about Simon dying, I mean. You weren't to know.'

Beatrice remained quiet, watching her sister as she plucked up the courage to say more.

'The thing is, Bea, the way things are at the moment, Adam can't manage without the work from Simon's business. Adam always made sure he got on with him, even though he didn't like him much.' Rosie hesitated. 'We don't know what will happen now. What if they decide to move the work somewhere else? Or what if the business gets sold or closed? I don't know how we'll cope.' Rosie had tears in her eyes.

'Oh, Rosie,' said Beatrice. She leaned over and squeezed her sister's hand. 'Is the garage in trouble?' Rosie nodded, whilst staring into her mug. 'Why didn't you say something before? I assume this hasn't just happened?'

'No. It's been getting worse for a while now. With all this uncertainty, people are cutting back and Adam's been getting less work. He spends hours phoning around trying to drum up new business, but it's always the same answer – people are getting essential work done, that's all.'

'Why wouldn't Adam let me pay for servicing my car? I'm happy to. I'd have paid someone if I'd still been in London.'

'You know what Adam's like,' said Rosie. 'Besides the cost of servicing your car isn't going to make much difference.'

Beatrice moved to sit next to her and took her hand. She gave it a gentle squeeze. 'It's that bad?'

'We can pay the bills and put food on the table, but there's nothing spare.' Rosie sniffed. 'I've even been thinking about stopping the girls going to Brownies. I don't know how I'd explain it to them; they love going.'

Beatrice felt ashamed she hadn't realised they were in trouble. Rosie was usually so open, but now, when she thought back there were signs. Why hadn't she said something? Embarrassment?

'Look, I've got some money left over from my redundancy. Not a lot, but it will help I'm sure.'

'Don't.' Rosie shook her head. 'Adam would hate that. You know he would, he's the "great provider" after all. Don't let on I told you, please? Anyway, we can manage as we are for now.'

'I'd really like to help.'

'It's good of you, but we'll have to sort ourselves out.'

'What about if I helped the girls?'

'What do you mean?'

'I could pay for them to go to Brownies. It's not much, but it would be one less thing to worry about.'

'Bea, I couldn't.'

'Why? It's not for you. It's for them. Please let me, Rosie, even if it's just for a few months. It will stop me feeling like such a bad sister and aunt. You'll be doing me a favour.'

'I suppose it is for them.' Rosie sniffed.

'Good. We're agreed then.'

'I didn't say...'

'No.' Beatrice interrupted her. 'That's it. All sorted. End of discussion. Besides, you sent James my way and, now he's going to be my lodger, I'll have a bit more money.'

Rosie sighed and rubbed her face with both hands as if trying to erase the tiredness. 'Thanks, Bea. I'm sorry I got snippy. The money problem is getting me down a bit. And you saw how Adam was at dinner tonight. He's like that most of the time now. Nothing either I, or the girls, do seems to snap him out of it. They know he's being different and it's starting to affect them.'

'What have you told them?'

'Just that he has a lot on a work, which is making him a bit quieter than usual.'

'That can't be easy for any of you.'

'No, but we just have to keep going. What else can we do?' Rosie wiped a tear from her eye.

'Adam must be very worried. If things get better maybe he'll go back to normal.' She patted Rosie's hand. 'One small bit of a silver lining is that I talked to Marina Bayfield today. I think she's going to let the business run as it is for a bit, with John Jakes in charge.'

'That would be good news. Adam has met John a few times, when he's dropped his car off, and gets on well with him. I can't imagine he'd want to change where the vehicles are serviced.'

Beatrice pulled herself out of the chair. 'Well, I'd better get home, I've got a lot of research to do.'

'How's it going with Cassie?'

'Nothing definite yet, but I'm sticking with it.'

Rosie walked with Beatrice to the front door. Beatrice bent down to give her sister a quick kiss on the cheek and surprised herself by turning it into a hug. 'Thanks for tea. Tell the girls I'll see them soon.'

'I will do. Beatrice?'

'What is it?'

'Don't you ever think about her? Mum.'

'Oh, Rosie.' The urge to leave was strong but Beatrice knew her sister needed her. She reached for Rosie's hands. 'Every day. I miss her. I can't get used to her not being around, even after all this time.'

'Me too. I wish she was here to talk to, about the garage, Adam and the girls.'

'I'm sure she'd have given you some good advice. I know I'm a poor substitute, but if you do need to talk, let off some steam, you know how to find me.'

Rosie kissed Beatrice's hands, gave them a squeeze. 'Bye for now,' she said and quickly closed the door.

Beatrice sniffed, ran her fingers across each eye and returned to her car.

When I was fifteen we lived in a ground-floor flat, part of an ugly rectangular block. The council did minimal maintenance. The rooms were dark and damp. The smell of mould in my tiny bedroom was overpowering. In the winter I had a choice of trying to breath only through my mouth or freezing. We had a small garden; the ground was uneven and prone to turn to mud. The grass grew in ragged tufts.

An old lady lived next door with her cats. The cats were friendly and when I was home alone I would stroke them. A big ginger one called Marmalade was my favourite; sometimes he'd let me pick him up and hug him. I loved the vibrations of his body when he purred.

The cats would come into our garden to do their business and it was my job to clean up after them. Mother told me to throw the mess back over the low fence. I did, but I did it behind a bush the old lady had. It was a small act of rebellion against her and I didn't want to antagonise the neighbour, or Mother would have one of her arguments and we'd have to move again.

Another of my jobs was to have food ready for when Mother came home from work. One day I'd been held up in school by a detention. I was late home. Mother went outside to enjoy the last of the sunshine whilst I served up the meal, and from the kitchen I heard her angry shout.

'What the bloody hell!'

The whole street must have heard it.

I rushed out into the garden in time to see her throwing a stone at Marmalade who was scrambling over the low fence, claws scraping on the wood. I was grateful when the stone whacked against the fence and the cat disappeared from sight.

Mother turned to me, took off her shoe and waved it at my face, the stink made my features scrunch up in disgust.

'You might well pull a face,' Mother said. 'It's your fault. You're supposed to clean up their crap.' She shoved the shoe at me and my hands became covered in muck.

'*You can start by cleaning that and then you'd better make sure there's none left out here.*' *She strode into the house and slammed the door shut behind her.*

There was no point trying to tell her about the detention, besides I did feel guilty. If I hadn't encouraged him by stroking and hugging him, then maybe Marmalade wouldn't come into our garden so often and been seen at the wrong moment.

By the time I went back inside, she'd tidied the kitchen. A slice of bread and margarine was on the table with a glass of water. I put her clean shoe away, washed my hands and sat down to eat. She stood watching.

'*You're not going to let that cat get away with it, are you?*' *Her voice was hard.*

'*I don't know how to stop them,*' *I said.*

She stood quietly for a while, thinking. '*I do,*' *she said.*

I had to do it: I had to do whatever she said. I knew I couldn't refuse, so I wanted it over quickly. The following day I stayed home from school. Mother rang to explain my absence as illness.

I knew our neighbour's routine was to let the cats out of the house and then she'd go off to town or to see friends.

Mother had left a tin of cat food and rat poison for me to use...

I wrapped the body in plastic bags, worried about leaking. I spent the afternoon lying on my bed, doing nothing, just staring at the ceiling, feeling the presence of Marmalade's body in a box outside my room. I heard the bang of a door through the thin walls as the old woman came home. Later I heard her calling repeatedly for the cat who would never come home and I remembered what it was like to hold him and bury my face in his fur as he purred.

Chapter 16

John Jakes was sitting at his desk when Kerry showed Beatrice into the room. She recognized him from Marina's photos. He stood and reached over the desk to shake Beatrice's hand. He was a few inches off six foot, a bony spare man. His short, wavy, black hair was brushed back off his face emphasizing the length of his nose and prominent cheekbones.

'Would you like a drink?' John asked.

'Water, please.'

John poured two drinks from a bottle taken from a mini fridge tucked into the corner of the room. There was very little other furniture; a desk, chair, a couple of filing cabinets and a single bookcase. The desk was uncluttered, everything in order. A solitary picture stood in a frame on the desk; John with a woman and two children.

John returned to his seat. 'What can I do for you? I saw Marina yesterday evening. She said I should tell you anything you want to know and let you have access to any business records you want.'

'Although I am now working for Marina, I should have been working for Mr Bayfield.'

'What do you mean?' John sat back in his chair. 'You're a private investigator, aren't you?'

'I am.'

'We didn't have any work for you.' He paused and shook his head gently. 'Not that I was aware of anyway.' He frowned.

'Mr Bayfield called last week, asking to see me. We arranged to meet on Monday. When I arrived I found him. He was dead.'

John gulped at his water. 'So, you don't know what he wanted to see you about?'

'Not yet. Marina has asked me to find out.'

'It could have been business or personal then?'

'I'm keeping an open mind.'

'How can I help?'

'You and Simon were friends. You'd known each other for a long time. Other than Marina and his mother you must have known him better than anyone else.'

'I suppose so. We were at school together for A levels. I'd moved up to Lincoln after finishing my GCSEs. I was the odd one out in sixth form – everyone else had been in school together for years. Simon took me under his wing, made sure I was ok.'

'Was it a rough school?'

'Oh no,' said John. 'No more than the average anyway. My dad had died. That's why me and mum moved; we had to find somewhere cheaper to live. Simon could see I wasn't coping well and we became friends.'

'How did you come to be working here?'

'After A levels I went off to university to study business. Simon didn't do very well in his A levels. He was too busy making money from all his part-time jobs and schemes. He was bright enough, but he wasn't interested. He wanted to be earning, he said, not wasting time for three years. I don't think he wanted to leave his mum either.'

'They were close, then?'

'Very. I remember after our exams we went on a holiday. We'd both saved up for it. He called his mum every day, sometimes twice. We had a good time, but I could see he was desperate to be back home at the end of it. It was only two weeks, but it was too long for him.'

'And what about you?'

'I enjoyed being away.' John smiled at the memory. 'I knew I'd love university. Once the results were through I didn't see much of Simon. I was too busy getting ready to be off, but he was happy for me: said he hoped I did well. Whenever I came back to see mum, which wasn't often in all honesty, Simon and I would catch up. He used to joke that once I'd done my degree I would be able to come and work for him.'

'He didn't think he'd end up working for you?'

115

'Not Simon.' John shook his head. 'He was always clear in his own mind which of us was destined to be the boss.'

'Did that bother you?'

'No. Not at all. He wasn't unkind to me about it. He just had a clear idea of how his life was going to be. In fairness, I never thought I'd be his boss either.'

'So, when you finished university you came to work for him?' asked Beatrice.

'Not straight away. I did some sales work for a few years. We kept in touch. Then after a few years, he said his business was up and running and he was looking for help. Someone with sales and marketing experience, and someone he could trust. Would I be interested?'

'And you were?'

'Yes. I wasn't enjoying my job at the time. I met up with Simon and he told me all about his plans for the future. He knew what he was doing and had made it his business to understand the industry. It came along at the right time for me. Jennifer, my wife, was furious with me for taking the risk, but she's come to realise it was the right thing. I always knew Simon would be successful.'

'Was Simon worried about anything in the weeks leading up to his death?'

John shook his head. 'No more than usual. He was concerned about the protestors who were stirring things up around the Sunrise development. He could handle them, but he didn't like the bad publicity they created.'

'Is the business doing ok? Financially, I mean.'

'Yes. It's fine. We're on target for sales and costs. The planning permission over Sunrise is taking a while, but we knew it would. Of course, there has been a lot in the press in recent months about fracking, which is helping us. Makes solar energy seem more attractive.'

'Would Simon have told you if he was upset or worried about something?'

'To do with the business? I'd have thought so. Which is why I'm puzzled about him wanting to hire you. He never mentioned anything, and I would have expected him to.' John ran his fingers through his hair. 'Are you sure he didn't say what it was about?'

'I'm sure.' Beatrice regarded him carefully for a moment. Was he worried about what Simon might have said or found out? 'Do you think Simon would have mentioned if he was concerned about something in his private life?'

'Well, I suppose he'd be more likely to keep it to himself then. But Simon was very happy with Marina. They suited each other. I really can't imagine that there was anything there.'

'Marina told me Simon had begun to try to lose weight. Is that something he talked to you about?'

'No, he never said.' John rubbed his chin thoughtfully. 'He had stopped smoking though. That did surprise me. I'd always known him as a smoker, until a few months ago, at least. Then he just stopped. Before that he'd often cut short our meetings to nip outside for a cigarette. It took me a few days to notice. When I finally realised he'd stopped, it seemed a bit late to ask about it. I suppose he might have wanted to lose weight too. Marina would know.'

So, Simon had given up smoking, and maybe lost weight. Perhaps he had started to think about the future and his health. 'How careful was he with his medication,' she asked.

'Obsessive, I'd say.'

'When I found him his pill bottle was empty.'

John stared at her before answering. 'He must have taken the last ones, then. It wasn't like him to get low though. Did he take the whole lot? Could he have killed himself?'

'Do you think he was capable of it or had reason to?'

'Not Simon. He loved life. I can't believe he'd want to die. I meant by accident.'

John was the third person close to Simon who said he was very careful with his pills. John also said he was happy in his personal life and her time with Marina hadn't suggested a problem with their marriage. It was more likely the reason he wanted Beatrice to work for him was to do with the business, and she knew John and Simon hadn't seen eye to eye on one thing at least. 'I understand that you had a bit of a disagreement about the Sunrise development.'

John sat back in his chair, frowning. 'Who told you that?'

'Is it true?'

John ran his fingers through his hair, which was starting to look messy. 'Disagreement is putting it a bit strongly.'

'So, what was it?'

'We just thought we should go about it slightly differently. Simon wanted us to take all the risk on by ourselves. I thought we should share it with another firm, especially with the current financial uncertainty. At least we could spread the risk.'

'He didn't agree?'

'No. He said he'd been building up to going it alone on the whole of a development. This was his chance to do it and he wasn't going to let anyone else muscle in on his plans.'

'There wasn't any hope of you changing his mind?'

'Once Simon had made a decision that was it, as far as he was concerned.'

'Didn't it bother you?'

'No. It wasn't me that would lose out if it went wrong. I'm an employee. It was Simon's money at risk, not mine.'

'Except that it was yours at risk in a way, wasn't it?'

'I don't understand.'

'You said that you're an employee. But you're not just that now, are you?'

'Marina told you about the will?'

Beatrice nodded. 'Were you aware Simon had left you a share of the company? Before Marina told you, I mean?'

Beatrice waited.

'Simon paid me a fair salary for my work. If we had a particularly good year, I'd get a bonus too. I was happy with what I got. It was more than I ever thought I'd get in any job.'

'Go on.'

'I was talking to him once about the future. About what we'd both do when we retired. He was talking about cruises and the other holidays he and Marina would take. I told him I'd have to be a bit more careful, not being as well off as him. And he said something like – "I'll see you right, don't worry". I thought I might get a nice pay off from the firm when I retired. I didn't know he'd put me in his will though. If I'd thought about it at all, I'd have assumed he'd leave everything to Marina, and his mum if she were still alive. Though I don't suppose he thought she'd outlive him.'

'You were very lucky, to have such a good friend,' said Beatrice.

John made an indistinct noise.

'You don't think so?'

'He was a good friend, as long as it didn't stop him getting what he wanted.'

'What do you mean?'

'Nothing particular. It doesn't matter.' John stood and offered his hand. 'I've another meeting and have to get off.'

Beatrice scrambled to her feet, surprised at the sudden dismissal. She shook the offered hand. 'Thanks for your time.'

'You're welcome. Ask Kerry to give you the records you want. She can explain how they work.'

'Most of the business records are kept electronically now,' said Kerry as she opened a file explorer on her computer. Beatrice could see multiple folders marked up as invoices, cash book, VAT returns and so on. All familiar terms from her previous work. There would be paper records somewhere to back up the contents of the files.

'That looks like a lot of information,' she said to Kerry.

'Oh, yes. But it's ok once you know what you're doing. Mr Bayfield liked to keep everything organised and clear.'

'Mr Jakes said Mr Bayfield was responsible for the finances. Did he keep these files up to date himself?'

'No. He always got me to do it, but he checked them once a week to make sure I hadn't missed anything important.'

'He must have trusted you to let you do all that.'

'He did, yes.' Kerry checked over her shoulder to confirm the door to her office was closed still. 'I probably shouldn't tell you this, but his last PA was fired for fiddling the petty cash.'

'Really? That's awful.'

'I know. That's why he always checked. It really upset him, you know?'

'I can imagine. Did you know the previous PA?'

'Not much. I worked here for a few months at the same time as her. I tried to be friendly. You have to get on with the people you work with, after all. But I wasn't here very long before she was fired.'

'Kerry, did you know that Mr Bayfield telephoned me to ask me to work for him?'

'No. What was it he wanted you for?'

'That's just the thing, Kerry. I don't know. He said he'd tell me when we met, but he died before he could. Do you have any ideas?'

'No, I can't think of anything. There aren't any problems with the business that I know of,' Kerry replied.

'Do you think… is it possible he found out that the previous PA was up to the same thing again at a new job?'

'I suppose. But she wouldn't do that, would she?'

'What do you mean?' asked Beatrice.

'Well, Emily had been caught already. It would be stupid to do it again, wouldn't it?'

'Maybe, if he thought she was doing it again, stealing, he'd feel responsible for giving her a good reference which allowed her to get another job.'

'I guess he might.' She sounded doubtful.

'It was just a thought.' Beatrice shrugged and gestured at the computer records. 'Perhaps you could explain how these work to me? It's best to assume I know nothing.'

Simon Bayfield had understandably chosen the biggest of the three offices for himself. It was in the corner of the building and there were big windows on two adjacent walls. It was almost double the size of John's and Kerry's offices combined. The furniture was oversized too; suitable for a very large man. The usual desk and chair were positioned in the corner to afford the best light. Aside from several bookcases and a pair of filing cabinets, there was, at the opposite end to the desk, a low oval coffee table, surrounded by easy chairs.

She moved over to the row of bookcases and examined their contents. There were a good number of books on business, renewable energy and engineering. One bookcase was taken up solely with photo frames filled with images of Simon, sometimes with Marina but mostly without, shaking hands with a variety of people. Some were minor celebrities, the rest looked like business people or politicians: an array of women and men with "ready for camera" grins.

The filing cabinets were unlocked, which surprised her. She pulled open each drawer in turn and briefly glanced at the contents. They were business records, consisting of sales invoices and expense records going back several years. Beatrice didn't see how they could help her right now. There was no suggestion yet of any financial problem, so it wasn't worth spending time on them, even though part of her couldn't put aside her old work: she was quite curious to see if the records matched the company accounts and tax returns. Closing the final drawer, she turned to the desk and sat in Simon's chair. The surface of the desk contained only two items: a blank notepad was to the right of Simon's seat, a telephone to the left. The drawers were unlocked, and Beatrice went through them methodically. There were no papers or private items, just stationery in most, but in the final bottom one she found around a dozen chocolate bar wrappers. They were different shapes and sizes, but all were empty. It looked like Marina had been too optimistic when she had thought Simon was watching what he ate. It was difficult to know how long they'd been there, but Beatrice suspected Simon hadn't managed to kick all his bad habits.

The sight of a pencil in one drawer inspired Beatrice. She used it lightly on the surface of the notepad revealing indentations where Simon's pen had pressed hard into the pad. She held it to the light at an angle to try to read the writing. There was a jumble of random letters, stasaph, probably a mixture from different notes Simon had written. Feeling foolish she tore off the top sheet, put it in her bag and returned the pencil.

Chapter 17

The doctor's surgery was busy, so Beatrice waited patiently in the queue. The receptionist was irritated when she found out she didn't have an appointment, but reluctantly agreed to ask Dr Todd if he'd speak to her. Beatrice hadn't been waiting long, when she was told he'd give her five minutes. His room was down a narrow corridor and Beatrice's knock received a "come in" so she entered.

'Dr Todd?'

The short, slight man at the desk smiled at her. 'You must be Miss Styles. Marina told me you'd be in touch. Please sit down. What can I do for you?' His voice was clear and low. Beatrice could imagine it having a calming and soothing effect on his patients.

Conscious of the queue waiting to see the doctor she gave a short explanation of why she was there. She placed Simon's pills on the desk. 'I believe you prescribed Simon these?'

'Yes.'

'He had a large number of them according to his wife.'

Dr Todd frowned. 'And what is your point?'

'Sorry. I'm not questioning whether you should or shouldn't have prescribed so many, I'm more interested in why. This conversation is strictly between us.'

Dr Todd stared at the container before answering. 'Simon was very anxious about his health, which didn't do his condition any good. He wanted enough medication so he could have it in several locations. That way he would always know he had some nearby.'

'That's what Marina said. Is it a dangerous drug?'

'Not at all. It's non-addictive and extremely difficult to overdose on by accident, so I saw no problem with helping him.'

'This glyceryl trinitrate is for angina, I understand.'

'That's right.'

'How is it used?'

'If a patient feels an angina attack start then he or she takes one of these pills and lets it dissolve under the tongue.'

'So, they only take it if they are having an attack, not as prevention?'

'Yes. One pill is usually enough to ease the discomfort, but if it doesn't work, the patient can take another.'

'And they keep going until the pain stops?'

'No. If the second one has not lessened the attack then taking another will do no good at all. In those circumstances the patient should telephone for an ambulance.'

'Do they get told that?'

'Oh yes. Definitely. It's made very clear. I imagine the pharmacists remind them too.'

Beatrice thought for a moment. Simon's pill bottle was empty when she found him. Had he forgotten his instructions and kept taking pills in the hope that they would work? 'If someone takes these pills, but the attack goes on to kill them, will it show in the autopsy how many they'd taken?'

'Please bear in mind that I am not an expert in pathology, but, as I understand it, there is a chemical reaction to the medication in the body and there would be a trace of that. It might depend on how long after death samples are taken as to whether it is measurable. But, broadly speaking a pathologist would be able to give an estimate of the amount taken, though it may not be very accurate. There are a number of complicating factors.'

'You must have been upset to find out about his death.'

'Very. We'd played golf together on the Saturday. He was his usual self. Quite cheerful in fact.'

'Did he tell you if he was worried about anything?'

'Like what?'

'I don't know. Simon wanted me to do some work for him, but never got the chance to tell me what it was. Did he mention anything to you?'

'I'm not sure. There had been something on his mind when we played the week before. I remember him saying something about disliking liars. He was annoyed about something. The last time I saw him though he was in better spirits. I got the impression he'd decided on how to deal with whatever it was that had been bothering him.'

'So it could be that hiring me was what he planned to do. Can you remember exactly what he said about liars?'

Dr Todd shook his head. 'I was just left with an impression of what he said.' He looked at his watch. 'I'm sorry, but I have patients waiting.'

'On a completely unrelated note do you know of a safe way I can dispose of these?' Beatrice took a small packet from her handbag. It was the one she had found in Cassie's bedroom.

Dr Todd unwrapped the pills. 'Do you know what they are?'

'No. But I suspect they're something illegal.'

'Not yours, I presume?' He frowned.

'No. I found them. I'd rather not say where, I'd just like to get rid of them safely. Do you know what they are?'

'No, probably ecstasy cut with goodness knows what else. Leave them with me.' Dr Todd slipped the package into his desk and locked the drawer. 'I'll take care of it.'

Outside the surgery, Beatrice stopped to consider what Dr Todd said about autopsy results. It seemed Simon had an angina attack, as he had done on previous occasions, and had taken out his pills. Was the tub empty when he opened it? That didn't seem likely. He would have instinctively known the difference in the heft of a full or empty bottle and Marina, his mother and John Jakes had all said he was obsessed with his pills. Had he instead taken everything that was in the bottle, because he'd realised the tablets weren't working? If he couldn't reach the phone and the pills were all he had, wouldn't he have taken them? After all, there would be nothing to lose by that point, even though, according to Dr Todd, he must have known after the first two tablets that they weren't going to help. It was the pill bottle being completely empty that was bugging her. She needed to know why.

She called DC Susan Wilde, which went straight through to voicemail.

'Hello, DC Wilde. It's Beatrice Styles. I thought I should let you know, Marina Bayfield has asked me to investigate why her husband wanted to hire me. Apparently he never mentioned it to her. I've been researching angina and I can't get out of my head how his pill bottle was empty. I just had a thought, I don't know if you'll know the answer, but did the autopsy on Simon show how many he'd taken? It's probably not important, but it's been bothering me because everyone I've spoken to said he was so careful with his medication. I hope you don't mind me asking, I didn't know how else to find out: if it helps I could get Marina Bayfield to call officially and ask. Let me know, please? Thanks.'

Beatrice found James in the living room, watching Coronation Street on the TV. He turned down the sound as she entered the room.

'Hi,' he said. 'I thought I'd watch a bit before I go out.'

'I wouldn't have guessed it was your cup of tea, what with you being a Londoner. Isn't Eastenders more your thing?'

'No way. Far too miserable. All that moaning and sleeping with each other's partners. Besides, Mum was from Manchester. She used to love watching this. I hope it was ok for me to use it?' he gestured at the TV.

'That's fine, feel free to use it whenever you like, as long as I'm not in the middle of watching something myself, of course.' She grinned at him.

'I'm off out into town in a bit,' said James. 'Do you fancy coming out for a drink?'

'Thanks for the offer, which I would love to take you up on, but I've got some work to do still today. Lots of research.' Part of her wished she was less conscientious. 'If I'm going to make any use of tomorrow, there's things I need to know.'

'Another time then?'

'Yes, that would be good. I'm going up to my office now so can you make sure you lock the door on your way out please?'

'Will do. I'll probably see you tomorrow then.'

'Goodnight.' As Beatrice climbed the stairs, she heard the volume of the TV increasing. An evening out with James would have been nice, but she really did have a lot to think about and find out: thank goodness for the internet, which would speed up her investigations enormously. Time was of the essence, particularly for Cassie, whose case Beatrice decided she had to prioritise. Simon wasn't going to get any less dead, after all, but Cassie, well, wherever she was, Beatrice hoped she was ok.

Firstly, she read Cassie's English book. Most of it was dull teenage stuff, but there were a couple of pieces, written within recent weeks which radiated sadness. One was a story of a lonely princess who was kept away from the world by an evil wizard. The princess longed to break free and one day saw her chance. She snuck away and never returned to her old home again. It was a simple tale, child-like but used a lot of emotive language. As did a poem written about freedom, which talked of escape, soaring, liberty and independence. It wasn't proof of anything, but it might clarify Cassie's emotional state.

Looking online, she could find no trace of Cassie: at least under her own name. It was unusual for a teenager, but without much privacy at home, Cassie would have found it difficult. Besides, it appeared that Sunita was her only close friend. She found details of child rescue alerts: lists of all the things the police would do and the agencies they'd contact. The police would have probably classified Cassie as medium risk. They would have checked CCTV, questioned potential witnesses, talked to her friends, and the school. What Beatrice hadn't realised was that they'd probably contacted social services and alerted other police forces, especially those in neighbouring counties. It seemed they did more to find a child, than an adult they didn't consider high risk. When her mum had disappeared the police said they couldn't do much for a missing adult. There were no signs of foul play and the fact it was totally out of character carried no weight with them.

Cassie had told her parents she would be at work, then at Sunita's house, when neither of those things were true. The unknown was whether she had planned to be back home Saturday, but something or someone had prevented her.

Deciding she wasn't tired enough to sleep, Beatrice spent some time researching the Bayfield case. By the time she finished, she had a much better understanding of angina and Simon's business, which appeared often in the papers. He was a wealthy and successful person: well connected to prominent locals and business people. He and Marina looked like they were very involved in a Lincoln based charity for disadvantaged children. She wondered if it was Marina's doing.

Finally, Beatrice opened the pictures of Simon's body on her phone. She shivered as the images recalled some of the feelings she'd had on finding him. Forcing herself to look, she took care over each photo. It was much as she remembered. Simon lay on the floor near the doorway his eyes open and staring. The pill bottle lay to the side. Beatrice enlarged the photo with the best view of the bottle. She could just make out some of the writing. The partial lettering in the photo matched up with glyceryl trinitrate: she'd learned it was a very common prescription for angina. There was nothing about it or the dose that was unusual or could have caused Simon any harm. From the photos, the office looked like a standard set-up, with a desk, chair, filing cabinet and a couple of bookcases. It was neat and tidy.

There was nothing else she could do until the next day, so Beatrice shut down the computer. She planned to prioritise finding Cassie the next day and needed to rest. She decided to watch a film to take her mind off Simon's dead body and her mother. She picked the cat up from where she had fallen asleep on the windowsill and carried her downstairs, looking forward to snuggling with her on the sofa.

Chapter 18

Saturday 19th May

Sitting at her kitchen table with a steaming mug of coffee Beatrice checked her phone and saw she'd had five calls from a local number. Someone was very keen to speak to her. She'd better find out who. After a few rings the phone was picked up.

'DS Fisher,' barked the voice on the other end.

'Ah. DS Fisher.' Bugger, she thought. 'This is Beatrice Styles, I seem to have missed several calls from this number. Did you want to speak to me?'

'Yes, I wanted to speak to you. Stop bloody interfering in my cases. Keep your nose out.'

'I beg your pardon?'

'I'm talking about Cassie Saunders. This is police business and we don't need you sticking your nose in where it's not wanted and buggering up our investigation.'

'The Saunders asked for my help.'

'I don't care. It's a job for the police not some useless woman getting in the way. I don't know what makes you think you've got the right to interfere. Drop it, or there'll be trouble.'

Beatrice swallowed, unsure how to respond. Whatever she said it was unlikely to pacify Fisher.

'Hello? Are you still there?' he bellowed down the phone.

'Yes, I am.'

'So you heard me then. Keep out of my business. Bloody amateurs.'

A ringing tone sounded in Beatrice's ear. He'd hung up. It was probably just as well she hadn't had the opportunity to tell him what she thought. There was a good chance she'd have said something she'd later regret. She stored his number in her contacts so she'd have some warning if he called again. She wondered how he'd found out about her looking for Cassie. Had Susan told him? Had he found out she'd given police information to her? What would he think if he found out about being hired by Marina or her questions to Susan?

James came in and poured himself a coffee. His hair was wet from the shower and he smelled fresh and clean.

'Are you ok?' he asked.

'I guess so.'

He sat down opposite her, giving her a querying look.

'I just had a call from that Sergeant, the one I told you about. He said I should keep out of police business and stop looking for Cassie.'

'Are you going to?'

'I don't know.'

James drained the rest of his coffee. 'Sounds like you need to have a good think. I'm off out. I'll probably catch up with you later. Maybe we could have that drink?'

'That would be great.' Beatrice smiled at him. As he passed on his way to the front door, he placed his hand on her shoulder and squeezed gently.

After he'd gone Beatrice could still feel the warmth of his hand. He'd been kind, but hadn't pushed his opinion on her. He was a really nice guy. Attractive too. She shook her head. There was no point pursuing that thought. She really wasn't his type.

So, what am I going to do, she thought. Give up? Stop looking for Cassie and hope the police found her? She considered the Saunders. She'd told them she'd help. Was she going to let them down? Just because Fisher had warned her off? Susan Wilde had been right: if she was going to remain as a PI, she'd have cases the police were also involved in all the time. If it wasn't Fisher telling her to keep out of police business it could easily be another officer. She either had to stop, apologise to the Saunders and Marina and find another career, or get on with it regardless. But she couldn't give up on Cassie, the way the police had given up on her mother. The Saunders needed to know what had happened to their daughter. Beatrice knew first-hand what it was like to be left not knowing, always wondering. They deserved better than that, even if it meant some friction with the police.

She'd been told dismissively that her mother was an adult: she must have wanted to leave home and not contact them. Beatrice knew in her heart, that although their mother was grieving for her husband, as much as she and Rosie were for their father, she never would have willingly abandoned them like that. Well, she could do for Cassie and her parents what the police wouldn't do for her and Rosie. She would carry on and she would find the girl. No matter how long it took. And if that meant having to deal with Fisher on the way, well so be it. She stood up, took a deep calming breath and went upstairs to her office, with a new sense of determination. Half way up the stairs her phone beeped. A text. Thankfully not from Fisher, but from Sunita. It looked like the girl had finally decided to talk.

Chapter 19

'I got your text. You said you wanted to meet, so here I am.' A couple of the people around the tables glared at Beatrice, like she'd committed a crime.

'This is the quiet area of the library,' whispered Sunita.

'Well, you wanted to talk,' Beatrice whispered back.

'Let's go somewhere else.' Sunita packed her books into her bag. Beatrice followed her out to the front of the library.

'Where to?' she asked.

'I don't know.' Sunita muttered.

'Come on. Follow me.' Beatrice had an idea of somewhere they could go for a chat, not too far away.

'I thought you youngsters are supposed to be fit?' Beatrice saw Sunita glare at her as she tried to catch her breath. 'We've only come part way up the hill.'

Beatrice had decided they'd be able to talk in a cafe she'd been meaning to try. It was on Steep Hill, in a section known as The Strait. She realised she was walking too quickly for Sunita to keep up, so she slowed down. She wanted the girl onside and willing to talk. If she didn't get anything useful out of her today, she'd have to think about going to the police, telling them she suspected Cassie had a phone and Sunita probably knew the number. It would be better for everyone if it could be avoided, but finding Cassie was too important to ignore it.

At the cafe, Beatrice indicated Sunita should go in first. She followed the girl, ducking as she stepped through the doorway. It took her eyes a few seconds to adjust from the bright light outside to the darkness indoors. Blinking a couple of times, Beatrice looked around. The room was small; half a dozen tables with seats and a serving counter at the back. A couple of the tables were occupied.

An archway led through to a kitchen area and a set of stairs rose on the right-hand side of the room. The walls were decorated in a mixture of Mod and London-themed posters. Behind the counter was a thin man in a chef's overall.

'Hi,' said Beatrice. 'I'll have a white coffee thanks, no sugar. Sunita?' She turned waiting for a reply.

'Hot chocolate, please.'

The man rang the drinks into the till and Beatrice paid. 'Is it ok if we go upstairs? We need to have a private chat.'

The man paused, then nodded. 'I'll put the lights on.' He put the drinks on a tray, which Beatrice picked up carefully.

'Thanks,' Beatrice smiled at him. Then she looked at Sunita and nodded her head towards the steep stairs. Sunita sighed dramatically but made her way up them. Beatrice followed gingerly as the wood creaked and groaned under her feet. When they got to the top Beatrice steered the girl into the far corner of the room. She wasn't comfortable again until they were sitting down near the window. The room occupied part of the roof space of the building and had been designed with people shorter than Beatrice in mind.

'What is this place? Is it new?' Sunita was clearly not impressed with the décor. Beatrice had to admit it had seen better days and, even with the lights on, it was a dark room.

'I've no idea how long it's been here. I only moved to Lincoln a few weeks ago myself. I saw it the other day and thought I'd give it a go. What do you think?'

Sunita didn't answer and Beatrice left her to stew for a bit. Hopefully she'd soon find the words or the nerve to tell whatever it was she knew about Cassie's disappearance. She watched as the girl placed her hands around the hot mug, peering into its liquid surface, as if she was trying to draw something from it, courage perhaps.

Beatrice reminded herself to be gentle. She was missing her best friend, after all. 'What do you know about Cassie's disappearance?' Sunita refused to meet her gaze. 'Look, I can't promise anything, but I'm not going to try to get you into trouble. I'll keep you out of it as much as possible, but surely you can see that the important thing is finding Cassie? And making sure she's alright?'

Sunita continued staring into her mug. Beatrice thought she saw tears on her cheeks.

'After all, what's the worst that's going to happen? Your parents will be angry, if they find out you knew about her leaving. That's it. And what do you think the worst that could happen to Cassie is? A young girl out in the world alone?'

Beatrice wanted to shock some sense into her. Couldn't she see how self-centred she was being? Did she even care about her friend? Beatrice held herself in check, hoping that a few moments to think would get through to her.

'She isn't alone.' Sunita's voice was low and quiet.

Beatrice breathed out slowly, trying to keep calm. 'Who is she with?'

'I'm not sure.'

Beatrice felt like screaming at her, but kept her voice low and steady. 'Please, just tell me what you know.'

Sunita finally looked up. 'There's this boy she liked. I don't know his name, honestly. He's in a band in town. Cassie used to go off and watch him play.'

Beatrice thought back to Cassie's diary, the initials she'd written with the love heart. 'Do you know the band?'

'No. Well, I'm not sure. She also went on about how good a group called Acoustic Dreams were. It might be that one.'

'What makes you think she's with him?'

'I had a message from her, she sent me a picture.'

Beatrice clenched her hands under the table. 'When?' She kept her voice even.

'Two days after she disappeared, the Sunday.'

'What's the boy's name?'

'I told you I don't know.'

'I thought you were best friends.'

'We are, well, we were. But she liked acting all mysterious about him. I wasn't even sure he was real until she left. I thought she could have been just trying to make herself look good.'

'Do you know anything else about him?'

'He sang. I think.' Sunita shrugged.

'Where did Cassie meet him?'

'At the Cat & Fiddle on the High Street. They have live music there some nights.'

It explained the notes 'C&F'. 'That's a help. Can you show me this message you got from her?'

'No.'

'Why not? I'm only trying to help Cassie.'

'Because I can't. It was on Snapchat.'

'So?' Beatrice assumed it was some kind of online social media.

'How old are you?'

Beatrice raised her eyebrows.

Sunita sighed like she was explaining something obvious to a dummy. 'You can send pictures and messages on Snapchat, but once you've looked at them, they disappear.'

'What's the point of that then?'

Sunita rolled her eyes.

'Can you remember what it said?' Beatrice spoke as patiently as she could.

'Just something about how I'd be jealous if I knew where she was.'

'What do you think she meant by that?'

'I don't know. Look I'm trying to be helpful, I really am.'

Beatrice sighed. 'I know. What's prompted the change in heart?'

'I haven't heard from her since last Thursday. It's not like her. I've sent her messages, but she hasn't read them. I'm getting worried.'

'I'll check out what you've told me, but if you think of anything else make sure you let me know, ok?'

'Er, there is one other thing.'

'Go on.'

'I saw the photo, the one the police were using.'

'And?' Beatrice frowned.

'It's not right.'

'I don't understand. It's one her parents gave the police.'

'But, when she went out, to town, she'd go into the toilets and change. Put make-up on. And sometimes a wig.'

'So, she'd look a bit different?'

'Not a bit – a lot.'

Beatrice began to see what Sunita meant. 'Enough so that people wouldn't know it was her?'

The girl nodded.

'Do you have any photos of her looking like that?'

'She sent me one, as well as the Snapchat message. In the evening, on the Friday she left. She was more dressed up than normal and she'd cut her hair. If it hadn't come from her email address, I don't think I would have recognised her. It's on my computer at home. I'll send it to you.' Beatrice was surprised to hear that Sunita had a computer of her own and presumably felt able to keep photos on it private.

'When?'

'It will have to be later, when I get home. I'll do it as soon as I get in.'

'Don't forget. This could be important.'

'I know.'

Beatrice was irritated by Sunita's actions. She was just a kid, worried about how her family would react to how she'd covered up for Cassie, but the police had lost valuable time in tracking Cassie down. She may have been ok a week ago, but what had happened since then? Where was she? Why had she stopped sending messages to Sunita?

'You said you'd been texting?'

Sunita nodded.

'So Cassie did have a mobile phone?'

'Yes.'

'Her parents said she didn't.'

'They didn't know about it, did they? She's only had it a few weeks. They never let her have any privacy. If they knew she had a phone, her dad would want to know what she was doing on it.'

'Can you send me her number?'

'Sure.'

'Now, please.'

Sighing, Sunita pulled her phone from her bag and tapped away.

135

Beatrice checked her own phone and read it back to Sunita, who confirmed it was correct. Beatrice dialled the number. It cut straight to voicemail, an electronic voice asked her to leave a message. She hung up.

'I've tried it over and over,' said Sunita. 'I've left messages, but she hasn't called.'

They sat quietly for a few moments, both deep in thought. Clearly Sunita had more freedom than Cassie, and had more of a typical teenage life, even if it seemed she wasn't allowed out at night in town. In an effort to hold her close and keep her safe, had Cassie's parents just ended up pushing her away, making her easy prey to a smooth talker?

'I hate her, you know.' Sunita's words cut through Beatrice's thoughts.

She looked across at the girl in surprise. 'Who? Cassie?'

'No. The great Dr Banerjee.'

Beatrice wasn't sure what to say. Why was the girl talking about family problems? 'Sunita, I'm sure your mother is doing what she thinks is best for you.'

'She doesn't care about me.' Sunita spoke with real venom in her voice.

'That can't be true.'

'She's not my real mother.'

Beatrice paused in lifting her mug to her mouth. 'Oh. I didn't realise.'

'Dad remarried after mum died. I wish he hadn't.'

'What happened to your mum?'

'Cancer.'

'I'm sorry.'

The girl shrugged.

'How old were you?'

'Six.'

'You remember her then?'

Sunita nodded as tears suddenly and silently poured from her eyes.

'Here.' Beatrice handed the girl a napkin and watched as she wiped her eyes and noisily blew her nose.

'Cassie was my only friend and now she's gone.'

Beatrice felt out of her depth. What on earth was she supposed to say to Sunita, a mixed-up kid? But she didn't have anyone else. 'What are your plans when you finish your GCSEs?' She thought back to what Cassie's form teacher had said. 'Have you thought about going to college?'

'She says I have to stay on at school. They get the best exam results. She says it would be better for me.'

'And what does your father think?'

'He doesn't talk to me properly about it. He just goes along with whatever she decides.'

'And how about you. What do you want?'

'I don't really know.' Sunita shrugged and wiped her eyes again. 'I guess I'd like to go to college. I might make some friends there. People who don't know me from school.'

'I'm sure you would.' Beatrice considered what Mrs Samson had said about the differences between college and school. Sunita would probably benefit from the change as much as Cassie would. A chance to reinvent herself. 'Perhaps you should think some more about it.'

'There's not much point is there? I have to do as I'm told.'

'You could try talking to your dad.'

'He'll go along with her. He always does.'

'Perhaps if you explained how important it is to you, he'd listen. What's the harm in trying?'

Sunita shrugged again.

'No one else is going to do it for you, Sunita. If you don't care enough to do something, how do you expect anyone else to?'

'But he won't listen.'

'It depends on how you approach it. If you go in shouting about how you hate your… Dr Banerjee, it would all sound like a teenage tantrum. If you take the time to think it through, and put your point of view calmly, but clearly, you'll stand a much better chance. Your dad needs to understand why you'd rather go to college than school.

It's ok for it to be about friendships as well as your future.' Beatrice didn't want to get dragged further in to the family's problems. 'I'm sorry, I've got to go now. If you think of anything else, or if Cassie gets in touch again, call me, and don't forget the pictures. Ok?'

'Sure.'

'I mean it, Sunita. She could be in trouble.'

Chapter 20

Arriving a couple of minutes late, Beatrice entered Burton village hall as quietly as she could. It was a modern building which stood out against the older houses she'd seen on the way in. The weather was warm and the doors had been left open to encourage a draft, so she was able tiptoe in and slip into a seat near the back. The room wasn't huge, but had seating for about 100 people, and it was nearly full. Beatrice was impressed with the turnout: there was a lot of strong feeling about the solar farm.

A table was set out at the front of the room for the committee. In the centre seat, she could see a slim, elegant-looking woman, with short, highlighted hair. Stella Bright presumably. They'd spoken when Beatrice telephoned her the day before and Stella had invited her to join the protesters' meeting. Four other people occupied chairs either side of Stella, with an empty seat at one end.

Stella glanced at the watch on her wrist and called the meeting to order, peering at the laptop open in front of her. There were the formalities of apologies and agreeing of the minutes of the previous meeting, before the main discussion began.

'Moving on then,' said Stella, her voice loud and clear in the hall. 'We come next to the direct action we discussed at the last meeting. Firstly, we will update on the demonstration and stall in town planned for Tuesday. Alan, can you fill us in please?'

The man on Stella's left stood up and cleared his throat. 'The Scouts have agreed to lend us the tent they use for rallies as our stall, and we've managed to borrow a couple of folding tables to put the petition and information about the development on. We've alerted the police and agreed with the council that we can be in Market Square. I've got a list of volunteers who will look after the stall during the day, but I still need a couple of people to help with putting the tent up and setting the tables out. We plan on doing that at eight thirty. It should only take an hour.'

Some hands were raised and Stella looked across toward the empty chair at the end of the table, tutted and typed the names into her laptop. A few seconds later a figure hurried down the side of the hall and slipped into the empty seat. Stella glared at the late comer. Beatrice looked across to see the new arrival and was surprised to see the bowed head of Kerry Honeywell.

'Yes, what is it Mrs Fielding?' asked Stella.

Beatrice looked back at the audience. A hand had been raised by an older woman near the front of the room. The woman stood with some difficulty, leaning on a wooden walking stick.

'Excuse me, Mrs Bright, I don't like to interrupt, but I have an important point to make.'

'Can't it wait until 'any other business'?' asked Stella.

'No, it can't,' said the old woman. 'It's relevant to this discussion.'

'Very well, but please keep it brief.'

'Mr Bayfield has died. Don't you think it's inappropriate to be holding a demonstration? I'm not suggesting we cancel, just think about postponing it. Out of respect.'

There were murmurs of agreement around the room. A man in front of Beatrice muttered, 'She's got a point.'

'Committee have already discussed this,' said Stella, 'and decided to go ahead. Everything is in place, time and money have been spent in getting ready.'

'It's not going to look good in the newspapers, is it?' Mrs Fielding was persistent.

'If we move the protest we'll lose momentum, we won't get as many people attending. Our supporters have planned around this date, which was set weeks ago.' Stella sounded annoyed. 'As far as the newspapers are concerned, I'll speak to them and explain how sad we all feel about that man's death. But, it is important for us to continue our work before the planning committee can grant permission. It's not going to be much use protesting after the decision is made, is it?' she challenged.

'On your head be it,' said Mrs Fielding, retaking her seat.

Stella shrugged and moved the conversation on to the next point. Beatrice suspected very few people dared to stand up to her: Mrs Fielding was one of the brave ones.

The meeting continued and there was more detailed talk about a letter campaign and the objections to be used. Some of the arguments were unfamiliar to Beatrice; loss of valuable farmland; traffic; lack of privacy due to CCTV installation; glare from reflected light; and noise from the substation. Beatrice also hadn't realised it would take ten years for the plants that were supposed to screen the site to grow large enough to do the job. She began to appreciate some of the protestors concerns. Stella promised to circulate a list of suitable objections for their letters, to those who hadn't already written.

'They need to see how strongly so many of us feel about the farm,' said Stella. 'We need everyone to put in formal objections to the planning office, as well as letters to our MP and the local councillors.' There were lots of mutters in the hall at Stella's comments and many heads nodding in agreement. 'I know that some of you have already done so, but I can't stress the importance of this enough. It doesn't matter if you send the same letter to all of them. The important thing is volume. We would prefer actual paper letters too, emails are too easily ignored or deleted.'

The meeting finally wrapped up, but not before, it seemed to Beatrice, everyone in the room had been given the opportunity to make complaints about the solar farm, no matter how repetitive it was. As she waited to speak to Stella, she wondered how to handle Kerry being there. Could she be working against the development, despite her job at Bayfields? Did Stella know Kerry worked for the 'enemy'?

Beatrice walked towards the front of the hall and saw Kerry's face turn pale as she approached. So she was there incognito.

'Mrs Bright, hello. I'm Beatrice, we spoke on the telephone.' They shook hands.

'Hello, how very nice to meet you. I'm glad you could make it. We're always happy to have new people joining the cause. Let me introduce you to the committee. This is Alan, Jenny, Fred and

Louisa. The young woman on the end there is Kerry. She isn't part of the committee, but she helps us out when she can, taking notes, drafting letters, that sort of thing.'

Beatrice smiled in Kerry's direction. 'It's nice to meet you all. I have to say, I'm impressed with the turnout you had tonight.'

'People around here are very unhappy about the solar farm.'

'I can see.'

Kerry spoke up. 'Stella, I'm sorry but I need to go now. I'll type up these notes and email them to you.'

'Thank you, Kerry.'

Beatrice watched the girl hurry from the room.

'I'm afraid I must get off too, Mrs Bright,' said Beatrice. 'Perhaps we could talk in more detail about the campaign sometime soon?'

'I know, why don't you come on Thursday morning to my home, say ten o'clock? I live in the village, in the house behind the church called The Willows. You can't miss it.'

'Thank you, that would be great. I'll see you then.'

Beatrice walked quickly to the car park, hoping to catch up with Kerry, but she'd vanished.

'You're new here, aren't you?' On older woman came alongside Beatrice.

'Oh, hello. It's Mrs Fielding isn't it?'

'That's right.'

'I live in town, not too far away.'

'So not close to the solar farm? Why are you here then?'

Beatrice smiled at her directness. 'I moved here a few weeks ago, heard about the development and was interested in what was going on. Just finding out more about the area and what's happening. How about you, do you live here?'

'Been here all my life.' She shifted her weight.

'I'm sorry, I shouldn't be keeping you standing here talking.'

'That's ok, love. I'm not as young as I used to be,' she chuckled. 'You can walk along with me to my house if you'd like.'

'Would you like to take my arm?'

'Thank you, but I'm fine if I take it steady.'

'Have you been involved in the campaign since the beginning?' asked Beatrice as they walked.

'Oh yes. I don't object to the solar farm itself mind, we all use electricity, it's just a daft place to put it. There's plenty of places it could go without using farmland. We've got old airbases we don't know what to do with.'

'Do you think there would be fewer people against it if they did that?'

'Well, some people will complain about anything, but I reckon most folks would see the sense of it.'

'Have you known Mrs Bright long?'

'Madam, you mean?' Mrs Fielding snorted. 'She's one of the new lot in the village, in her big posh house, playing lady of the manor.'

'She's doing a lot of work for the protest group.'

'Oh aye, I'm not knocking that. Someone's got to do it and I'm too old for that sort of thing these days. She sticks up for the village well enough. You should have heard her. She gave him a piece of her mind and no mistake.'

'Who?'

'The dead man, Mr Bayfield. I saw him: early last week it was. He came to speak to her, tried to persuade her it wouldn't harm the village. She told him though.' Mrs Fielding chuckled. 'Oh yes, she told him alright.'

'Really. What did she say?'

'Well, he said something like "and we both know what you're up to, but it won't happen". She told him he was too used to getting his own way, but she'd stop him. He stormed off then.'

'You don't like her though?'

'She's a funny woman. Puts on a good act of being everyone's friend. But I bet she doesn't like not getting her own way either, that one.'

'What makes you say that?'

'Nothing I know for certain, she just strikes me as a bit hard, you know? The sort that would be prepared to sell their own grandmother if there was something in it for them. I've met her type before.' Mrs Fielding paused outside a small but well kept terraced cottage. 'This is me. It's been nice chatting to you.'

'I enjoyed it. Take care.'

As she walked back to her car Beatrice's phone buzzed. It was a text from Sunita saying she had sent an email with the photos of Cassie. She switched the 4G signal on and accessed her email account. As promised, there were several pictures of Cassie on a night out. The final picture was of the day she disappeared. In it her hair was styled in a short, layered bob. It looked rough, as if she had cut it herself. She'd also changed the colour to a dark brown. If she'd been to a hairdresser in Lincoln they would have recognized her and alerted the Police. Her restyle completely changed her look: she appeared a lot older, more mature. Her makeup was subtle, but changed the shape of her face and eyes. Sunita was right, she'd become unrecognizable. No wonder she disappeared so effectively.

Beatrice called Susan's number having quickly dismissed the idea of contacting Fisher. It went straight to voicemail so she emailed the photo and Cassie's phone number, asking if the number could be traced and maybe Cassie found on CCTV, now they knew what they were looking for. She followed the email with a text saying she'd sent an important email on Cassie.

She was getting more anxious about the girl. The fact she had stopped messaging Sunita meant something had changed for Cassie and it was unlikely it was for the better.

'Come in.'

I entered the room to find a man sitting behind a desk, pieces of paper laid out in front of him. He was wearing a suit and tie, and thick-rimmed glasses.

He checked my name off a list and looked me up and down. I could feel his judgement. He made me ashamed of my charity-shop shirt, trousers and scuffed shoes. He pointed to a chair and I sat down.

'Why do you want to work in the library?' The man in the suit sat back in his chair and smirked.

My throat was dry. I couldn't tell him the real reasons: it was near the flat where Mother and I now lived, the work looked easy, it was indoors and warm. 'I think... I like books. Reading. I want to work with books.'

He raised his eyebrows. 'What are your favourite books?'

I scrambled in my mind to remember the ones we'd read at school. 'To Kill a Mockingbird. Rebecca.'

He sniffed. I had the feeling he knew why I'd said them.

In your application you've left the section headed previous experience blank. Do you have any work experience?'

I shook my head. I wasn't going to get the job. I already knew it. So did he. He'd made up his mind within seconds of me walking into the room. Why was he putting me though the pretence of an interview? Asking questions when he didn't care about the answers?

'So what are you going to do about it?' Mother had asked later.

I knew she'd ask. I'd been thinking about it on the way home. 'I don't know yet,' I replied. 'But I'll think of something.'

She nodded her head in approval.

I did think of something...

I waited, I was patient and did my research. I joined the library and started visiting once a week. I didn't read the books I took out: I used my time there to plan what I was going to do and, once I'd decided, to prepare. I wanted to get back at the man in the suit but I never saw him again. Perhaps he'd been there just for the interviews.

The blaze could be seen for miles according to the newspaper reports.

I guess that's what happens when you combine a building filled with paper and a fire alarm system whose wiring had mysteriously become disconnected. The police suspected arson, but there was no evidence.

I watched from nearby, out of sight, as the flames consumed the building. It was late at night and the fire was already established by the time the fire engine was called. It was all destroyed. I only wished the man in the suit had been inside.

My clothes had picked up the stench of smoke and when I returned to our flat Mother came out of her room to see what I was doing. She sniffed at the air.

'You've been busy,' she said.

I nodded.

'I don't suppose they'll be turning anyone else down for a job then will they.' She started to turn away, then changed her mind. Then she said words she'd never said to me before and I felt alive.

'Well done.'

Chapter 21

Monday 21st May

Beatrice had spent Sunday catching up and gathering her thoughts. She had even managed some unpacking, cleaning and a hot bath. She'd had a pleasant dinner of roast chicken with James, during which they chatted easily and learnt more about each other. He was good company and she felt comfortable in his presence. She found him attractive, but knowing he wouldn't be interested in her meant she didn't get flustered, as she usually did around men she liked. It felt more worth the effort to be cooking for two instead of one and she found the whole day relaxing and was able to take her mind off work. On Monday morning she refocused, beginning the day by reviewing and updating her files. Then she planned her next steps.

Until Susan got back to her about Cassie's phone and picture, there wasn't much more she could do except follow up with the Cat & Fiddle pub. After a quick check on the internet and an unanswered phone call, she decided she'd have to wait until the evening when the pub reopened. She had to hope that Susan would let her know the results of the search for her phone despite Fisher telling Beatrice to keep out. In the meantime, she'd focus on trying to find out why Simon Bayfield had wanted to hire her, which meant going back to the business.

'Thanks for not telling Stella about me. It would be awful if she found out,' said Kerry.

'You're welcome,' replied Beatrice. They were in Kerry's office drinking tea. Kerry had looked worried when she came down to meet Beatrice at reception, but back in her office had soon become her usual cheerful self.

'She looks a bit fierce. I don't imagine she'd be too pleased to find out you worked for the other side.'

'No, I'm sure she wouldn't. It would look bad for the business too.'

'I was surprised to see you there,' said Beatrice. 'Why are you helping them?'

'It was Mr Bayfield. He asked me to find out about what they were up to. He thought they were planning something big to try to stop Sunrise and, if he had someone on the inside, he could keep ahead of them. He was very worried about it. He thought no-one would know me, so I could join the group and report back to him.'

'How long have you been doing it?'

'A couple of months.'

'Did you find anything useful to tell Mr Bayfield?'

'Not much. Just that they were planning on organising things like letters to the MP and local councillors, an online petition and a Facebook group. I belong to that too, so I can see what they're posting. Mr Bayfield couldn't join it himself. I used to show him on my profile.'

'How was that useful to him? Aren't they the sort of things all these groups do?'

'I guess so. But I was able to tell him when things were happening, so he could take action before if he wanted.'

'What sort of action?'

'Well, like with the letters to our MP. Mr Bayfield had met him before at some political gathering, so he went to see him, and I suppose he got him on side, in support of the development. He probably did the same thing with the councillors too. And I told him about the stall that's going in town tomorrow. You know, the one Stella mentioned at the meeting.'

'I see,' said Beatrice. 'So how come you're still going there, now that Mr Bayfield is dead?'

'I thought Mr Jakes would want the same information, so I carried on. It seemed a bad idea to just drop it. Stella would start asking questions and might find out I work here.'

'Wouldn't she find out eventually?'

Kerry shrugged. 'I thought I'd just gradually stop turning up and, once the planning hearing is done, it will be over then anyway.'

'I suppose you're right. Well, thanks for the tea. I'll see you around.' Beatrice stood up.

'Hang on a minute. Look, I don't know if I should be telling you this...'

Beatrice lowered herself back into the chair. 'What is it, Kerry? Is it about Mr Bayfield?'

'No. Mr Jakes. That's why I don't know if I should tell you. He could fire me if he found out.' Kerry frowned.

'Does he need to know? What is it?'

'It could be nothing.' She lowered her voice, 'Mr Jakes has meetings sometimes.'

'And what worries you about them?'

'He doesn't say who they're with. He just blocks the time off in his calendar and tells me not to book it up. And sometimes he's on the phone with the door closed and stops talking if I have to go in to his office and speak to him.'

'Is that unusual?'

'He doesn't do it all the time, just now and then.'

'Has he got any more of these mysterious meetings planned in?'

'That's what made me think of it. I came in this morning, checked the calendar and saw he's put one in for Wednesday.' She showed Beatrice on her computer screen.

What could the meeting be for? Was it connected to the business, or maybe John was having an affair. Either way she'd have to find out, in case it was connected to what Simon was worried about. Beatrice made a note in her diary. 'Thanks for telling me, Kerry. Don't worry I don't see any need to mention it to him.'

John was busy working when Beatrice poked her head around the open door, but he put his papers to one side and beckoned her in. She closed the door behind her.

'What do you think about Kerry and the protest group, Mr Jakes?' asked Beatrice, sitting down in the chair opposite him.

'Please, call me John,' he smiled. 'What about her?'

'Do you think it's a good idea? It makes her vulnerable don't you think? If they were to find out.'

149

John shook his head. 'I'm sorry, I don't know what you're talking about.'

'I went to the anti-Sunrise protest meeting on Saturday, to find out about what they were doing and to speak to the organiser, Stella Bright. When I got there, I found Kerry is part of the group.'

'Oh. I'm surprised, but maybe she was just interested in them the same way you are.'

'She wasn't just in the audience, she was helping the committee they've pulled together.'

'What?' John frowned.

'Yes. I spoke to Kerry about it and she says she's been doing it for a couple of months: Simon had asked her to spy on them and report back.'

'Why would he do that?'

'To get inside information, she says, so he could try to counter whatever they organised.'

'What use would that be?' John shook his head. 'Look, Simon had professional advice on what these kinds of protestors do and the objections they make, as well as his years of experience from working in the sector. There's nothing Kerry could find out that Simon wouldn't have already accounted for. Here, let me show you this.' John unlocked his desk drawer and pulled out a file. 'Here is our project management document showing the risks to the development.' He handed it over to Beatrice. 'If you turn to the third page you see the section for 'Public Engagement'. This was written before the development plans became public. As you can see, Simon knew well-organised protestors had the capacity to potentially stop or delay the project. He had plans in place to prevent that. Even before we applied for planning, Simon and I had done a lot of work.'

Beatrice examined the document closely. It looked very detailed. There was a column for actions to take which was long and specific, including listing multiple interactions with councillors, the local MP and the planning department. Against most of the items, dates were added, almost all for several months ago.

'I presume the dates are when you and Simon did the things listed?'

'That's right,' said John. 'I've got another version on the computer focusing on things for us to do from when the planning request first went in. This one was mostly for the pre-planning work.'

'Thank you,' Beatrice handed the document back and John locked it away. 'So, I guess I come back to the question of why Simon asked her to go there. Perhaps it was the same reason he called me. Maybe Kerry found out something that he wanted me to look into further.'

'Possibly, but I can't imagine what. They can make a lot of noise, but the important thing is knowing where the decisions are made and who by. I'd better tell that girl to stop it anyway, before she gets found out. It will make the company look bad, spying on them. If the papers get a hold of it, they'll put some sort of spin on it.'

'Wait, can you do me a favour please? Don't mention this to Kerry yet. Let her carry on for a few more days.'

'Why? I'm not sure that's a good idea.'

'I'm not certain, but as I said it may have something to do with what Simon wanted me to investigate. I've found nothing else and I'm seeing Mrs Bright on Thursday.'

'I suppose a few days won't make much difference, but after Thursday, I don't want her near that group. If you find out anything that affects the business I want to know about it.'

Chapter 22

Marina was grooming a large chestnut horse when Beatrice pulled up in front of the house. She climbed out of the cool of the car and walked over to the pair.

'Hi,' she said.

'Hello.' Marina glanced briefly over at her before turning back to the horse. 'I wasn't expecting you.'

'I tried calling and then I thought, as I was near, it would be a good chance to come and see you.'

'Did you need something? I'm sorry, but I have to finish brushing before I put him into the stables?'

'I dropped by because I needed to give you this.' Beatrice handed over her bill for the work she'd already done. Marina looked at it briefly then tucked it into her jodhpurs. 'And I thought I should update you on what I've found out so far and see if the police have finished with Simon's office here.'

Marina paused her work and turned to her. 'Yes, I should have called you. They said now they've officially closed the case I can take the tape off. Can you do it, when you have a look?'

'Yes, of course. I'll come back later in the week, if that's ok with you? I've got some other things to be doing first.'

'It's fine. Are you still looking for that girl?'

'I'm afraid so.'

'Her parents must be so worried.' Marina spoke quietly and continued to brush the horse using circular motions. After a few more strokes she selected a different brush and began yet more brushing. It looked like a lot of hard work. They remained in silence until Marina spoke again. 'Why don't you tell me what you've found out so far?'

'I still don't know why Simon wanted me to work for him. I searched his office at the business and spoke to the people there, but he hadn't told anyone about me. Kerry thinks he'd been worried about Sunrise, and it could have been that. John said he was too, but was surprised Simon wanted to hire me and he didn't know why. Do you think if it was about the business he would have discussed it with John?'

'It would depend. He trusted John, but if it was something he was going to do anyway and he thought John would argue with him about it, then he'd go ahead and get on with it.'

'I see.' Marina's description fitted with what she'd learned about the man: he knew what he wanted and did whatever he needed to get it.

'Do you?' Marina brushed the horse with more vigour and he stepped away from her hands. 'He was the same in his personal life.' She stopped brushing and bent her forehead onto the horse side, gently caressing his flank in apology.

'I'm sorry?' asked Beatrice.

'If he made a decision about something and he thought I'd disagree, then he wouldn't tell me until it was too late. Like spending a chunk of money on that bloody Lexus.' She indicated Simon's car, still parked where it had been on the day Simon died.

Beatrice recognised the anger of someone grieving. Anger at being left alone without the person she could most rely on for support. She knew Marina was simply letting off steam.

'I'm sorry.' said Marina. 'I did love him, but...'

'It's ok. I understand.'

'He was a good man. I don't know what I'm going to do without him. I don't have any family now.'

'Did you never want children of your own? Sorry, that's too personal. You don't have to answer.'

'It's ok. It doesn't really matter now anyway. I wanted children, but Simon couldn't have any. I looked at all the options, including fertility treatment and adoption: but Simon wouldn't agree. He thought it was a reflection on him. He didn't want people to think he was less of a man. I wish I'd insisted, then maybe this wouldn't be so hard.' Marina took a deep breath and smiled. Embarrassed she turned away, continuing to groom the horse.

'I went to a meeting on Saturday with the anti-Sunrise protest group.'

'Really? Why?'

'John said it was Simon's main concern, so I thought it was worth checking out. They seem well organized.'

'Well they would be wouldn't they, with Stunning Stella in charge.'

'You know her?'

'Oh yes, we're on the board of a local children's charity. It's what rich men's wives are expected to do, to contribute.' Marina led the horse into the stable. Beatrice stood by the door watching her organise water and food.

'What's she like?'

'Stella? She's ok really. Just fancies herself as lady of the manor. Talks about the village she lives in like she was born and bred around here.'

'She wasn't?'

'No.' Marina closed the bottom part of the stable door. They both began to walk to the house. 'She and her husband came from London. Rumour has it they lost some money and had to sell their house to meet debts. They came up here because it's much cheaper. Stella needs a big house to show everyone how well she's doing. Up here they could still have that.' Marina sat on the front step of the house and pulled off her riding boots. 'Cup of tea?'

'Yes please.' They went through to the kitchen. 'They're going to have a stall in town tomorrow, collecting signatures on a petition to try to stop the development. There might be some publicity.'

'Great. That means the press will come sniffing around again.'

'They might. I'm sorry. Do you want me to talk to the police and see if there is anything they can do to stop it, given the circumstances?'

'Thanks, but no. It will only be a postponement anyway.'

'A woman at the meeting spoke up and did try to persuade Stella to hold off because she didn't think it would look good in the papers.'

'I can imagine how that went down. Maybe the press will think it's tactless. Who knows?'

'You could always speak to them yourself? Help them spin it that way.'

'Seriously?' Marina placed two mugs of tea on the table and they sat down.

'It's only a suggestion. I have contact details for a reporter at the Weekly. You could always give him a call.'

'Give me his name and number. I'll think about it. It would be satisfying to scupper her plans.'

Beatrice scribbled a note on her pad and placed it on the kitchen table. 'Did she know Simon well?'

'Not especially. They met at functions and charity events. You tend to see the same faces at these things.'

'I was told Stella and Simon had a heated argument last week.'

'Oh. He said he'd gone to try to talk some sense into her. They're both stubborn. I can imagine they had a row. Neither of them would be bothered by doing it in public either. I don't understand why she changed her mind, but Simon thought it was worth trying to get her to change it back.'

'I'm sorry, you've lost me.'

'Sorry. I didn't really explain, did I. About eighteen months ago, when Simon began planning the solar farm, Stella was all for it. Later, she became set against it; claimed it was for environmental reasons. She's the one who set up the group to try to stop it.'

'I wonder why?'

'Simon said it was because she was an idiot. So next time we met at a charity board meeting, I asked. She said she'd looked into it more and come to realise how bad the solar farm was going to be for the local environment. She felt she had to try to stop it for the sake of the villages.'

'Interesting.' Beatrice stood up. 'I'd better go. Thanks for the tea. I'll give you a ring when I'm ready to search Simon's office.'

Beatrice drove from Marina's straight to Simon's mother. The old woman was the same as when they had first met. She wore the same sort of clothes and sat in the same chair. Beatrice refused the offer of tea, handed over a copy of her bill and briefly explained what she had found out so far. Mrs Bayfield seemed to understand and asked a few questions.

'In the circumstances perhaps you would like to reconsider hiring me? I'm not sure there is anything for me to find.'

'Are you still working for that woman?' It was clear who she meant.

'Yes.'

'Then you will carry on working for me too.' She narrowed her eyes as she stared at Beatrice. 'I suppose you've told her all this already.'

'Yes, because of the direction I was driving from. I came here as soon as I finished with Marina.'

The old woman sniffed. 'Is there anything else to tell me?'

'Not for now, no.'

'Very well, you can go.'

Beatrice was pleased to leave and felt relief as the door closed behind her. Then she felt guilty because Mrs Bayfield had lost her son, her only living relative.

Her phone beeped. It was a text from Pete Hayes. *Just had a call from Marina Bayfield. Thanks.* Beatrice typed a quick reply. *My favour was bigger than yours. You owe me now.*

Her phone beeped again straight away. *We'll see!*

Chapter 23

Tired, Beatrice knew she still had to follow up on the lead about Cassie. She'd finally managed to get through to the Cat and Fiddle and had been told the landlord would be available to speak to her after seven o'clock in the evening. She ate at home, then walked down the hill to the pub. A small group of young men stood outside smoking. They moved aside to let her pass.

Beatrice ducked under the low lintel as she pushed the heavy door open. The noise of a badly-played electric guitar assaulted her ears. She took in the room quickly. It was brightly lit, with tables and chairs set in front of a low make-shift stage. It was functional but not comfortable looking. The room was about half full, with most of the people trying to carry on conversations over the noise of the amateur guitarist. The bar took up one side of the room where a middle-aged woman stood looking bored. As Beatrice approached, the woman's face brightened.

'Hello, love. What would you like?'

'Hello,' Beatrice almost shouted. 'I'm here to speak to the landlord, Dave.' Beatrice grimaced, as a particularly bad chord was destroyed on the stage.

The barwoman smiled in sympathy. 'Don't worry, he'll stop in a minute and some other deluded fool will come on. It's open mike night. Helps draw folk in on a quiet evening.'

'Oh, good.' She smiled at the woman. 'Something to look forward to.'

'Dave likes to give the kids a chance, but I don't think this one will be back.' They both looked across at the thin young man on the stage. He was attacking the guitar with plenty of enthusiasm and energy, but very little skill.

'They all think they can win X-Factor these days,' said the barmaid. 'It's a shame.' She turned back to Beatrice. 'Anyway, Dave will be down in a few minutes. Are you having a drink whilst you wait?'

'Orange juice, please,' bellowed Beatrice into the unexpected silence. The guitarist had stopped, and the audience sat quietly. Stunned, Beatrice assumed. After a pause, there were a few slow claps, and the lad shuffled off stage, his head bent low. Beatrice wiggled her fingers in her ears, hoping they still worked.

'Alright, Julie. He's finished then, thank God.' A thin, cheerful looking man had appeared behind the bar, nodding at the barmaid. Julie placed an orange juice in front of Beatrice and took the proffered note.

'This lady says you're expecting her, Dave.'

'Oh, right.' Dave moved towards Beatrice. 'You must be the one who phoned this afternoon.'

'That's right.'

'A private investigator, you said?' He sounded sceptical, so Beatrice handed him a card, which he looked at carefully.

'What can I help you with?'

'I understand that you've got a band here called Acoustic Dreams.'

Julie quietly slipped Beatrice's change onto the bar in front of her, then discreetly moved away.

'Well, we had. They played a few weeks, but moved on.'

'Why was that?'

'They wanted more money, didn't they. They weren't too bad, but you can see for yourself how many I get in unless there's a decent band on. I can't afford to pay much, even if I'm full on a weekend. They all think they're God's gift to music these kids.'

'Do you know where they went to?'

'No, sorry. Can't help you, love. What they done then?'

'Possibly nothing.'

'Why are you after them then?'

Beatrice fished in her pocket for her phone. She pulled up photo of Cassie in school uniform. 'Do you recognise this girl?'

'Isn't that the one from the papers? The one that went missing?'

'Yeah, that's her. Did you ever see her in here?'

'No chance. Look at her. She looks barely thirteen. I wouldn't let her in here without her parents.'

Beatrice swiped across the phone screen changing the picture to one Sunita had sent to her. 'How about this girl? Would you let her in?'

'Bloody hell. That's not the same kid is it?'

'Yep.'

'She looks so different. Much older. You can usually tell when the young ones dress up, trying to look the part, but her, she really does look like she's old enough.'

'It seems that she went out dressed up, so she could get in places like this.'

'Well, I tell you she wouldn't get in any clubs around here, even looking like that. They check ID on anyone going in these days.'

'What about here?'

'Well, I don't have anyone on the door, so she'd probably get in alright and not be out of place. Mind you, we'd have ID'd her if she'd tried to buy any alcohol. I'm not going to get fined or lose my license over some kid wanting a drink underage.' Beatrice suspected he wouldn't have thought to ID Cassie, but let it pass.

'Have you seen her here? Perhaps when the band were on?' she asked.

'I don't recognise her, love, but it doesn't mean she wasn't here. They played Friday nights, so we usually had a bigger crowd in.' Dave turned around and called along the bar. 'Julie, could you come here for a minute?'

'What is it?'

'Have you seen this girl in here at all?' Beatrice showed her the second photo of Cassie. Julie peered at it, screwing her eyes up, as if it would help her see it more clearly.

'I don't know. Maybe.' She shook her head. 'I'm not sure.'

'She might have been in on the same nights as a band called Acoustic Dreams.'

'Oh, them. I'm glad they've gone,' said Julie.

'You didn't like them?' asked Beatrice.

'The music was ok. It was the lead singer. He was a bit of a creep, if you ask me.' Julie wrinkled her nose as if she'd encountered a bad smell.

'But you don't remember seeing her with them?' Beatrice asked.

'No. Sorry. I'd be busy behind the bar or collecting glasses. I tell you what though, Matt might know.'

'Matt?'

'He's the guitarist in one of the other bands,' said Julie. 'Nice lad. They played Fridays too. He's more likely to have noticed if the girl was around, whilst he was waiting to go on. What do you want to know about her for anyway?'

'She's missing and she's only fifteen.'

'Oh no. Missing? That's terrible. Her parents must be beside themselves.' Julie turned to Dave. 'Have you got Matt's number?'

'I dunno. I suppose it might be in my phone.'

'Well, you must have it. How else do you book them? Go on have a look.' Julie nudged Dave into action.

'Alright, alright. I'm doing it, aren't I. Keep your hair on.'

Julie rolled her eyes, whilst Dave looked slowly though his phone contacts. 'Here it is,' he said at last.

'I told you you'd have it,' said Julie, pleased at being proved right.

'Can I have his number please?' asked Beatrice.

'Can't do that. I'll tell you what, I'll give him a ring and see if he'll talk to you.'

Ten minutes later, Beatrice was sitting at a table in the pub, as far away from the bar as possible. Another guitarist had come on stage, but was playing soothing acoustic music that didn't make her eardrums pound. Opposite her sat a young man, around twenty years old. Matt had agreed to meet with her and, living just around the corner, he'd offered to come at once, for the promise of a pint. He was pale skinned with blonde hair, clean-shaven and of stocky build. He was smartly, but casually dressed.

'How can I help you?' His voice was clear and pleasant to listen to.

'I'm a private detective.'

'Dave said.'

'I'm looking for a young girl who has gone missing from home.'

'What makes you think I know something about that?' He sat back in his seat frowning.

'I don't know you do, but it is possible you might be able to help me. Can I explain?'

'Yes, sorry, I didn't mean to snap. Go ahead.'

Beatrice showed him the photograph of Cassie dressed up. 'This is the girl. It's possible you might have seen her.'

'Yes, I have definitely.'

'Really? That's great. What can you tell me? Where and when did you see her?'

'She came in here sometimes, on a Friday evening. Not every week, but now and then. Me and my band do Fridays here regularly. Helps pay the bills whilst I'm at university.'

'Can you remember when you last saw her?'

'I'm not sure. It might have been a couple of weeks ago. I can't say for certain.'

'Did you ever talk to her.'

'Yeah, a couple of times. We chatted about music a bit. She seemed interested in how I learnt to play the guitar. Asked if I knew any female guitarists. I thought she wanted to learn.' He sipped at his drink.

'What did you think of her?'

'She was a funny kid. A lot younger than she looked: she didn't fool me about her age. She reminded me of my little sister. I liked her though.'

'What made you think she was younger?'

'She asked me to get her a lager once. I said I would if she had some ID. Of course, she didn't have any, did she. That's when I was sure she wasn't eighteen. I asked her how old she really was.'

'Did she tell you?'

'Eventually. I agreed not to tell Dave. She thought he'd throw her out. I told her though, as long as she stuck to juice or water and didn't cause any trouble he wouldn't mind. She stayed away from me after that though.'

'Cassie went missing just over two weeks ago. Did she ever say anything that could give a clue as to where she might be?'

'You think she left home on purpose then? Or do you think she was grabbed or something?'

'It seems possible she left of her own accord, but I'm keeping an open mind.'

'Look, well, it might be nothing, and she never said anything to me, but once she started avoiding me, she started moping around after the lead singer in another band. They played here a few times, but they don't anymore.'

'Acoustic Dreams?'

'Yeah, that's them. I told her to stay away, but she just laughed at me.' Matt shook his head.

'Why did you say that to her?'

'Well, she was just a kid. Besides, I didn't like the look of him. I wouldn't want my sister hanging around with someone like that.'

'Did you ever see them together?' Beatrice asked.

'No, but that doesn't mean she didn't spend time with him. When he was off stage, I was on it, so I'd probably not notice.'

'Do you know why they stopped playing here?'

'They said something about Lincoln being too small for them. They wanted to get back to a proper city, they said.'

'Where was that? Did they say?'

'Sheffield. If it was so great, I don't know why they came over here in the first place.'

'Do you know where in Sheffield they were from? Or what their names were? Anything you can remember at all would be helpful.'

'You think she's probably gone off with them then?'

'It is possible. It's the only lead I've got.'

'I don't know where in Sheffield they're from. They talked about playing pubs in the centre though. The lead singer was called Mike. I don't remember the other two, they usually kept to themselves. I'm not sure they liked the other lad either.'

'It's not much to go on, but better than I had this morning. Thanks for your help, Matt. If you think of anything else will you give me a call, please?'

'Sure. You could look on the internet of course. They're bound to have something online to advertise the band.'

'Thanks, I'll check it out.'

'Good luck. I hope you find her.'

As she left, Beatrice waved to Julie and Dave, who were both busy behind the bar.

She'd gone for a walk after leaving the pub, to think things through and clear her head, so it was after eleven by the time Beatrice got back home. The house was quiet. James had thoughtfully left a lamp on in the living room, so she managed to enter the house without crashing into anything for a change. Perhaps I ought to get a timer, she thought. That way I can always have a light on when I come home late. And I don't have to rely on James thinking about it.

She locked the front door and checked the back, which was already locked. The cat's eyes stared at her through the window and Beatrice could hear it's plaintive meow. Sighing she let it in. It slipped through the narrow gap of the open door and, instead of being grateful to her for letting it in, the cat decided to meow even more loudly.

'Ok, ok. You're hungry, I get it.' She put out some food and water, and went back to the living room. She dropped onto the sofa and pulled out her mobile phone. It had already logged on to her home Wi-Fi network, so she began to search for Acoustic Dreams. It took a while and was more difficult on the small screen of her phone than it would have been on the computer, but she couldn't be bothered to go upstairs and switch the machine on. She found some promising looking links, but finally accepted she was too tired to carry on tonight. She book-marked her search results and made her way upstairs.

The cat followed, so Beatrice had to go back down and shut her in the kitchen. At least the floor in there was easy to clean in the case of accidents, she thought, deciding she'd have to get a litter tray if she was going to continue to let the cat in. Wearily she climbed the stairs again, hoping this time to be able to go to sleep.

Chapter 24

Tuesday 22nd May

The next morning, after a lie-in, Beatrice felt much better. James had already left for work so, after a quick bowl of cereal, she went up to her office and followed up on her search for the band. They didn't have their own website, but she was able to find a pub in Sheffield which listed them on their bill for a music night, which took place some months ago. She also made a start of looking at the business records of Bayfield Renewables. It would take several hours to go through them in any detail, so she spent half an hour familiarising herself with them. When she was ready for a break, she decided to call DC Susan Wilde.

'It's me. How are you?' she said, when the call was finally answered.

'Hi. Currently I'm keeping myself extra busy, staying out of Fisher's way.'

'Why? What's he up to now?'

'He's seriously pissed off at you: and me by association.'

'Why?'

Susan sighed heavily. 'It's the fact you found Cassie's phone number and those photos. Our boss, Inspector Mayweather, had a bit of go about why he didn't get them.'

'So I can look forward to another angry call from him then? It's not really his fault though. Sunita wasn't keen on giving them to me. It was only Cassie going incommunicado that finally pushed her into telling the truth. Even if Fisher hadn't annoyed the whole family, I don't suppose she would have said anything to him.'

'The thing is, Beatrice, he blames you, no matter how unfairly.'

'Great.'

'What did you phone me for?'

'I wanted to check to see if you had any luck with the information I gave you. Or will that get you in trouble as well?'

'I checked with Inspector Mayweather and she said I could speak to you, since you found out more than we did. Fisher's not happy with it, but he'll have to live with it.'

'What have you found out?'

'The phone was last recorded being used when Sunita said. It was somewhere in Sheffield at the time. She didn't phone any other numbers.'

'So, that's probably where she is now.'

'Assuming she hasn't moved on. It's out of action now, so we can't use it to trace her. We've put an alert on it, so if she does use it again we'll get some location data.'

'And the photos?'

'We had some PCs review the CCTV footage. We've traced her to the train station where she got on the service for Sheffield. She looked like she was with three young men. We don't have ID on any of them.'

'What's your next move?'

'We've already done it. We've alerted Sheffield police and sent all the details across. They'll circulate the information through their officers and hopefully one of them will find her. If they do they'll let us know.'

'You and Fisher won't go to Sheffield then?'

'We can't. Sheffield is a large city. There is no way the two of us could search effectively. We don't know if she is still there and, even if she is, where would we start? We need to let Sheffield do their job. They know what they're doing, Beatrice.'

'It doesn't seem enough.' It reminded Beatrice of the lack of action by the police when her mother went missing. Some of the same feelings of helplessness resurfaced. 'Isn't there anything more you can do?'

'No. Think about it realistically. Without anything more specific to go on, they have a much better chance of finding her than we do by wondering around a city that size.'

Beatrice considered telling Susan about the band Cassie had been seen with. What would they do about it? Tell South Yorkshire police and leave it to them? It wasn't good enough. She'd follow it up herself, that way she'd know it had been done properly. 'Did you get my message about Simon Bayfield's autopsy?'

'I did.'

'And?'

'We've closed the case, Beatrice. The autopsy showed he died of a heart attack. He had angina for goodness sake. What's to be gained by asking more questions about it?'

'Weren't you at all bothered about why he had no pills left? You know how they work right?'

'Of course. We do know how to do our jobs.'

'Sorry. But everyone I spoke to said how careful he was. There's no way he would have been without his pills. Look, if the autopsy showed he took what could have been left in the bottle then that clears it up doesn't it? Maybe he just carried on taking them in the hope they'd help. It would put Marina's mind at rest. At the moment, she's got a dead husband and is struggling to understand why.'

Beatrice listened to the silence at the end of the phone. 'You've got the report, haven't you? Would it hurt to take a look?'

'I did look.'

Beatrice smiled to herself. 'What did it say.'

'Nothing. It said nothing about the pills at all.'

'Is that normal?'

'Not really. If he had a high dose of any substance it would normally be flagged.'

'So what does it mean?'

'It could be the pathologist saw what he expected to see, given Mr Bayfield's medical history, so didn't feel the need to highlight it.'

'But you're not sure?'

Susan sighed. 'No. I'm not sure.'

Beatrice allowed the silence to stretch again, hoping if Susan's interest was piqued enough she'd make the next logical step.

'I suppose I could phone the pathologist and ask about it.'

Smiling Beatrice replied, 'Well, that would be the way to be certain, wouldn't it?'

'If Fisher finds out, we'll both be in trouble.'

'I'm already in his bad books.'

Susan sighed. 'Leave it with me, I'll get back to you. So, what are your plans now?'

'I'm going to go to Sheffield.'

'I thought you might. You know it will probably be a waste of time? Why don't you wait and see what South Yorkshire come up with? We're thinking about running another public appeal for Cassie with the new photos. It might give us some new leads to follow up.'

'I can't just sit around waiting, Susan. I need to do something.'

'It's your choice. If you do go, keep in touch and let me know what you find.'

After sitting for a while and thinking, Beatrice dialled the number for the Sheffield pub she'd found earlier. It rang out for a long time before a breathless voice came on the line.

'Hello.' The woman sounded annoyed.

'Hi,' said Beatrice, hoping she sounded friendly. 'Is that the Admiral Henry?'

'Yes.'

'I was wondering if you could help me. I'm looking for a band called Acoustic Dreams. I understand they've played for you and I thought you might have a contact number for them.'

'What the bloody hell do you think this is? We're a pub not a bloody booking agent.'

The phone cut out and Beatrice was left looking at her mobile in surprise. She had anticipated some difficulties – like maybe they would be wary of giving out information or it might take time to find them – she hadn't anticipated outright rudeness. She'd been naive. She briefly considered calling straight back and trying again, but it was unlikely to help matters and could make them worse. Cassie had been in Sheffield, and could still be there, so it was time to plan a visit. If she turned up in person, she might have more chance of tracking down the band, and in particular the lead singer. If Cassie wasn't in Sheffield anymore, then maybe he would know where she had gone.

The market square was busy for a Tuesday afternoon. The scout tent had its front and side panels rolled up so it was more of a gazebo than a tent. A table was laid with leaflets, with colourful posters stuck to its sides: Save our Villages! Stop the Destruction! they shouted out. Stella and two other women stood with clipboards and pens, waylaying any passersby, trying to coax them to sign the petition. They were having limited success.

Beatrice had left the market with a cat bed, litter tray and an assortment of treats and toys, and was making her way back home. She wanted to leave James well equipped to look after the cat, should her trip to Sheffield require an overnight stay. So wrapped up in her search for Cassie, she'd forgotten it was the day of the protest. There wasn't much chance she'd be able to cross the square unnoticed.

Sure enough, Stella turned around at just the wrong moment and caught sight of Beatrice. 'Hello,' she called out, striding towards her. 'Here,' she held out the clipboard, 'you can sign the petition.'

'I've already done it,' Beatrice lied. 'Online.' She didn't want to leave her address for anyone to see.

'Oh, ok.'

'How's it going?'

'Not very well really.' Stella spoke in a low voice. 'It would be better if we were here on a Saturday, but the police said we couldn't because there's another event on. So disappointing. We're still very far off our target of 5,000 signatures.'

'Never mind. I'm sure you'll get there.'

'The press are coming soon. That will help.'

'Oh, yes?'

'I had a call from a reporter, Mr Evans. He'd heard about our group and wants to interview me about the protest. Once we get in the papers, I'm sure there'll be a lot more people signing up.'

Beatrice thought about warning her that Peter Evans might not be as on her side as she was obviously assuming, but a hard look in

Stella's eye dissuaded her. 'I've got to be off now, I'll see you Thursday.'

'Oh, yes. Lovely.' Stella waved, then immediately turned her attention to a couple crossing the square who were clearly trying to avoid catching the eye of any of the clipboard holders.

'David,' Natalie called up the stairs. 'Beatrice is here.' She'd opened the door eagerly, before Beatrice could knock and immediately invited her in. 'Come on through to the lounge. Would you like a drink?'

'No thanks. I won't stop long, I just came to update you.'

David joined them. Natalie perched on the edge of the sofa, David sat next to her. They clasped each other's hands tightly.

'Do you have any news?'

'A little. Let me explain.'

Natalie nodded as she wiped her eyes.

'As you probably know from the police, it seems that the Friday Cassie went missing she had arranged to take the evening off work, to go into town. She collected her wages from the restaurant, then caught the bus. I believe she had also gone prepared to leave home.'

'But why? I don't believe you. Why would she do that?' asked David.

'Only Cassie can answer that, I'm afraid.' Beatrice glanced at her watch. 'I need to show you something.' She handed them a printed copy of the picture she had been given by Sunita.

'What's this? One of her friends?' asked David. 'Someone she was with?'

'No. That's Cassie.'

'I don't understand.'

Natalie took the photo and examined it closely. 'She looks so different. I wouldn't have recognised her.'

'I think that's why no one came forward in response to the police appeals. They wouldn't have seen Cassie as she normally looked to you. She probably looked more like this, with much shorter hair. You'll see it looks like she cut it herself.'

'But why would she do that? There's nothing wrong with the way she looked before.' David looked confused.

'Girls like to dress up when they go out. They often try to look older than they are. Especially if they want to get into clubs or bars.'

'But what do you mean "go out"? Cassie wasn't like that,' protested David. He looked bewildered. 'She is a good girl. She's not like that.'

'I'm sorry, but I think she did.'

'Where are you getting this information? Who is telling lies about Cassie?'

'David please.' Natalie put a restraining hand on her husband's arm.

'I'm sorry this is upsetting you, Mr Saunders, but you asked me to find Cassie. That's what I'm trying to do and I am very sorry this is so painful to you both, but I have to get at the truth if I'm to have any chance of finding her. As for where I am getting my information, I'm afraid I can't tell you.' Beatrice hoped the obvious link with Sunita wouldn't occur to them. They would achieve nothing by being angry at the girl. 'The most important thing is to find Cassie.'

'I'm sorry,' said Natalie. 'David's just surprised by this. We both are. It's such a shock.'

'I've shown you the picture because the police may decide to use it in an updated appeal. There's a chance we'll get more information on her movements and who she may have been with.'

'But it's been so long, will people remember?'

'Possibly not. I do have information that suggests Cassie may have gone to Sheffield though. It's my intention to go there later today and to search for her.'

'Sheffield? But why?'

'Cassie became friendly with the singer in a band and she may have gone with him to Sheffield. It's a big city,' said Beatrice. 'I'll start making enquiries there. In the meantime, the police here have contacted their Sheffield colleagues, who will be looking out for her. They've been sent copies of this photograph, so they'll be able to recognize her.'

'I want to come with you. I can help,' said David.

'I don't think that's a good idea.' Beatrice hesitated. 'If Cassie sees you she may disappear again.'

'She wouldn't do that,' David insisted.

'I'm sorry, but Cassie left for a reason. We don't know why, but she hardly knows me, so even if she recognises me it probably won't matter. Besides, you should both stay here. The police may need to talk to you again and there is always the possibility that Cassie will try to contact you. If she does get in touch, phone me on my mobile straight away. I need to go now: I have a few things to do before I leave for Sheffield. I'll be in touch as soon as I can.'

'Thank you, Beatrice,' said Natalie. 'Please bring Cassie home, if you can. Tell her we can sort it out, whatever the reason was that she decided to leave. It doesn't matter, it will be ok.' Tears fell down her cheeks.

'I'll do everything I can. I promise.' Beatrice stood up and showed herself out of the house, leaving Natalie and David hunched on the sofa, clinging to each other.

Chapter 25

Beatrice parked in a multi-storey in the city centre which she'd researched before leaving Lincoln. It was only a short walk away from the Admiral Henry and near a Premier Inn hotel, where she was sure she could get a room, if needed. She checked her watch. It was three o'clock. The pub should be open and quiet.

After parking her car, she continued on foot down and under a large roundabout, whose centre was open to the sky. She could hear the traffic above her. A group of young men, scruffily dressed, were hanging about. They looked Beatrice up and down as she passed. She returned their gaze steadily, wondering if they would say something to her – try to demonstrate their ownership of the public space. Perhaps they saw something in her expression, because they decided to ignore her and she walked past without incident.

The Admiral Henry was a large squat building. It stood a little way back off the busy main road going East out of the city centre. The entrance was at the front of the pub; wide double doors leading into a hallway. A further set of doors took Beatrice into the main part of the pub. It was very dark inside and her eyes took some time to adjust. A wooden U-shaped bar protruded out into a large room. Opposite the bar was a small alcove into which had been crammed a set of drums. Two very large speakers were set either side, pointing out into the room.

Beatrice approached the long side of the bar. An older man was behind it, pulling a pint of bitter. He had thick black hair and a long, droopy moustache hung off his brown face. As Beatrice reached the bar, he finished pulling the pint and presented it to the large man standing next to Beatrice.

'Cheers, Len.'

The drinker was probably in his forties, the same height as Beatrice, but twice her width. He looked very strong, but under his t-shirt bulged a belly announcing his interest in beer. As he turned to face Beatrice he smiled, looking her up and down with interest.

'Eh up, love. Aren't you a sight for sore eyes.'

Beatrice frowned.

'Don't mind him. He don't mean any harm, do you, Kevin?'

'What me?' The big man looked genuinely shocked. 'Sorry, love. I didn't mean anything by it. I just meant it was nice to see someone a proper size around here, instead of all these tiddlers.'

He gestured at Len, who rolled his eyes in response.

'Can I get you a drink? You know, to say sorry like. I didn't mean to offend you.'

'It's alright, duck,' said Len. 'He really is harmless. Besides, if his wife ever thought he was up to summat, she'd murder him.'

'Too right,' agreed Kevin. 'She can get real angry given half the chance. So what'll it be?'

'Ok. Fair enough. No offence taken,' said Beatrice, smiling at his sincerity. 'I'll have a lemonade, please.'

'Ice and lemon?' asked Len.

'Yes, please.'

'My name's Kevin and this 'ere is Len, the landlord.' He held out his giant hand.

'Beatrice.' They shook hands.

'What brings you to this neck of the woods? You're not a local, I can tell by the accent. Just moved in the area have you?'

'No, I haven't.' Beatrice hesitated. She was reluctant to reveal why she was in Sheffield in front of Kevin. She had hoped to speak to the landlord alone, but the two men sounded like they had lived here all their lives. Perhaps they could both help her. 'I'm here because I'm looking for someone and I thought you might be able to help me: I think she's probably been here.'

'Sorry, love,' said Len. 'We get a lot in here, especially on student nights. I don't know most of my customers these days.'

'Now then, Len,' said Kevin. 'Let's hear the lass out. You never know, maybe we can help.' He nodded at Beatrice. 'Go on then. Tell us what it's about and p'raps Len will loosen up a bit.'

173

As far as she could judge from a few minutes' acquaintance, they were decent enough. They'd be more likely to help her once they knew why she was looking for Cassie. She explained who Cassie was, how she'd run away from home and why she thought the girl might be in Sheffield and have been at the pub.

'You think she went off with this lad then and has come here?' asked Kevin.

'I think it's a real possibility. That's why if I can find him I might be able to find Cassie.' Beatrice handed Len a photo of the grown-up looking Cassie. 'Have you seen her?'

He looked at the photograph carefully, shaking his head. 'Not me. Mind you, on music nights I'm usually stuck behind the bar. We get pretty busy. Kevin here does a bit of glass collecting, so me and the wife can get on with serving.'

His wife must have been the woman who'd hung up on Beatrice earlier that day. She was glad it was her husband she was dealing with instead. 'How about you, Kevin?' she asked.

He took the photo from Len's hands and examined it closely, tilting it to see it better in the lights from the bar. He frowned. 'I'm not sure. I might have done. She does look a bit familiar. I don't go many places, except work, home and here, so chances are I've seen her here if anywhere. I can't say so for certain though.'

Beatrice turned to Len. 'Do you have a number for anyone in the band? They're called Acoustic Dreams.'

'Oh, it's him is it?' said Kevin. 'That slimy git.' He turned on the landlord. 'I told you, Len. I told you he was no good. You shouldn't let him in. I'm sure he was dealing drugs in the gents that time. You wouldn't listen.'

The outburst explained where the drugs in Cassie's room had come from.

Len sighed. 'I know, Kevin, but who else can I get? The regulars expect music on a Tuesday. Even that lot are better than nowt.'

'Do you have a number?' repeated Beatrice.

'Aye. Somewhere. Give us a minute.' Len went to the back of the bar and pulled out an old shoebox from a cupboard. He spent several minutes shuffling through its contents, which appeared to

Beatrice to consist of business cards, beer mats and odd scraps of paper.

'Here we are,' said Len, brandishing a stained piece of paper. He put the lid back on the box and stowed it away in the cupboard. Len approached Beatrice holding the paper out to her. 'That's his,' he said.

Beatrice took the paper. It had a mobile phone number scribbled on it, alongside the band name and the name 'Mike Evershed'. It looked like she was getting closer to tracking him down. 'How about the rest of the band. Do you have details for them?' she asked Len.

'No. Just his. The other lads don't tend to stay around long once they've realised what he's like. He sorts gigs and the money out himself.'

'What you gonna do then?' asked Kevin.

'I thought I'd give him a ring, try to get him to meet me. Maybe say I was interested in booking the band.'

'You should get him to come here,' said Kevin. 'Don't think you should meet him on your own.'

'I don't want no trouble here,' said Len. 'I've got music night to prepare for.'

'Never mind Len, love. You call him, get him down here. And if he won't talk, you give me the nod. I'll persuade him. I've girls of me own, and I don't like his sort.'

'Thanks, but I don't know if he's involved and I wouldn't want you to get in any trouble.' Beatrice was tempted though. Mike was her only lead and maybe Kevin could help her.

'He's bound to have done summat wrong. Besides, I don't need to hurt him to make him talk. Trust me.' Kevin grinned and downed the rest of his pint.

Thirty minutes later Mike arrived. He burst through the doors with an arrogance which immediately annoyed Beatrice. She was the only woman in the pub, so he came right over to her.

'Hello, darling.' He looked her up and down with a sneer on his face. 'Been looking for a real man?' He leaned in close.

Kevin grabbed him by the neck from behind. 'Now you listen here you little shit, you and me are going over in that corner there with this nice woman. And we're going to have a friendly chat and you are going to be polite. If I hear any more crap like that out of you, or if I think you're telling lies then it's going to quickly become an unfriendly chat. Do you understand me?'

Beatrice watched, alarmed as he shook the lad.

Mike cleared his throat, his single word came out as a whisper. 'Yes.'

'Good,' said Kevin. 'Let's get going then.' He pushed Mike towards the corner table. 'And don't even think about making a run for it.'

'When they reached the table, Kevin pointed the scared lad right into the corner and sat down next to him, blocking any possible escape. Beatrice took a seat opposite. Her heart was beating a little fast after Kevin's unexpected intervention, but she had to make the most of the opportunity to talk to Mike. There was no point stopping Kevin now and she wouldn't get another chance. She sincerely hoped that innocent Cassie hadn't been under the influence of the shifty looking young man.

'Where's Cassie?' she began.

'Who?' He was belligerent, glaring at her and Kevin in turn.

'How many girls called Cassie do you know? Cassie Saunders.'

'What's it to you?'

Kevin growled. 'Just answer the bloody question, 'fore I lose my patience with you, my lad.'

'Ok, ok. Look, I don't know where she is, do I? I can't help you.'

'When did you last see her?' asked Beatrice.

'I don't know.'

'Oh, come on,' said Beatrice. 'You're not going to try to pretend you didn't bring her here with you when you left Lincoln, are you? The police have photos of you with her at the train station.'

'The police! You're with them?'

'No, I'm not. But if you don't answer my questions I'll get them here. And I'll hand over a certain packet I found in Cassie's room which will no doubt have your fingerprints on it.'

'I didn't give her any drugs'

Beatrice leaned forward. 'I never mentioned any drugs, Mike. Now answer my question.'

'I didn't bring her here. She wanted to come. It was her idea, not mine.'

'Really?'

'Yeah it's true. She was fed up with those parents of hers, wasn't she? You can't blame her. Stuck in that place in the middle of nowhere. Have you seen it? There's nothing to do.'

'Come on, when did you see her last?'

'I told you I don't know.'

'I'm gonna wallop you in a minute.' Kevin's voice boomed.

'Look, I really don't know. I was stoned, wasn't I?'

'You must have some idea. Was it yesterday? This week? Last week? Think about it.'

'Last week, I think.'

'She didn't stay with you for long?'

'I suppose not. It felt long enough though. She kept banging on about finding somewhere better to live. It's not like I've got any money.'

'Cassie was paid just before she left home. What happened to that?'

'We spent it, didn't we. She didn't have much.'

'What on?'

'This and that.'

'Drugs you mean?' said Beatrice.

'Some of it, I suppose.'

'Bloody idiot,' mumbled Kevin. 'If you didn't spend all of your time worrying about getting your next score, you might be able to find yourself somewhere decent to live.'

'What's it got to do with you? It's none of your business.'

Kevin pushed his face close to Mike's. 'It's my business, if I say it is.'

'Where were you staying with Cassie?' asked Beatrice.

'We had a room in a squat in Nether Edge.'

'Where exactly.'

177

'One of them terraces on Vincent Road. Fifty-four, I think. It has just been sold to a developer though, so we had to move on.'

'I didn't think it was that easy to get rid of squatters.'

'It is if you value your health, isn't it.'

'What do you mean?'

'What do you think I mean? Look, a couple of big blokes came around. They threw our stuff about a bit and said we had a week to clear out or else.'

'Or else what?'

'A nice stay in hospital of course.'

'So you moved on.'

'Yeah. I wasn't getting into any bother with them. I'm not stupid.' Kevin snorted.

'Did Cassie go with you?'

'Yeah, but she bloody moaned about the new place too. Said it was even worse than the first. God that girl could go on. Drove me mad, she did.'

'Was she right? Was it worse?'

Mike shrugged. 'She didn't even give it a try. Left the same day.'

'Did she say anything about where she was going when she went?'

'Not to me, she didn't. We had a bit of a row and she grabbed her bag and stormed off.'

'When was this, Mike?'

'How many bleeding times do I have to tell you? I don't know.'

'When did the men visit and tell you to leave? You must have some idea of that or how would you know when to be out by?'

'Friday. Yeah, they said be out by Friday.'

'Did you leave straight away?'

'No. I was there a couple more nights 'til I found the new squat. '

'Was it day or night when Cassie left?'

'It was night, wasn't it. We went to the new place late, so no one could see us going in. We hadn't been there five minutes before she was off again about the smell and what a state the place was. I was lucky to get it before someone else did. Bloody ungrateful, she was. We argued, and she stormed off.

'Could Cassie have gone back to the old place when she left?'

'Might have I suppose.'

'You did know she was fifteen, didn't you?'

'So? What's your point?'

'You let a fifteen-year-old girl go off on her own, late at night, in a city she doesn't know, with no money and nowhere to go.'

'So bloody what? That's up to her.'

'How old are you, Mike?'

'None of your business. Look, I've answered your stupid questions and now I'm off.' He made to get up. Kevin reached up, grabbed him by the neck and forced him back down into his seat and spoke threateningly into his ear.

'Answer her.'

Beatrice glanced nervously over at the bar. Len was busy with a tea towel, giving a glass the best polish it had probably ever had in its life.

'I'm twenty. So what?'

'The point I'm making, Mike, which you seem to be too dense or stoned to appreciate, is that Cassie is underage. If you were in a relationship with her you are in a lot of trouble.'

'Nothing wrong with being friends with someone younger is there?' He looked smug.

'There's a law against having sex with them when they're fifteen though. And you're twenty. That's a big difference to the courts.'

'They're all at it at her age. Besides, you can't prove anything like that. If she says we did then she's lying, isn't she.'

'Perhaps. We'll see about that. The police could at least make your life very uncomfortable.'

'If they find me. I was gonna move on anyway.'

'I assume you live off benefits, Mike.' A wary look came into the young man's eyes. 'And you have to report to the job centre and prove that you're looking for work or they'll cut your money off. I think the police will know to start looking there.'

'You bitch! You set the police on me and I'll have you.'

Kevin pushed him back down with considerable force. 'Watch your language.' He gestured with his head to Beatrice to indicate they should move away a little to talk in private. They stood a few meters

179

from the table, making sure they were still positioned so Mike couldn't escape.

'What are you gonna do now?'

'I think I'll go to the first squat and see if anyone there has an idea where Cassie might be. She could have gone back when she left him. As far as I'm aware it's the only place she knew of in the city.'

'They could've all left the squat. Could be no one to ask.'

'I know. I'm hoping someone will still be there though. The two men he mentioned gave them a week which isn't up yet. It's something to try at least. If she's not there, I'll try showing her picture door-to-door in the area. Someone may have seen her.'

'Fair enough. I'll keep laddo here for half an hour, which should give you enough time to get up there without him interfering.'

'Kevin, you've been a great help, you really have, but I don't want to get you into bother. He's the sort that will make trouble for you if he can.'

'It's no problem. He's a little shit, excuse my language. You go look for her. If you don't have any luck at the squat there's places for homeless in town, you know, charities. She might have gone to bag a room there. You can find them on the internet or ask at the library.'

'Thanks, Kevin. Thanks for everything.' They shook hands.

'Just do me one favour.'

'Of course.'

'Let me know how you get on. You've got me worried about the girl now.'

'I will. Here's my card. How should I get in touch with you?'

'I'm usually here propping up the bar. And don't forget, it's your round next time.'

Chapter 26

It took twenty minutes for Beatrice to arrive in Nether Edge, at the street Mike had told her about. She was glad of the GPS mapping App she had on her phone which had led her there. Vincent Road consisted of two rows of Victorian, terraced houses. It was narrow, made worse by the rows of cars parked along both sides of the street: there were no driveways or garages. Beatrice walked slowly along its full length.

Judging from the multiple letting agent signs, this was a student area. The houses looked in reasonable condition, but clearly not loved and cared for in the same way a family home might be. The one house in the street that stood out from the rest was a badly run-down mid-terrace. It had a 'sold' sign outside and the ground floor bay window and front door were both boarded up. In appearance, it reminded Beatrice of her own house in Lincoln, though this one was in much worse condition with its grubby façade, rotting wooden window frames and peeling paint.

An alleyway led down the side of the house. Beatrice ducked into its darkness, surmising that the squatters would have found a way in through the back, out of sight. At the end of the dark alley there were two gates, one for each of the houses either side of the passage. Beatrice chose the one belonging to the squat and tried the latch. The gate didn't budge. It was about six foot in height so Beatrice reached over the top, felt around and found a bolt. She drew the bolt back and tried the latch again. This time the gate opened.

Stealing a quick glance behind her to check she wasn't being observed, Beatrice slipped through the gate and closed it quietly behind her. She found herself in a small paved yard. It was empty apart from an overflowing and pungent black wheelie bin. Beatrice put her hand over her nose to reduce the stink of rotting food. Clearly someone had been living here until relatively recently. She moved away from the bin and took a good look around. These rows of terraced houses were normally built back-to-back, but this particular row had a factory wall at the end of its short yard. There were large windows set into the factory façade but they were positioned high up and were glazed with frosted glass. There was no one to overlook Beatrice's investigations and it probably made it more attractive as a choice for a squat.

At the back of the house there was an off-shot kitchen with a window and a door. Beatrice rattled the door handle without much expectation; it was firmly locked. The only other option was another window on the main wall of the house. Beatrice was surprised it hadn't been boarded up like those at the front. Perhaps the owner thought the visible signs from the street would deter anyone from coming into the back, especially if the bolt on the gate used to have a padlock.

Beatrice used both hands to shield out the light and pressed up against the window to peer in. If the layout was the same as her own home, this was probably the dining room. She could see no furniture, but leaflets, newspapers and other rubbish were strewn all over the floor. There were no signs of anyone sleeping in the room though. Beatrice examined the window more closely. The men who had warned the squatters off had said they would be back on Friday, which hopefully meant they hadn't yet restricted access to the building. If that was the case, this window would have been the way in and out for those taking advantage of the empty house.

It was a typical wooden sash window. She knew they normally had a fixing in the house to stop the window being slid up from the outside. She peered at the middle bar across the window but couldn't see clearly enough to determine if it was locked. She pressed her hands flat against the glass, pressing in at the same time as pushing upwards. The bottom half of the window slid up a couple of centimetres. Beatrice wiggled her fingers into the newly created gap and pulled upwards. The window opened a bit more before sticking. She couldn't get it to move any further.

It looked like enough room for her to squeeze in, though it would be tight. She rummaged in her handbag and pulled out her phone, switching it's torch on. She zipped up her bag securely then lowered it though the window and placed her phone on top of it. She then ducked into the gap and proceeded to go head first through the opening. It took some effort, and at one point Beatrice thought she might be stuck. It was awkward for her to bend her long limbs through the gap, but she eventually managed it and was in the dining room, wiping her hands, which she'd had to use on the floor to stop herself falling head first onto it. She tried to not think about when it had last been cleaned and whether rats had been running freely in the house.

Putting her bag back across her body, she looked around. The room was reasonably well lit, with the light from the window and kitchen area, but she held her phone ready, expecting the rest of the house to be darker. She headed towards the living room. The stairs in the house rose sharply upwards between the dining room and living room. Beatrice shone her torch up them to check no one was there. She stood listening for a moment. All she could hear were muffled sounds of traffic. There were no sounds from inside the house: it was either empty or its occupants had heard her entrance. Perhaps they thought she was the threatening men returned to throw them out, and they were hiding.

She stood at the doorway to the living room and swept her torch across the whole room. Once she saw there were no people inside she stepped further in, examining it more carefully and methodically. As she entered, the smell hit her nostrils: the stale bitter smell of unwashed bodies and damp cloth. There was rubbish in this room too, but also in the far corner was a grubby looking mattress: bumpy with stuffing coming out of it. Beatrice walked slowly over to it and looked more closely. What she had, at first glance, thought was a pillow, was actually a bag. A rucksack.

Beatrice held it up in the light of her torch. It was hard to tell the exact colour in the artificial, low light but it fitted the description of Cassie's. She opened it up and looked inside, shining the torch into it. It looked like it contained some clothes and a mobile phone. Beatrice pulled out the phone and tried to switch it on. It was dead: the battery most likely having been drained. Beatrice put the bag down on the floor and reluctantly placed her hand on the disgusting mattress in the large dent where a person would naturally lie. It felt slightly warm to her touch. Could Cassie be here? Had she heard Beatrice open the window and hidden? Or had she left just before she had arrived? Or had someone else been here? Someone who had stolen her bag?

Beatrice knew she'd have to search the rest of the house to be sure. First she returned to the dining room and closed the window. If someone else came into the house whilst she was looking around, at least the noise would alert her. It's not like she could make a quick escape though the gap. If there was someone else here who wasn't Cassie, she'd just have to face them.

At the top of the steep staircase there were three open doorways and one closed door, all positioned around the small landing. Beatrice went through the open one on the right first. It was a bedroom, it's boarded-up window facing to the front of the building. A wardrobe had been built into the alcove created by the chimney breast which ran up through the house from the fire place in the living room below. Beatrice shone her torch around the room to confirm it was unoccupied. She then went over and carefully opened the wardrobe doors. Empty.

The next doorway led to the bathroom, its only contents a dirty bathroom suite. The surface of the sink was wet. Beatrice tried the cold tap and water splashed into the bowl. Either the building owners had forgotten to get the water turned off, or the squatters had found a way to get it back on again.

The third open doorway led to a small, empty room. There was plenty of the ubiquitous rubbish here too, but nowhere to hide.

Beatrice went back onto the small landing and reached out to the closed door. She paused a moment, thinking. Judging from the size and layout of the other rooms this either opened onto a cupboard, or to stairs into the attic. It could be either. It was also the last place for her to look. So, if anyone was in the house right now, which the warmth of the bed and the wet sink would suggest there was, then they could be right behind this door. Beatrice hadn't noticed from the street if the house had attic rooms, but she hadn't really been looking. Feeling a little annoyed with herself for not having paid attention earlier, Beatrice took a breath and pulled the door wide open.

There were no hidden surprises, instead a narrow staircase rose up and curved away around a corner. Light must have been coming from some windows in the room above because Beatrice could see clearly. She switched off her phone-torch and tucked it into her pocket. She wanted her hands free for the unexpected. She didn't think she had anything to worry about from Cassie, but it could just as easily be one of the other squatters, who would probably be a lot less friendly about her intrusion.

Beatrice ascended cautiously, checking no one was about to jump out on her. She arrived safely at the top of the stairs. The air was fresher at the top of the house, but it was warm in the room.

It was a large space, running almost the full length and width of the house. Two Velux windows sloped in the ceiling, one each at the front and back. There were five small panels set into the walls at a low level. Beatrice had seen things like them before. They were access panels into the parts of the roof-space that were too low to have much use in the room. They could still be used as storage spaces though. One of the panels looked as though it wasn't in place properly.

A noise from below distracted Beatrice. She stood still, listening. Was it Cassie? She heard the front door of the house opening. Whoever it was had a key. The door closed again and she heard indistinct voices. There were at least two of them. Deep male voices. She glanced around the room again. No, definitely nowhere to hide. She heard heavy footsteps on the lower staircase. Beatrice briefly contemplated the eaves and the open panel. She'd never fit.

'They'd bloody well better have gone.' The voice of one of the men came clearly up into the attic room. They'd reached the landing. She heard the heavy tread of two people searching the rooms on the floor below, then one set of footsteps stopped at the bottom of the attic stairs. Beatrice carefully took out her phone and selected Susan from her contacts. She held the phone at her side, her thumb hovering over the call icon, ready to dial.

The sound of boots on the uncarpeted stairs Weeklyed around the attic. Beatrice backed nervously away from the top of the stairs. A large, white, shaven head appeared, closely followed by a wide body. It took a couple of seconds for the newcomer to notice her. When he did he stopped and turned his head and shouted towards the lower floor.

'Steve. Come on up here, mate.' He called, then grinned. 'Looks like I've made a new friend,' he muttered to himself.

Beatrice didn't like the expression on his face. She knew the type; most women did. He was the kind of man who only worried about what he wanted. She pressed her thumb onto the surface of the phone and hoped Susan would answer quickly. She kept the phone by her side so the man wouldn't know she'd made a call and take it off her.

Steve had now come into the room. He was smaller than his companion, but didn't look any more pleasant. 'Well, well,' he said. 'We seem to have a trespasser, Malc.'

The weak ringing Beatrice had been focussing on stopped and she heard the faint, tinny voice of Susan. Beatrice cleared her throat. She hoped the microphone was good enough to pick up her voice.

'Hello,' she said. 'I hope you don't mind me coming in. The door was open.' The men exchanged a disbelieving look.

'I'm looking for a young girl who was staying here. I was told she's still here.'

'Not if she knows what's good for her,' growled Malc. 'People who know what's good for them don't go into other people's houses.' He stepped forward.

'I'm working with the police,' Beatrice blurted out. 'The girl is only fifteen. The police think she's been kidnapped,' she improvised.

'What the...' Malc took another step towards her, but Steve placed a restraining hand on his arm.

'Hang on a minute, mate,' he said. Steve turned to Beatrice. 'We've got nothing to do with kidnapping kids.'

'She was seen here. I just came to check if she's still around.'

'Well, she isn't,' said Steve. 'You'd better leave.'

'Wait!' A muffled voice cried out from inside the eaves. It was followed by a scrambling noise. The loose panel fell to the floor with a bang and a grubby face gazed out. 'Wait for me,' Cassie emerged from the hole. She hurried over and stood behind Beatrice, peering around her at the two men.

'It seems I got what I came for, so we'll be leaving now.' Beatrice took a step towards the stairs and stopped. Malc and Steve were blocking the way and they didn't look like they were going to move. She held her phone up to them. The screen showed an active call to Det. Wilde: she was glad she had put Susan's job in along with her name. Steve's eyes narrowed and he looked uncertain.

Beatrice put the phone to her ear. 'Detective Wilde. I'm here.'

'Beatrice are you alright?'

'I'm in Sheffield, with Cassie. I found where she was staying. It's fifty-four Vincent Road The owners are here and they're going to let us leave now. Aren't you?'

Steve grunted and moved away from the stairs, pulling Malc along with him. Beatrice grabbed Cassie's arm and steered her to the stairs, sending her down first. She kept the phone to her ear and went down the steps one at a time, standing sideways so she could keep watching the men.

Cassie had stopped on the first floor landing.

'Get downstairs, grab your bag and go out of the front door,' hissed Beatrice. 'I'll be right behind you.' They both hurried down the stairs.

'For God's sake, Beatrice.' Susan was angry. 'What the hell is going on?'

'Hang on.'

Out on the street, Beatrice was relieved when the front door of the squat closed with a loud bang behind them. She looked up to see Steve and Malc staring down at them from the first floor window. She took a firm hold of Cassie's arm and walked quickly away.

'I've got Cassie,' she told Susan. 'We're ok, but we need to get away from here. I promise I'll ring and explain as soon as I can.'

Chapter 27

Beatrice kept them walking for ten minutes before she eased up outside a scruffy café. 'This will do,' she said. 'You hungry?'

Cassie nodded and followed her inside. The unhappy man behind the counter looked up and frowned as Cassie entered. Beatrice pointed to a table in the window and told Cassie to sit, before walking up to the counter.

'I don't want any trouble in here,' said the man.

Beatrice looked back at Cassie. Out of the dark of the squat she looked even worse. Her hair was a mess, all knotted and greasy. She looked and smelt like she hadn't had a shower since leaving home.

'She's with me. She won't be a problem. We just want some food. Please.'

'Are you paying?'

'Yes,' sighed Beatrice. She opened her wallet and showed the man her money.

'Alright then.'

'Can we have two teas and two cooked breakfasts – one vegetarian?' She'd give Cassie the choice of which to have.

'I'll bring them over.'

'Thank you.'

Beatrice allowed the girl to eat in peace, watching as she threw the food into her mouth, barely chewing before she swallowed. The bright light by the window illuminated the patches of dirt on Cassie's face. Her left cheek had a purple tinge to it. A bruise, perhaps? Beatrice went to the counter to order more tea. As she waited for the fresh mugs, she wondered how to approach the subject of her running away. How could she persuade the young woman to go home, without creating a confrontation?

Beatrice returned with the drinks and allowed a silence to develop. Cassie seemed content to stare out of the window.

After a couple of minutes, Beatrice spoke. 'Do you remember me?'

Cassie shrugged.

'My sister Rosie lives near you in Sudbrooke.' Beatrice watched Cassie blow on her tea to cool it. 'How have you been, Cassie?'

The girl shrugged again.

'Why did you leave?'

'It was better than staying.'

Having seen the squat, Beatrice didn't think she was referring to the comfort of the Saunders' home. 'Why? What was so bad about living with your parents?'

'You wouldn't understand.' Cassie turned back to the window, her eyes following the people walking by on the busy street.

'I saw your bedroom,' Beatrice persisted. 'Not exactly a typical teenage room. It was very neat.'

'Mum tidied it.'

'You didn't want her to?'

'It didn't matter what I wanted. She said I couldn't keep it tidy enough, so she'd have to do it for me. Mum always likes things in their place. What were you doing in my room?'

'Your mum and dad asked me to look for you. I wanted to see if there was anything to show where you'd gone.'

'Why?'

'I'm a private detective and they want you home.'

Cassie stared at her.

Beatrice broke the silence. 'How come you don't have any posters up? No favourite musicians or film stars?'

'Dad didn't want me putting pin holes all over the wall. He said if I wanted pictures I had to save up to buy proper frames. I didn't earn that much from waitressing.'

'Not really the point of posters either.'

'No.' Cassie gave a brief smile.

'They let you have a job though.'

'They didn't want to. It took a lot of arguing. It was only when I said they were worse than Sunita's parents they changed their minds.'

'Was that why you left? Because you thought they didn't let you do what you wanted?'

Cassie nodded and large tears rolled down each cheek. She hurriedly brushed them away. Beatrice found a packet of tissues in her bag and handed them over.

'And now you've tried living away, perhaps you think it wasn't as bad as you thought?'

'Maybe.' Cassie was watching the passersby when Beatrice saw her body tense: her shoulders rose, her body became rigid and she shrank back in her seat.

'What is is?' Beatrice looked out of the window. Some way down the street a figure that looked familiar was standing by a lamppost, smoking: Mike.

Beatrice reached over and squeezed her hand. 'It's ok, Cassie. I can take you home. I won't let him hurt you again.'

Cassie's eyes widened and her mouth opened then closed. She swallowed. 'I can't go back. Not after running away. They'll want nothing to do with me.'

'That's not true. They want you home. They're the ones who asked me to find you.'

Cassie shook her head.

'What's the alternative?' Beatrice nodded in the direction of the smoking figure.

Cassie shrugged. 'How do you know about him?'

'I've met him. How do you think I found you?'

Cassie stared out of the window.

'You know can't rely on him,' said Beatrice, pointedly looking at Cassie's bruised cheek. 'He looks out for himself.'

Cassie covered her cheek with her hand. 'He didn't stop me doing what I wanted.'

'Come on, Cassie, he let you go off alone because he didn't care.'

'He did care!'

'Well, maybe in the beginning.' Beatrice doubted it. 'Think about it Cassie, he's twenty: he got you to leave you home, give him your money, encouraged you to take drugs, hit you and made you live in a squat – all because it suited him. It was never about what was best for you.'

Cassie's eyes widened and her mouth fell open. 'You know about the drugs?'

'I found them in your room.'

'Oh no! There's no way I can go back then. Can you imagine how they'll be because I've taken drugs? I'll never be allowed out.'

'I didn't tell your parents, Cassie. I got rid of them. There's no reason for me to mention it now I've found you.' She looked at the hunched figure. 'I'm not going to force you to go back home.' But I'll make sure the police know where you are, she thought. 'You need to make a choice, and it has to be yours. It's between Mike - a selfish, drug-taking layabout - and swallowing a bit of embarrassment, going home to the two people who love you most in the world. A boy who persuaded you to leave your home because he fancied you, or your mum and dad, who have spent the last fifteen years taking care of you, whose only fault I can see is being over-protective. '

'But they won't want me back when they find out I'm pregnant,' Cassie covered her face with her hands.

Beatrice sat open-mouthed. 'Pregnant? Are you sure?'

'I couldn't afford a test.'

'How long since you had a period?'

'Six weeks.'

'You've only missed one?' It was possible she wasn't then.

'Yes. But I'm always regular.' Cassie looked away, embarrassed. 'I feel different now.'

Beatrice stared about of the window, watching people hurrying by. This was a bigger mess than she'd expected. 'Well, if you are pregnant, Cassie, how do you think you're going to manage by yourself? Do you think Mike's going to help you?'

'I don't know.' She sniffed. 'I'm scared.'

'Of course you are. But I am certain your parents love you, Cassie. Whether you are pregnant or not, the best place to be is with them.'

'But I can't tell them.'

Beatrice looked at the child in front of her. To Cassie the thought of telling her parents might be enough to prevent her going home. And then what? Although she didn't like the idea of getting so involved in the lives of her clients, she couldn't leave her in Sheffield. If Cassie wouldn't go home willingly, Beatrice knew she'd have to call the police. Perhaps she could still persuade her.

'Cassie, would you like me to tell them?'

'Would you?' She looked up eagerly at Beatrice.

'I think it would be better if you told them, but if you are really sure you can't, I'll do it for you.'

'Are you going to phone them now?'

'I think it is best in person, don't you? Besides, we should stop off on the way back and buy a test. There may be nothing to tell them.'

Cassie nodded. 'Ok.'

'You'll come back then?'

Cassie nodded.

'Good. It won't be easy, but it will be ok. You can get through this, trust me. Once I've taken you home, I'll let the police know you're safe.'

'The police?' Cassie's face paled behind the dirt and she shrank back in her seat. 'I thought you were bluffing with those men.'

'They've spent a lot of time and effort during the last couple of weeks trying to find you.'

'I didn't know,' she spoke quietly.

'What did you think your parents would do when you didn't come home?'

'I didn't think about it.' She shrugged.

She really is just a child, thought Beatrice. Only focused on herself. Beatrice hoped the test would show Cassie wasn't pregnant. The girl couldn't look after herself. It was hard to imagine that she could look after a baby as well. But if she was, there'd be concrete proof Mike had broken the law and she'd be happy to see him face the consequences.

He was still out there when they left the cafe. Beatrice took a firm hold of Cassie's arm and steered her away from him. She could feel his eyes on her as they walked away.

Beatrice took a deep breath and knocked on the door. David opened it. He stepped out of the house and around Beatrice to look at her car. His face fell when he saw it was empty.

'I thought you might have found her,' he said.

'Can I come in?'

'Of course.' He stood back.

Beatrice went straight through to the lounge. David trailed behind her.

'Can I get you a drink?'

'No thanks. Is Natalie here?'

'She's upstairs having a nap. She had a bad night.'

'Could you get her, please?'

'She's resting; she needs her sleep.'

Beatrice reached across and put both hands onto David's shoulders and looked into his eyes. 'David, go and get Natalie and I'll speak to you both.' She turned him around and pushed him gently towards the hall. She was relieved when he didn't argue anymore and went to fetch his wife. They came down a few moments later, Natalie looking confused with dark circles around her eyes. Her clothes were crumpled as if she'd been sleeping in them.

'What is it?' Natalie's voice shook, sounding frightened. 'Where's Cassie?'

Beatrice took Natalie's hand, led her to the sofa and gently told her to sit, which she did. David promptly sat next to his wife and they clasped hands tightly. Beatrice sat in the chair opposite them.

'The most important thing to tell you is that I've found Cassie and she is safe.'

Natalie's hand flew to her mouth and she sobbed loudly.

'Are you sure?' asked David. 'Have you seen her?'

Beatrice nodded.

Natalie took a deep breath to calm herself. 'Where is she?'

'I've taken her back to my house for now. She's getting cleaned up.'

'We don't care if she's clean. She should know that.'

'Cassie asked me to come here and explain some things to you before she comes home. In fact, she's worried that you might not want her home.'

'That's ridiculous. How could she possibly think that?' Natalie's knuckles whitened as her grip on David's hand increased.

Thirty minutes later Beatrice left the Saunders' house with a bag of clean clothes for Cassie. She promised she'd be back as soon as she could with their daughter. Once they understood the situation, Beatrice had been surprised at how quickly the couple had accepted the idea of Cassie being pregnant. They'd even begun talking about how they could organise it so that Cassie could go back to school whilst they looked after the baby. Beatrice had worried about Cassie going into all that, as if her choices weren't important. Beatrice advised them to listen to their daughter and what she wanted, or there was a chance she wouldn't hang around. The Saunders' appeared to take it on board and Beatrice knew she'd done all she could. It was up to the family themselves to try to understand each other better.

After dropping a clean and very nervous Cassie off home, into the arms of her tearful parents, Beatrice drove to the police station at Nettleham. She asked for Susan at the reception desk, but it was Fisher who came to speak to her.

'What do you want?' He spoke loudly. 'Interfering again, are you?'

'Good evening, Sergeant Fisher. How are you? I'm very well, thanks for not asking.'

'Why don't you clear off? Your little friend isn't here so there's no point you hanging around.'

'I came to give you some information, but if you don't want it, that's fine.' Beatrice turned back to the receptionist. 'Is Inspector Mayweather in please?'

'She's not here,' Fisher butted in.

'Ok. I'll come back tomorrow and speak to her then. At least she'll be interested in what I have to say.'

'What do you want her for?'

Beatrice looked carefully at the angry man in front of her. Perhaps they had just got off on the wrong foot and she should try to improve relations. She stepped closer to Fisher and spoke in a quiet but clear voice. 'I came to let you know that I've been to Sheffield looking for Cassie Saunders. I found her and I've taken her home to her parents. You can stop searching for her now.'

'Oh, right.' Fisher rocked back on his heels, surprised.

'I appreciate you'll need to talk to her. May I suggest that you leave it a day or so before you question her. She's very upset right now.'

'Was she taken, or did she choose to leave home?'

'A good question, Sergeant.' Beatrice smiled at him. 'I suspect there was a great deal of persuasion by someone, but ultimately Cassie chose to go of her own accord. You'll probably want to speak to the revolting specimen who did the persuading.' That was an encounter she'd enjoy seeing. 'If Cassie doesn't tell you about it herself, let me know and I'll come in and explain. Someone needs to take that lad down a peg or two, and I think you're just the man for the job. Goodnight.' Beatrice left Fisher looking after her open-mouthed.

Chapter 28

Susan and Beatrice were upstairs in the café. Susan had sent a text early that morning asking to meet Beatrice urgently. Beatrice suggested the cafe on the Strait. They arrived within moments of each other, ordered food and drinks, then went upstairs for privacy: the owner had recognised Beatrice and switched the upstairs lights on without being asked. It made her feel as though she belonged there.

'Well, you've started a big row,' said Susan, when they were seated.

'What do you mean? About Cassie?'

'No. Simon Bayfield. I phoned the pathologist about how many pills Simon had taken, like you asked.'

'Why did that cause a row?'

'It didn't by itself, but it turns out there was no trace of glyceryl trinitrate in his system.'

'Is that normal?'

'No. The pathologist said given the estimated time of death and when the samples were taken, there should have been some.'

'He had none at all?' Beatrice frowned. It wasn't what she'd expected.

Susan nodded.

'But the people closest to him said he always had his medication on him and he was really careful about it.'

'I know. Which means we, the police, should have been asking more questions before closing the case. The pathologist is insisting it was obvious from the report that Simon was on prescribed drugs, and there should have been some trace, which would be recorded in the report. He says he shouldn't have to "state the bleeding obvious"'

- his words - to a detective Sergeant of almost thirty years experience.'

'And what does Fisher say?'

'He says the pathologist shouldn't assume that whoever reads his reports will have thirty years of experience – it could be "an idiot DC" for example.'

'He's got a point, I suppose.'

'Pardon?'

'What? Oh, I mean about the people not having all that experience, not about any DC I know being an idiot.' Beatrice grinned.

'That's better.' Susan sipped at her coffee. 'I think they're both right in part,' she said. 'I know the pathologist had a lot on – there was the car accident he had to deal with. He had too many bodies and everyone wanting answers straight away. On the other hand not every detective is a scientist and the pathologist knows that. He should have spelled it out clearly. And Fisher shouldn't have missed it either. Our Inspector's none too pleased. Fisher had assured her it was a heart attack and told her the autopsy confirmed it. No matter how much he tries to lay the blame on the pathologist, it's him our inspector can have a go at, whilst the pathologist is safe in his hospital.'

Susan sighed. 'It's just one of those things. I expect what happened was he did a thorough job of the examination, but didn't have time to check the report thoroughly. Fisher probably made it clear to him he was expecting natural causes – well you saw the body – and, because he found nothing to disagree, the report was likely checked over quickly. If the pathologist had known Simon should have taken some pills shortly before he died, it would have rung alarm bells. As no one told him, his failing to highlight the absence of medication is understandable really.'

'And instead of just saying they're both responsible, you've got a testosterone fuelled pissing contest about who was most wrong.'

'That pretty much sums it up, yes.'

'Fisher's even more fun to work with than usual now?'

'He's not too bad, I told you. It's mostly bluster. Might be best if you avoid him for a bit though. You did well finding Cassie, but it hardly shows him in a good light, so you're not his favourite person right now.'

'I wasn't planning on asking him out on a date.'

'Why ever not? He's such a fine figure of a man and so charming.'

They burst out laughing.

Beatrice returned to the matter in hand. 'What's next? With Simon's murder, I mean. Now that we know it's murder.'

'Come on, Beatrice, that's a big leap. We don't know it's murder – only it's a remote possibility. We have some suspicious evidence, or rather the absence of evidence, but it's not conclusive.' Susan finished off her coffee. 'There's not enough information or any grounds to act on. I might be able to persuade Fisher to let me ask some more questions. In the meantime, I think you'd better keep digging. It would be good to know why he needed a private investigator. I'll have to talk to the bosses and see what they want me to do. If anything.'

Their meal was served and they spent the time whilst eating talking about their personal lives, getting to know each other better. Beatrice found out Susan was a single parent to a thirteen-year-old son and liked to read and walk. She'd joined the police force three years earlier, thinking about the future, when her son would be leaving home. She wanted a career she could develop in. Beatrice talked a little about her past, but beyond mentioning her father's early death and the fact of her mother disappearing she didn't go into detail about them. Susan was sensitive and didn't ask too many questions. Once they finished eating they returned to Simon and his death.

'Let's suppose, just for a bit, that he was murdered.' Beatrice raised her hand to stop Susan's objections. 'I know it is unlikely, let's just say "what if?" for now. If Simon was murdered, or helped to die in some way, however you want to put it, who are the suspects?' asked Beatrice.

'I'm not sure I should be talking to you about this.' Susan sipped at her fresh coffee.

198

'But,' said Beatrice, 'in any investigation surely you have to ask yourself "what if?" and think it through?'

'I suppose so.'

'Think of it as a thought experiment.' Beatrice grinned.

'Oh, alright then, ' Susan replied. 'Let's start with suspects. The spouse is usually number one on the list.'

'Right. Marina certainly stood to gain from Simon's death. She gets his share of their very large house and rental business, a majority share in the Bayfield Renewables, which is solvent and has very healthy reserves.'

'Plus, she gets an income from the policy Simon took out just over a year ago,' said Susan.

Beatrice frowned. 'She told me they had insurance over the mortgage, that's all.'

'We found papers in his office for income insurance too. It pays out around two thousand pounds a month.'

'That's pretty wealthy by most people's standards. It must have cost a lot.'

'It's a strong motive and she had easy access to Simon's pills. Who would he have trusted more than her?'

'I suppose.'

'You're not convinced?'

'I guess I'm not,' Beatrice said slowly. 'She seemed genuinely upset to me. I agree she had the access and what looks like a motive on paper, but she doesn't want to run the business and it seems she doesn't know what to do without him. Did she know about the income insurance policy?'

'She says she didn't, in which case there would be less of a motive, but if she did...' Susan shrugged.

'Is there any way to find out?'

'I can contact the insurance company and see if I can find out how the policy was arranged and if Marina was involved at all. If Simon went through a broker or a solicitor then they might know if she'd been told about it.'

'Another point in Marina's favour is that she hired me.'

'Of course no one who hired you could be a murderer!'

Beatrice laughed. 'She does have excellent taste, but I meant if she hadn't hired me then it's likely the police would have just put it down to natural causes and stopped investigating.'

'That's true as it turned out, but she might have expected us to pick up the lack of glyceryl trinitrate in his blood stream and start asking questions. Don't look at me like that. It was an honest mistake. In the normal course of events we would have followed it up earlier.'

'We're agreed she's a suspect then?'

Susan nodded.

'Ok. The next one is John Jakes. He stood to benefit from Simon's death. He inherited a substantial share of the business. It's not a controlling share, though he might have expected Marina would ask him to run it as he saw fit.'

'He and Simon disagreed over the solar farm,' added Susan.

'More specifically about how it was to be financed,' said Beatrice. 'I wonder who John thought they should work with on the development?'

'Someone with a lot of money presumably?'

'Or someone who is already in the same area of business. A supplier or some other person they already had a working relationship with.'

'Are you suggesting we go through a phone book and question all the businesses in the energy sector.'

Beatrice shook her head. 'There can't be that many around here. Anyway I've got access to the business records. I can go through them and find likely leads.'

'Then John Jakes is a suspect?'

Beatrice nodded. 'Like Marina, Simon would have trusted him, and he would have had access to the pills. Who else?'

'His mother?' suggested Susan. They looked at each other and shook their heads.

'The protest group were causing him a lot of trouble, there could be something in that,' said Beatrice.

'True. If they expected the development would stop if Simon died, but surely they would assume it would carry on.'

'Maybe not,' said Beatrice. 'Simon was the real driving force behind it and John was worried about the risk involved. If it was up to him, he could decide to stop it. Marina certainly wouldn't push for it to go ahead.' Beatrice finished what was left of her coffee. 'I'm due to see Stella Bright tomorrow. I'll see what else I can find out. She was seen arguing with Simon last week and Marina told me she originally was keen on the development but changed her mind. I think I'll ask why.' Beatrice remembered today was the day of John's mysterious meeting. Perhaps she should follow him and see what he was up to?

'I think the best thing we can do,' said Susan, 'is to keep digging. We can meet again and compare notes and see if we are any further forward.'

'You've changed your tune.'

'What do you mean?'

'You didn't want to talk to me about any of this and now you're arranging another meeting.'

'You'd rather I didn't?'

'No. I'm glad you want to pool our findings. Right, I'd better be off. I've got the Saunders' final bill to work out as well as getting on with Simon's case.' She stood up, her head brushing against the ceiling.

'Beatrice, be careful won't you?'

'What do you mean?'

'It's unlikely Simon was murdered, but if someone else was involved in his death, they're not going to be happy with you asking difficult questions.'

Chapter 29

Beatrice had arranged with Marina to call at the house some time before midday and she arrived with plenty of time to spare.

'How are you?'

Marina looked tired and simply shrugged a response before passing her a coffee.

'Thanks. I'll go through Simon's office once I've had this.' She sipped at her drink. 'Have the police been in touch?'

'Not since Monday afternoon. Someone called to say they'd be able to authorise the release of Simon's body.' Marina's voice was flat.

'Nothing since?'

'No. Why?'

Beatrice had hoped the police would have been quick to update Marina, but it seemed not.

'What is it?' Marina looked her in the eye for the first time since she'd arrived.

'It's just since we last spoke things have become slightly more complicated.'

'How?'

'I asked the police about how many glyceryl trinitrate pills Simon had taken before he died. It was the empty pill bottle and the fact both you and Simon's mother emphasised how careful he was with his medication. It didn't seem right. I thought it was possible that he might have taken everything that was left in the bottle when the first ones didn't ease the attack.'

Marina shook her head. 'Simon knew that if taking two didn't work he should call an ambulance.'

'So I understand. Anyway, it turns out the autopsy showed he hadn't had any angina medication at all.'

Marina's eyes widened. 'But how? That's not possible. He always had pills. He'd have known if the bottle was empty. He never let them get empty. What does it mean?' The pitch of Marina's voice rose and it began to crack.

Beatrice reached across the kitchen table and gave her hand a squeeze. 'I'm not sure Marina. The autopsy confirmed Simon died of a heart attack. But it can't explain why there were no pills for him to take.'

'Do the police know about this? They must do.'

'Yes, though I'm not sure what they are going to do about it.'

Marina's shaking hands lit a cigarette and she took a long pull on it. 'I don't know what it means. I don't know what to do.'

'The police might come back to ask questions about Simon's pills and where he kept them. They'll want to know why he had so many in lots of places. You should think about what you want to say to them: you may want to warn Dr Todd.'

'Ok.' Marina nodded her understanding.

'Marina, I'd like to carry on a bit longer with the investigation to find out why Simon hired me, but I'll understand if you want me to stop.'

'No.' This time her voice was firm. 'I wouldn't know Simon hadn't taken any pills if you hadn't been around. I want you to carry on. I want to know why he hadn't got any left.' Marina sat up straight and wiped her hands across her face. 'When I spoke to Sergeant Fisher, he said they didn't need the office to remain sealed anymore.'

'I suppose they'll want it left alone now.' Beatrice didn't want another reason for Fisher to have a go at her.

'I don't care what they want. They took ages over the autopsy, didn't take me seriously when I told them Simon never ran out of pills, and clearly didn't even pay attention to the autopsy results. They just wanted to close it down from the start. As far as I'm concerned they had their chance. Take what you need. There'll be files on his computer for work: take copies if you want. There are memory sticks in his desk you can use. I have to go out soon.' Marina stood up and stubbed her cigarette out aggressively. Then she collected a set of keys from the kitchen island. 'Can you post the keys through the front door once you're done please?' She handed them to Beatrice.

The feeling of trepidation as Beatrice approached the trees wasn't as strong as on her last visit, but it was still there, lingering. She strode confidently down the path, determined to push the apprehension away. once at the cabin she carefully peeled the police tape off and rolled it into a sticky ball. The lock worked smoothly and the door opened in front of her. She paused, staring at the floor where Simon had lain. It was just an empty piece of carpet: no scuff marks or stains to show the body had lain there. Beatrice took a breath and stepped inside. She left the door open to clear out the stale, unused smell which had developed, and walked over to the window to prop it open, dropping the tape into the waste bin on the way.

She noticed a muddy scuff mark on the floor, right where someone might have stood looking out of the window. Wondering if it had been caused by the police, she checked the photos on her phone. It wasn't clear, but it did look as though there had been a mark by the window when she'd found Simon's body. The soles of his shoes seemed clean. Had someone else been in the office that day? It had been so dry, where had mud come from? Was it the fields at the back of the office?

She looked at the rest of the room. The bookcases only contained a small number of books and some pictures: Marina and Simon together, and separate ones of Mrs Bayfield looking proudly at her son. There were none of the women in his life together.

There was nothing on the desk, apart from the computer and a telephone: she checked, it had a dial tone. It explained how Simon could work even with the bad mobile reception under the trees. But why didn't he phone an ambulance when he had his attack? Was he in too much pain? Did it happen too quickly? If his pill bottle was empty, surely he'd phone for an ambulance straight away: he knew the seriousness of his condition.

The phone was on the corner of the desk, it's cable hung down then pulled taught around the back of the desk, across the floor to a socket set in the wooden wall on the left. Beatrice stared at it. It was as far away from where Simon had fallen as it could be. She closed her eyes and pictured Simon's desk back at the business. There the telephone had been on the left, suggesting Simon was right-handed: he could pick up the phone in his left hand and write notes with his right. So why was the phone on the right side here? Surely the cable would get in the way if he wanted to get to the filing cabinet? Beatrice moved the telephone to the left. The cable now had slack and lay flat on the floor, no longer in the way of anyone moving around the room. Had the police moved it? She checked her photos again: no, it was where it had been on the day Simon died. Interesting.

Beatrice sat down and switched on the computer. While it loaded, she began to search through the desk. There were stationery items in the top drawers, including several memory sticks. She found nothing else until she came to the bottom drawer. Inside was a carrier bag, rolled up tight around its contents. She lifted it out carefully and placed it on the desk with a dull thud. Beatrice peered in the bag. To her surprise it contained a large, solid lump of chocolate. The mass was made up of lots of separate bars that had fused together in one melted pile. She drummed her fingers on the desk as she considered the chocolate. She'd found empty wrappers at the business and now what appeared to be their contents at Simon's home. Why would he do something like that? Why buy the chocolates, or get Kerry to buy them, and then not eat them? And if he wasn't going to eat them, why not just throw them in the bin intact?

The computer was ready, so she began a methodical search of its contents. Almost all the files related to the business: documents and contracts relating to Sunrise, as well as business accounts going back several years. There was a file of personal letters written by Simon, mostly relating to donations he'd made to charities and replies to letters asking for his financial support from individuals and businesses across the local area. It looked as though Simon received a good number of requests for help every year and was selective about those he answered or sent money to. Beatrice took a memory stick, the largest capacity she could find, and began copying the files across. She left the computer to work and moved to the filing cabinet. It was locked. She retrieved the keys from the door lock. There was a small one which fitted the cabinet.

The drawers weren't very full. There were copies of items she'd seen on the computer, mainly contracts, presumably those he felt it was important to have hard copies of at home. Beatrice quickly checked through each document in turn, scanning every page. In the second drawer she came across a file for Sunrise. She took it to the desk and flicked through its contents. Pausing suddenly, she realised that she had caught a glimpse of Stella Bright's name somewhere in the file. It had taken a few seconds to register it being there. She turned back the pages of the file more slowly. She found it. The document was a copy of a land registry entry. It was for a large piece of land on the northern edge of Lincoln. The document showed it had been bought by Stella Bright eight months ago. She turned back through more pages. Yes, she'd remembered correctly, the initial scoping documents for the Sunrise development were included. She read them carefully paying close attention to the date they were written. It was very interesting and coupled with what Marina had said about Stella suddenly going cold on the project, it made sense.

Beatrice glanced at her watch. John would be leaving for his mysterious meeting in another hour and she wanted to find out what he was up to. She put the Sunrise file on the edge of the desk, planning to take it with her and look again at home. She checked the rest of the filing cabinet, the only other thing of interest she found were the business petty cash records for the previous year. She didn't have time to think about them, so she added them to the Sunrise file for later.

She finished copying the electronic files onto further memory sticks and picked up the papers she wanted to take. She locked the office and slipped the keys through Marina's letter box. Checking her watch again, she concluded she just had time to buy a sandwich from the nearest shop before getting to Bayfield Renewables.

Chapter 30

She had driven past the entrance to the business earlier and had noticed John's car, so knew he hadn't already left. Had Simon found out about John's meetings and that was the reason he'd wanted to hire her? It would explain why John had known nothing about her appointment with Simon. Or at least he claimed he didn't know. Beatrice finished the last bit of her sandwich and washed it down with water. Had John known, whatever his secret was, it was about to be found out? Had he taken Simon's pills in the hope he would have an angina attack? Beatrice shook her head. No. If you wanted to kill someone, it was an incredibly unreliable method. The chances were Simon would have realised he'd got an empty container and pick some up from his multiple sources.

Just then, John's dark blue Mondeo left Bayfield Renewables, turning away from Lincoln. Beatrice allowed a reasonable distance to develop, then pulled out. There wasn't much other traffic on the road and she felt very conspicuous in her red car.

He drove several miles before turning onto the road for Gainsborough, a large market town. There was more traffic on the busy route so she felt less exposed, but more worried about losing sight of him. A mile or so outside the town, John turned into the entrance of a light industrial estate. Beatrice slowed, allowing him to get ahead. When she turned into the estate, the Mondeo had disappeared. Roads branched to either side of her and she took the left turn, beginning a methodical search for John's car. After around ten minutes she saw it in the car park, outside a large unit. The hatches to the loading bays were closed so she couldn't see inside, but the business was called Diamond PV Limited. She parked up and used her phone to quickly search for some information. As she suspected, it was a manufacturing firm, specialising in solar panel units, both domestic and industrial. It was presumably a supplier for

Bayfield, though not one she recalled seeing mentioned in the papers. But why would John be secretive about meeting a supplier? At least, according to Kerry he was. She moved her car to a shady part of the car park, away from the entrance.

John left half an hour later. Once he was out of sight, Beatrice walked purposefully towards the business.

'Good afternoon,' the young man behind the reception desk said, as she entered. 'How can I help you?'

'Hello,' she replied, leaning casually on the tall desk. She smiled warmly. 'Can I speak to John Jakes please. I understand he's here for a meeting.'

'I think he may have left already.'

'Oh. Is it possible to check?'

'I'll see what I can find out.'

'Thank you.'

The receptionist dialled a short number and waited for it to be answered.

'Good afternoon, Mr Prothero. I'm sorry to disturb you, but I have a woman here who is hoping to speak to Mr Jakes.' He placed his hand over the receiver. 'Can you tell me your name please?'

'Styles. Beatrice Styles.'

Her name was relayed to Mr Prothero and the conversation finished quickly. The receptionist smiled again at Beatrice, but he looked uncomfortable. He was about to speak when a tall, thin man in a very smart suit burst into the reception area.

'You have no business being here.' He spoke loudly and angrily. 'You can leave.'

'Mr Prothero, I presume?' Beatrice held out her hand to the irate man. 'I'm Beatrice Styles. I work for Mrs Bayfield.'

'I don't care who you are. This is private property and I'm telling you to leave. Now.'

'Is this how you treat all visitors? Potential customers?'

'You're no customer and if you don't leave in the next thirty seconds, I'll call the police. You're trespassing.'

Beatrice sighed, as if she were dealing with a child having a tantrum. She drew a business card from her handbag and placed it on the reception desk. 'My contact details,' she said. 'Just in case you change your mind and decide to speak to me.' She nodded at him curtly, smiled at the younger man, and left.

She drove away from the business and found a quiet spot on the estate. She was shaking a little. Mr Prothero had responded very aggressively to her, causing adrenaline to shoot through her body. He seemed to know her name. Had he and John Jakes talked about her? But why? Unless there was something secretive going on between them. Something they didn't want getting back to Marina.

Her heart rate began to settle as she calmed down. When Prothero had launched into his verbal attack, part of her had wanted to escape, another part had wanted to respond in kind. She thought, on reflection, she had handled it ok, remaining calm. She still felt embarrassed about her first meeting with Fisher though. He'd caught her at a bad moment and she hadn't responded well to him. Maybe she could go some way towards mending fences next time she saw him.

Beatrice drove home, deciding to have a good look at the business records again, in particular the file she'd taken from Simon's office. There was a lot to think about and she needed to spend the rest of the day going through financial records, documents and contracts. It would be just like being back at work.

There was nothing more she could do on the business records for now. The five hours she'd spent had been productive. There were some very interesting things in there, if you knew what you were looking for. Beatrice reached her arms up and stretched, then moved her head around in circular movements, to release the tension in her neck.

James popped his head around the office door. 'Fancy a drink?' he asked.

Beatrice, who had been deep in thought, looked at him in confusion.

'I'm going to the pub. Do you want to come?'

She smiled. 'Yes. Actually I'd love a drink. Can you give me ten minutes?'

'I'll be downstairs when you're ready.'

She now had more information about what was going on in and around the business, but the paperwork had raised more questions. She was prepared for what she needed to do the next day, and an hour down the pub with James and a pint of lager was just what she needed to take her mind off accounts, cash records, contracts and land deals. She packed away the papers and slipped a few pages into a blank file for easy access. She was going to have to ask some tough questions tomorrow.

I enjoyed watching him die.

I didn't like the redness in his contorted face or the animal noises of pain.

No. What I enjoyed was the look in his eyes as he realised what was happening, what I was doing to him. I liked the feeling of power I had over him: the power of life or death. I made sure he knew why he was dying. Why he deserved it.

As he stared at me, his hand reaching out for help, we both knew he was going to die. I had made the choice, not him.

The man who liked to have so much control over other people could now do nothing.

It took longer than I expected. When he finally accepted his fate he fell heavily onto his knees before collapsing completely. He curled in pain, clutching at his chest, calling out again in a low moan, then he became still and silent. His hands slipped to the floor, his eyes stared blankly.

I leaned over, making sure I was out of reach of his fleshy hands. I grabbed his shoulder and pulled so that he turned onto his back. There was no reaction. His eyes were open, but he couldn't see me.

I didn't want to touch him, but I had to be certain. I cautiously pushed my fingers into the warm flesh at his neck. I tried several places but he had no pulse. I'd done it.

Mother would be pleased. I was already looking forward to seeing her approval when I told her.

Chapter 31

Stella Bright's home in the village of Burton was very impressive. Built from honey-coloured stone, it was a substantial two-storey building, surrounded by large gardens. Beatrice knew from her checks online it had cost half a million just five years earlier. She briefly wished she had access to her old resources at HMRC, when it would have been possible to find out if it was bought outright or with a mortgage. Marina had mentioned possible money trouble, but their home didn't reflect that.

The doorbell, whilst being new, was of the old-fashioned kind that was pulled downwards. Beatrice could hear it ringing inside the house, followed by the sound of high-heeled shoes on a tiled floor. Stella greeted her warmly.

'Hello, Beatrice, isn't it? You remembered our appointment, I did wonder if you would. Do come in.'

'Thank you.' Beatrice wiped her feet on the mat, even though she knew her shoes were clean. She couldn't help but feel grubby next to the well-groomed woman in front of her. She was led through the impressively decorated hall and an elegant dining room, into a large conservatory at the back of the house.

'Please sit down. May I make you a drink?'

'Something cold would be lovely.'

'I have white wine or lemonade?'

'Lemonade, please.' Stella left to get the drinks, whilst Beatrice looked out into the garden, which was as well-groomed as Stella. It was warm in the conservatory, but a fan gently blew the air around making it feel cooler.'

Stella returned, and they sat opposite one another sipping their drinks, Stella drinking wine.

'You're interested in our group then?'

'Yes. I had heard about it and I couldn't understand why anyone would object to a solar farm. I thought I should find out more.'

'How did you find the meeting on Saturday? Helpful?'

'It was. The objections you went through were illuminating. There were certainly issues I hadn't thought of before.'

'I hope we've managed to convert you and you'll want to join our campaign. If you like, you could stay for the meeting I'm having here with the committee at eleven. You'd be very welcome.'

'Thank you, but I have appointment later.'

'Another time perhaps.'

'I understand you know Marina Bayfield?'

Stella looked wary. 'Oh. Yes. Yes, I do. We go to some of the same events. Charity stuff, you know?' She waved her hand dismissively. 'Why do you ask?'

'I was talking to her the other day and she told me that you used to like the idea of the solar farm and that you'd changed your mind about it.'

'I don't know what gave her that impression. I've always been interested in the environment, and the solar farm would have a huge impact locally.'

'She didn't seem confused. She was quite definite about it.'

Stella shrugged. 'How do you know Marina, anyway?'

'I'm working for her.'

'What, cleaning her cottages? I'm surprised.'

'No,' said Beatrice, filing away the fact that Stella thought she looked like she spent her time cleaning. 'I'm a private investigator.' Beatrice handed over a business card. Stella had turned slightly pale.

'Then you must know…, but…'

'I'm sorry?' asked Beatrice.

'It's nothing. Well, I can't think why on earth you want to talk to me. What are you supposed to be investigating?'

'I'm sure you're aware her husband, Simon, died recently.'

'Of course.'

'I believe you knew him personally.'

'Slightly. We met occasionally at functions, that's all.'

'I think you knew him better than that.'

'Whatever gives you that idea?'

'You were seen speaking to him about two weeks ago, here in the village.'

'As I said, I knew him slightly. If I saw him it would only be polite to speak.'

'It was more than that though, wasn't it? You and he were having a row.'

'You shouldn't listen to gossip,' Stella snapped. She put her drink down forcefully on the table.

'It's true though, isn't it.'

'If we exchanged words, and I really can't remember if we did, then it would have been about the development. We didn't see eye to eye about it.'

'From what I heard it was about more than that. He used the words "and we both know what you're up to, but it won't happen." Isn't that what he said?'

'I told you, I don't remember.'

'I think he was talking about a certain piece of land you own.'

Stella's hand shook slightly as she reached for her glass and took a large drink. 'What land is that?'

'The land Simon was considering developing right at the start of the project. It was owned by a local farm, but you bought it.' Stella didn't respond, her expression grew icy. 'I checked the dates,' Beatrice continued. 'It was in Simon's initial plans, then a few months later he changed the development site. What happened, Stella? Did you find out from him or Marina where he intended to put the solar farm? You thought you'd make a large profit off him. It didn't work out though, did it. I think Simon realised what you'd done and decided he wasn't going to let you. Did you ask him for too much? It's funny how it wasn't long afterwards you started the protest group.' Stella stared at her but didn't respond. Beatrice could see the woman was thinking. She was sure Stella had planned to make money off the development. Simon would have known she'd taken advantage and he'd gone so far as to change the site to make sure she didn't succeed.

'The part I can't figure out is why were you both arguing so recently. Why did he decide to see you that day?'

'You have no idea what you're talking about.' Stella stood up. 'I want you to leave. Now.'

Beatrice carefully placed her glass on the table and stood slowly. 'I've said what I wanted to. I'm going to keep digging and find out what you are up to.' She picked up her handbag and walked calmly and slowly back through the house, gently closing the front door behind her.

'Can I borrow your car?' Beatrice was in her sister's kitchen sipping tea.

'Why? What's wrong with yours?' Rosie had her back to Beatrice and was scrubbing hard at an oven dish.

'Nothing.'

'If you won't tell me, I'm not going to lend it to you.'

'Fine,' said Beatrice. 'I need to follow someone and I'm worried they'll recognise my car.'

'Who is it?'

'I can't tell you that. They've probably done nothing wrong.'

'So why are you following them then?'

'Because I want to check. So can I borrow it, please?'

'I suppose so.' The oven dish was put to one side and Rosie began to relentlessly scrub at a saucepan. Beatrice had never seen her sister put so much effort into washing up.

'Thanks. I'll bring it back as soon as I can. You can use mine if you need to go out.'

Rosie grunted.

'Are you ok?'

'Why wouldn't I be?' Her voice was tight: terse.

'That's why I'm asking. I don't know.'

Beatrice allowed the silence to stretch. She looked at her watch. She had to leave soon. 'Is it Adam?' she asked.

'No.'

'Then what is it?'

'I heard you found Cassie.'

'Oh, yes. Thankfully she's back home. I just dropped their final bill off. Thanks for getting me the work. It's good to have one case finished.'

'Good for you.'

'Why are you upset that I've found Cassie?'

'I'm not.'

'For goodness, sake Rosie, just tell me what I'm supposed to have done.'

Rosie spun around angrily. 'What you're supposed to have done is found Mum.'

Beatrice stared at her in stunned silence.

'You managed to find Cassie quickly enough,' Rosie continued. 'Why didn't you look for Mum?'

'Do you think I didn't try?'

'You never said.' Rosie paused in drying her hands on a tea towel.

'No. Because I couldn't find her.'

'Perhaps you didn't try hard enough.' She threw the towel onto the worktop. 'Was it because you thought I was her favourite?'

'Don't be ridiculous.'

'Really? So where is she then?'

'You don't understand.' Beatrice shook her head slowly from side to side.

'Understand what? What is there to understand?'

Beatrice avoided Rosie's glare.

'What aren't you telling me?' demanded Rosie.

'I spoke to the police. There was no sign of anyone else involved in her disappearance.'

'So?'

'Don't you see what it means?'

'What?'

'She chose to leave us, Rosie,' said Beatrice. 'That's why I didn't tell you I'd looked for her.'

'I don't believe it.'

'It's what the police believe: what they wrote in their files. She left under her own steam. I'm sorry, but she left us.'

'If she left then she had a reason. There's no way she'd go unless she had to: someone or something made her. She wouldn't just go!' A tear ran down Rosie's cheek.

'I didn't want to believe it either, Rosie. I don't think she knew how to cope with losing Dad and she had to get away.'

'To do what?'

Beatrice shrugged. 'To start again, I suppose. Where she wouldn't be reminded of him. You know how much she loved him.'

'She loved us too!'

'Yes, but not enough to stay.' Beatrice's voice was louder than she'd intended. The idea of their mother choosing to leave still hurt. 'I'm sorry, Rosie. I can't think of any other explanation for why she's never been in touch.' Beatrice stepped close to her sister and put her arms around her, offering what little comfort she could.

Beatrice was parked a short distance away from Stella's house by eleven fifteen, now cramped uncomfortably into a VW Fox, which was far too small for her, but wouldn't be recognisable. She'd left Rosie's upset. Her sister hadn't wanted to talk about it anymore and that suited her just fine. She'd not been able to stop thinking about it though. Rosie was right about one thing: she'd found Cassie when the police had failed. Was there more she should have done in searching for their mum? Had she been too ready to believe the police's view? She groaned out loud in frustration. She had to stop thinking about it and concentrate on the task in hand.

She'd had the impression, when talking to Stella earlier, that she knew Kerry worked for Simon, and she'd been about to suggest that Beatrice must know Kerry. Kerry had said she was there incognito, but was it true? Had she been passing on confidential information to Stella, helping the protestors? She was convinced Stella was up to something, whether it was connected to Simon's death, she hadn't yet decided. Perhaps it had to do with the development site. She was making enough fuss in the villages. Maybe she had hoped she could persuade Simon to change back to the original site, on the land she owned. Whatever it was, Kerry could be involved and might know. When Kerry had shown her John's meeting in the diary earlier in the week, she'd seen the girl had booked today off work. Perhaps she was going to be running errands for Stella. Beatrice had decided to follow her.

At eleven thirty, she saw Kerry leaving Stella's house in a hurry. No one else left at the same time: was she unpopular with Stella now because she hadn't told her about Beatrice? She wasn't worried about the younger woman: Her involvement with the group was going to have to come to an end sooner or than later.

The place Beatrice had chosen to park was away from the route she knew Kerry would need to use to get to the main road, so when she saw the purple KA, set off she followed shortly afterwards. Once they were on the main road, she was able to remain behind Kerry, putting several cars between them. It helped that the vehicle she was following was distinctive. Kerry didn't head towards town, where Beatrice knew she lived. Instead they turned away from Lincoln on the bypass, heading South. Beatrice briefly checked the dashboard, pleased to see there was half a tank of petrol. She continued following, where possible allowing several cars between them, relieved that Kerry's KA was as underpowered as Rosie's car. It meant she was unlikely to fall too far behind.

Kerry drove a few miles away from the city and then took a minor road. It was getting more difficult for her to stay behind without being seen in the flat countryside. She trusted the girl wouldn't even consider the possibility of being followed, after all, why would she? Kerry was out of sight on the bendy road for about half a minute, but Beatrice caught up with her in a pretty village, where Kerry turned left off the main street into what looked like a private driveway.

Beatrice drove past the turning and parked up. She waited a few moments, watching the entrance in her rear-view mirror, in case Kerry came back out. She didn't, so Beatrice painfully unfolded herself out of the car and stretched with relief. Then she walked back up the road to the drive Kerry had turned down. The village looked small and was very quiet, so no one noticed her as she peered around the grand gateposts. She could see a long drive led up to a very large house in impressive grounds. It was probably a manor house originally, certainly built by someone with a lot of money. A sign partially hidden by an overgrown shrub identified the place as a hospice. In the car park, about one hundred metres away, she could easily make out Kerry's car. Beatrice expected she was here to visit a sick relative or friend.

She walked away from the hospice towards the centre of the village, thinking over what to do next. When Kerry came out she could continue to follow her, or she could try to find out who she was visiting. Beatrice couldn't see there being any connection to the protest group, but decided it was best to make sure. She'd have to be heading back to Bayfields to meet with John Jakes, so she couldn't spend much more time focusing on Kerry. In the village there were few facilities, just a florist and a convenience store which sold sandwiches. Beatrice imagined the florist did well out of visitors to the hospice. As she sat on a low wall, she began to think of a way to get the information she needed.

Beatrice rushed into the reception area, her breathing exaggerated to give the impression of being in a hurry. 'Hi. Is Kerry Honeywell still here?'

'I don't know. I can check,' said the middle-aged woman sitting at the desk.

'It's just she left these flowers at the office. I know she was looking forward to bringing them, but things got so busy at work she left in a hurry. I saw how important they were to her, so I followed as quickly as I could, but got held up in traffic. Did I miss her?'

The receptionist smiled. 'That's kind of you. I'll just speak to the nursing staff.' She lifted the phone to make a call. A minute later she hung up. 'I'm sorry, it looks like she's left already. If you'd like to leave the flowers, we'll make sure Lynn gets them.'

'Thanks. I don't want to be a nuisance, but would you mind if I gave them to her on Kerry's behalf? It's just Kerry was so excited about them, they cost her a lot.'

'I can see. It's an impressive bouquet.'

'That way I can tell her Lynn definitely got them, because I handed them over myself. I'm sure that will make her feel better.'

'Ok, that's fine. It's room twenty-one, through that door on your right. If she's asleep, please don't disturb her, she needs to rest when she can.'

Beatrice hurriedly signed the visitors book with an illegible scrawl.

She found the right room easily enough: the name Lynn Davies was written on a label on the door. It was small, brightly decorated and with a faint smell of urine and disinfectant. There was only one bed and in it lay a tiny, sleeping woman. She looked peaceful.

Beatrice tiptoed over to the chest of drawers and gently laid the bouquet down. No doubt a member of staff would put them in water later. On the table she noticed two framed pictures. One was of Kerry, probably taken a few years ago. She was standing with an older woman in a park. Beatrice looked closely. There was a similarity between the two women, perhaps they were related? The second photograph was of the same woman, taken when she was much younger, standing on a beach next to a row of brightly coloured beach huts. Beatrice glanced back at the bed, if this was her then she was very ill. Judging by the photographs, she must have only been around fifty but looked much older now. What was the connection between the dying woman and Kerry? And what was it about the photograph that seemed familiar? She was sure she'd never seen it before, but there was something about it.

Whatever Stella Bright was up to, it couldn't involve this sick woman. She must be a relative of Kerry's. How awful for the girl, she thought.

Chapter 32

John Jakes was polite, offering her a seat and a drink, but seemed more reserved than when she had seen him last. He looked tired and preoccupied as he sat waiting for her to speak. Beatrice decided there was no point going for a soft approach.

'What were you meeting Oscar Prothero for?'

'I beg your pardon?'

'I think you heard, Mr Jakes.'

'Who said I met him?' John began to fiddle with his pen, taking the top off and putting it back on again repeatedly.

'Please don't insult my intelligence. I'm sure by now Mr Prothero has told you of my visit. He clearly knew who I was when he was being rather unnecessarily rude. As you'd just finished meeting with him, I think it's safe to assume you told him about me. What I can't work out is why you'd bother and why he was so angry with me being there. What was your meeting about?'

'Not that it's any of your business, but I was talking to him about supplies.' He threw the pen onto the desk.

'I think it is my business given that Marina has asked me to investigate anything to do with Simon or Bayfield Renewables. She'd think so.' John said nothing, but looked angry, his face becoming red. 'I already know,' Beatrice continued, 'Diamond PV Limited isn't an existing supplier and isn't intended to be for the Sunrise development either. So why were you there?'

'It's not important. I was just discussing a possible future project.'

Beatrice regarded him steadily and he glared back; defiant. 'I don't believe you,' she said. 'I think you've been meeting Oscar Prothero since before Simon's death. I also think you kept your meetings secret from him.'

'Why would you think that?'

'Because Simon didn't like Oscar Prothero, though that may be putting it too mildly. I know because I called Marina.'

John stared at her, his eyes moving rapidly in their sockets as he tried to think of what he could say to stay out of trouble.

'They had history together,' Beatrice continued. 'Simon thought Prothero had treated him badly on a deal. He didn't want to work with him ever again: didn't trust him. I think you knew, which is why you kept your meetings from him: I know yesterday wasn't the first time you'd met him. You knew Simon would be furious with you.' Beatrice banged her hand on the table. 'For the last time of asking, why were you meeting with Prothero yesterday? Why did you meet with him before that, even though you knew Simon thought he was dishonest? Why would you do that, John?'

'Oh God.' He put his head in his hands. 'Do you think he knew? Simon? Is that why he hired you? There was something off about the last couple of weeks before he died. He didn't seem himself.'

'No more lies, or I'll go straight to Marina. She was very upset when I spoke to her about you on the phone last night. If you come clean, you might still have a job.'

'But I own shares in the company.'

'It doesn't come with the guarantee of a job, you know that. So, tell me. I'm losing patience.'

John gulped from the glass of water on his desk. 'I already told you Simon and I disagreed about the Sunrise development.'

Beatrice nodded.

'I did think we should do it, that wasn't the problem, but I thought we were stretching ourselves, or rather the company too much. The upfront investment will take almost all the financial reserves in the company. It was too risky. If something went wrong there was a chance we'd lose the whole business. Simon didn't agree. We argued about it, but once he'd made up his mind, that was it. It carried on worrying me. If the company went under, I'd have no job. I couldn't just forget about it, could I? It was alright for Simon. He had money put by and his house.'

'And you decided to approach Prothero for money?'

'No.' John shook his head. 'He came to me. He said he'd heard about Sunrise and it sounded too big for one company. He asked about investing in it.'

'You began to meet?'

'Yes, to discuss how we could do it. I favoured approaching Simon, talking to him about the merit of having another business on board, sharing the risk.'

'What did Prothero think of that?'

'He wasn't keen. He said they'd fallen out in the past and Simon wouldn't want him, or his money involved.'

'How did he propose you get around that rather significant issue?'

'He suggested we enter into an agreement instead.'

'What kind of agreement?'

'Well, he'd loan me the money, I'd invest it into the development and when it began making a profit I'd repay him from my share, with interest.'

Beatrice stared at him whilst she thought over what he'd said. Could he be that stupid? 'I know about contracts,' she said. 'I know about due diligence reports and money laundering regulations. So, I know that what you have told me is another lie. Not least because Simon would question where you got the money from. What was the real plan?'

John remained silent again, his hands clenched and unclenched nervously, his eyes darted around the room. Beatrice sat forward in her seat as if she was going to get up and leave. 'I should warn you,' she said, 'Marina and I talked about involving the police.'

John paled. When he spoke, his voice was less confident than it had been. 'Oscar's business would supply the PV panels for the development instead of the supplier Simon wanted.'

'And they would be more cheaply made with a bigger profit margin for Prothero, I presume?'

'Yes.'

'Out of which you'd get a cut?'

'So what? I worked ridiculous hours, but didn't get overtime.'

'You told me before you were happy working for Simon and with what he paid you.'

'I was. Mostly. It's just my wife and I have started talking about retirement. She has lots of plans. I didn't know where we'd get the money.'

'I need to show you something.' Beatrice reached into her bag and pulled out several folded sheets of paper. She smoothed them out on the desk then turned them around so he could see. 'These are the latest abbreviated accounts Diamond PV Limited filed with Companies House.'

'Ok.' John ran his fingers down the page as he looked at the figures. 'They have a large turnover, make a profit. Oscar told me they have been investing in recent years, so a smallish profit is to be expected. He's trying to expand the business.'

Beatrice pointed to another page. 'Look at the balance sheet. The company is trading with no reserves. In fact, they shouldn't have paid a dividend out this year. They have no money to invest. It's barely making a profit at all, even if the accounts are to be believed.'

'But he said he had been investing in the manufacturing process, so it would be easier and cheaper in the future to produce the solar panels.'

'The assets on the balance sheet haven't changed. If he'd improved his manufacturing capability it would show in the accounts with extra plant or machinery purchased. If there ever was any money, it isn't in the company now. Where has it gone? When you look across several years, which I have done, the turnover has reduced and so has the net profit rate. Oscar Prothero is doing badly, despite his fancy suit and posh car. Or rather the company is.' She sat back in her chair. 'What I don't understand is how you thought you could get away with it.' Beatrice paused. 'Unless Simon wasn't around.'

John's face whitened.

'I mean, once you'd got solicitors and accountants involved they'd be bound to notice. It would come up as part of the due diligence process.'

John looked shocked as if something had just occurred to him.

'You can't be that naive? Surely?' said Beatrice.

He gulped down more water. 'Are you sure there's no money.'

'You've seen what I have. I'm as sure as I can be without seeing the detailed accounts and business records. It doesn't look good.'

'When we met yesterday he said it would be easier now Simon wasn't in the way and Marina was letting me run the business. I could sign an agreement on behalf of the company.'

'But no doubt he didn't want you to get the professionals involved?'

'He said we didn't need solicitors. We could have an agreement between ourselves.' John placed his head in his hands. 'I've been a fool, haven't I?'

Beatrice didn't answer. She folded the papers and returned them into her bag.

'Are you going to tell Marina?'

'We all make mistakes,' she replied. 'But it's what we do about them afterwards that counts.'

'That means you are.'

'I think it would be better if you told her. Don't you?' She stood up and prepared to leave.

'But nothing happened. I didn't sign it yet.'

Beatrice paused. 'He gave you a contract?'

'Yes. I have it here. I was going to look it over.'

'Can I see it?'

He reached into his briefcase and handed a thick pile of papers to Beatrice. 'This is what he gave me.'

Beatrice sat back down and began to leaf through the pages. It was a complex document and would take careful reading. 'I think I should keep this and pass it on to Marina. I suggest you go and see her today and explain. I'll speak to her once I've been through this. If you come clean and tell her the truth, maybe you won't be arrested for attempted fraud. I don't know how you could do this to your friend. All for money.'

John grunted.

'When we spoke before you told me Simon hadn't always been a good friend to you. What did you mean by that.'

'It wasn't anything important.'

'I'd like to know what it was though. It might help with Marina if I can tell her how cooperative you've been.'

John stared at the surface of the desk. Lost in his memories.

'Whatever it was, you clearly haven't forgotten,' Beatrice persisted.

'Simon liked to be in control, get whatever he wanted.' John ran his fingers through his hair. 'There was a girl I liked. A lot. But Simon decided he wanted her and even all those years ago he'd do whatever it took to get his own way.'

'What did he do, John?'

'He took her off me.'

'What do you mean? How?'

'It was a holiday romance. We'd met these two girls and paired off. Simon had first pick of course. But I liked Amanda. I thought she liked me. Simon grew tired of his girl. He'd had his fun and she was getting too clingy. He said she'd been asking about coming back with us and meeting his mum. Can you imagine?' John shook his head slowly from side to side. 'Well, Simon had had enough of one girl, so he decided we could swap.'

'Why would you agree to that? Why would they?'

'I didn't. He never bothered asking. He told me Amanda had given him a message about meeting me and when I got there she was nowhere to be found. I thought she'd stood me up. I waited for a bit then went back to our B&B. That's where I found him. And her. In our shared room. I'd really thought she liked me. I was wrong. Simon laughed at me and told me to give them some privacy. So I left them to it. What else could I do?'

'Where did you go?'

'To a pub the four of us had been in a few times. Simon's girl was there looking for him and she asked me where he was. I was pretty angry at him, so I told her.'

'How did she take it?'

'About as well as me. She sat quietly for bit, looking at me, not saying a word. She told me to finish my drink, then she took me by the hand and led me to a place she knew in the sand dunes.' John looked away embarrassed. 'She'd decided to use me to get her revenge on him. If she thought it would make him jealous, she soon found it didn't. We saw him in the pub again later that evening and she told him what we'd done.'

'What did he say?'

'"Congratulations."' John sneered as he answered. 'He actually seemed pleased.'

Beatrice thought about the incident. It cast a less than favourable light on Simon's character and John was still angry about it. Was a desire to get his own revenge and his love of money enough to make him do something even worse than fraud?

Simon's work office was the same as when she'd last seen it. Beatrice went over to the filing cabinet and began to leaf through the papers.

There was a knock on the door and Kerry popped her head around. 'Oh, it's you. I thought it might be Mr Jakes. Is there anything I can help you with?'

'No thanks, Kerry. Just checking something.'

'Do you know where Mr Jakes is? I need to remind him about a meeting.'

'He was in his office a minute ago.'

'He's not there now. He's probably popped out for a late lunch. I'd better see if I can catch him.' She closed the door.

Once Beatrice was alone again she continued looking at the records, checking the dates on what was there. Petty cash records going back five years were there, apart from the previous year. Those were in the back of her car: she'd taken them from Simon's home office. Why did he have them at home? What did he want with them that couldn't be done at the office? Was he afraid John would see him looking? Had he found out about John's meetings and become suspicious about what he was up to?

She closed the filing cabinet drawer and walked over to the window. In the car park she could see Kerry and John. They were standing by her car talking. John was animated, waving his arms about as he talked. Beatrice watched the pair of them until they began to head back. They both looked up at Simon's office and saw her. John stopped in his tracks and glared. His piercing blue eyes contrasted against his pale skin and wavy black hair. His face was contorted in anger. Kerry had stopped and was looking up too. Beatrice held her breath. An idea had come to her. A reason why Simon Bayfield might have been killed. But could it really be possible? Had a motive been in front of her all along?

Chapter 33

Beatrice waited until she'd heard Kerry and John's office doors closing before going back downstairs. Sandra was in reception.

'Hi, Sandra.'

'Have you finished then?'

'Yes, for today. Do you mind if I ask you something?

'No, go ahead.'

'Has Oscar Prothero ever been here?'

'Oh, no. Mr Bayfield would never allow it.' She looked around to check they were alone. 'They had a falling out, years ago. Mr Bayfield wouldn't have anything to do with him. He came here once, said Mr Jakes had invited him. It was a lie. Mr Bayfield had the security guard make him leave. Said he'd call the police if he didn't go.'

'Thanks. Do you know if Kerry has any family locally?'

'Her? She's never mentioned any. Not that she speaks to me unless she has to. She used to talk to Emily, our old PA. She would have known. Is it important?'

'No. I was just curious.'

Back in her car Beatrice couldn't get the idea out of her mind that she knew why Simon Bayfield was killed. The rational part of her couldn't believe it was a strong enough motive for murder, but it was personal and perhaps it made all the difference. She started the car, deciding to go home and plan her next moves. She needed to think out her idea. She briefly thought about going to see Rosie, but didn't want to get into another conversation about their mum. As she drove, her thoughts bounced between the two problems. Could Simon have really been murdered? Did she really do all she could have in searching for her mum?

She was distracted and not paying enough attention to the traffic. The lights ahead changed red and she had to stamp on the brakes to avoid crashing into the back of another car.

Except the brakes didn't work. The car wasn't slowing.

She pumped the brakes repeatedly, they didn't work. She pulled on the handbrake, put the car into second, then first gear to try to slow the engine.

When she hit the other car, the airbag exploded in her face, knocking the air out of her lungs. She sat for a moment, dazed. Sounds began to form in her ears. There was knocking on the window and a muffled voice.

'Are you alright?'

Beatrice pushed the remnants of the airbag to one side and undid the door. She tried to get out, but was held in place by the seatbelt.

A middle-aged woman peered in through the open door, frowning. 'Take your time. Must have been a bit of a shock.'

Beatrice un-clicked the seatbelt and climbed slowly out of the car.

'Are you alright?' the woman asked again.

'I will be, thanks.' Beatrice managed a weak smile. She hadn't been driving at much of a speed so the damage wasn't as bad as it could have been. 'Was it you I hit?'

'No. That's the driver over there.' A man in his twenties stood at the side of the road, on his mobile phone. 'I was behind you. I saw your brake lights come on, but you just kept right on.'

'They didn't work,' said Beatrice, almost as much to herself as the woman.

I'm sorry, I've got to get off. Here's my address for the police.' She handed over a business card. 'That's my work, but it has my mobile number: you can give them that.'

'Thank you.'

Susan arrived shortly after the uniformed officers in response to Beatrice's call.

'Are you ok?' she asked.

'Not too bad, thanks.' Beatrice rubbed at her shoulder where the seatbelt had stopped her body being thrown forwards.

'What did you want me for? The PCs can deal with an accident.
'My brakes didn't work.'
'What do you mean?'
'Just what I said. My brakes didn't work at all.' She looked down at the younger woman. 'They were perfectly fine this morning.'
'Well, something must have gone wrong. You should get it serviced regularly.'
'My brother-in-law is a mechanic. He serviced it three weeks ago. There was nothing wrong with my car until today, Susan.'
'Wait there.' Susan went over to one of the Traffic PCs and held a brief conversation with him. He lay down on the floor next to Beatrice's car and pulled himself underneath it. A minute later he came back out and said a few words to Susan.
'What is it?' Beatrice asked as the DC walked over to her, notebook in hand. 'I thought you said they could deal with it.' She gestured towards the PCs.
'Have you rung your breakdown service yet?'
'No.'
'Good.'
'What's going on?'
'It looks as though the brakes have been cut through.'
Beatrice stood still and considered. 'Could they have worn?'
Susan shook her head. 'It looks clean according to PC Williams. We'll take your car and get a proper look at it.' Susan folded her arms. 'Who have you upset?'
'Fisher?'
'Seriously, Beatrice.'
'I can't think of anyone who'd do something so awful. Except...'
'Except who?'
'Well, that kid Mike, who Cassie went off with. He threatened me. But he's with South Yorkshire police, so it can't have been him.'
Susan looked uncomfortable. 'Actually, they had to let him go, pending further investigation. He made some unsavoury comments to the arresting officers about you, I'm afraid.'
'But they let him go anyway? So where is he now?'
'We don't know. He's supposed to report back next week.'

'In the meantime he could be trying to kill me.'

'We can't lock people up when they haven't been found guilty of anything.'

'Have you warned Cassie and her family?'

'I'm going to. I'll tell them to be careful. Let me give you a lift home first.'

Emily Jones had a small flat in Lincoln. Beatrice had asked Marina for her details and when she called, the young woman agreed to meet without hesitation. The flat was just off the High Street, in a nondescript block a short walk from Beatrice's home. Emily had answered the door, muttered 'hello' and stood aside for Beatrice to enter the dark hallway. After closing the door, she led the way into a small living room that also served as a dining area. In the light, Beatrice was able to get a better look at Simon's ex-PA. She had dark eyes which stood out from her pale round face. Her straight, brown hair was tied back in a ponytail.

'Thank you for agreeing to see me, Emily.'

'How is she? Mrs Bayfield. I read in the paper about Mr Bayfield. It was such a shock, he was so young really.'

'Shall we sit?'

'Yes, please do.' Emily gestured at a well-worn armchair and sat on a matching one opposite.

'Mrs Bayfield is doing as well as can be expected in the circumstances.'

'She must be feeling awful. I thought about getting in touch, you know. Once I'd read about it. But I didn't know whether it would be ok.' She shrugged.

'Look, Emily, there's no easy way to say this so I'll just get on with it. Ok?'

Emily nodded.

'Marina has asked me to look into a couple of things to do with the business. I've come to talk to you about why you were fired.'

Emily folded her arms across her chest, hugging herself. 'I thought I was done with all of that. Besides, I'm sure she told you.'

232

'She did. And she also told me that she never really believed it could be true.'

'She said that?'

'Yes.'

'Oh.' Emily smiled.

'Can you tell me about the time leading up to you leaving your job?' asked Beatrice.

'What do you want to know?'

'Anything that you can remember. Whatever sticks in your mind. What was going on in the business, how everyone was, how the theft was discovered.'

'The business had been doing ok for a while. Mr Bayfield and Mr Jakes were pretty wrapped up in the plans for the new development.'

'When was this?'

'About ten months ago I suppose. It takes ages to get a development off the ground. There's loads of work to do even before you think about putting in a planning application.'

'Go on.'

'Well, there was plenty for me to do, what with the bookkeeping, invoicing, accounts and so on, so Mr Bayfield agreed we needed more help.'

'And that's when Kerry was hired?'

Emily nodded.

'How did Kerry come to get the job?' asked Beatrice.

'I recommended her.'

'How did you know her?'

'I'd met her about a month before. I was in town on a night out with some friends and we got talking. She said she was new to the area, doing temp work in an office and didn't know anyone. She said she hadn't got any family. I guess I took pity on her, so we arranged to meet up. We got friendly and met quite often. I thought she was nice, good company.'

'And when you needed extra help in the office you thought she'd fit in.'

'Yes. And I was right, she did. We worked well together. She helped take some of the pressure off.'

'Do you still see her?'

'Occasionally, but not so often these days. She's been busy with work, doing overtime. I'm sure we'll catch up again soon, once things quieten down.'

'How did John and Simon get on?'

'Very well, most of the time. I think John got annoyed sometimes, because Mr Bayfield liked things done his way. But he was the boss.'

'Did they ever argue?'

'Not that I heard.'

'Did Mr Bayfield ever show you any evidence to explain why he thought you were stealing?'

'No! Nothing.' Emily spoke angrily. 'I'd worked there two years and he wouldn't even give me a chance to show him it must have been wrong. I don't know how he could think I would do anything like that. I'm sure it was a mistake in recording. If he'd let me, I know I could have sorted it out. And now he's dead, so I'll never be able to convince him.'

'Did he say why he wouldn't let you explain?'

Emily shook her head. 'He said he was disappointed in me, he'd trusted me, and I'd just make up lies to try to convince him there was nothing wrong. He said if I went quietly he'd give me a reference.'

'And you agreed?'

'I had to. I could see there was no way he was going to listen, and I'd never get another job without a reference, so I had to go along with it, even though I knew he was wrong.'

'Can I show you something?'

Emily sniffed. 'Of course.'

Beatrice dug around in her bag and pulled out the scrap of paper which she'd taken from Simon's office. She held it out to Emily. 'If you hold it to the light you can make out some letters where the pencil has missed. Is that Mr Bayfield's writing?'

Emily took it over to the window, tilting the paper. 'Oh, I see it. Yes. That's definitely his writing. I don't know what it means though. It doesn't look like a real word.'

Beatrice stood up and took the paper from her. 'Thanks for seeing me, Emily. I appreciate it.'

'Do you think Mrs Bayfield would mind if I sent her a card?'

'I don't think she would.' Beatrice considered. Everything had become so much more complicated in the last couple of days but she hoped soon she'd fully understand the events surrounding Simon's death. Marina was going to be preoccupied with John too. 'Can you leave it until next week though?' Beatrice thought about telling the girl what she'd found from the petty cash records, that maybe Simon hadn't died thinking she was a thief, but it was all tied in to his death and she still needed more information to be sure.

Chapter 34

'Did John come and see you yesterday?' Beatrice asked Marina once they were settled in the living room with coffee.

'Yes.' Marina shook her head sadly. 'He told me he'd been colluding with Oscar Prothero over the Sunrise development and had planned a way to get money out of the business and into his own pockets.'

So he had come clean. She was relieved. 'What are you going to do?'

'I don't know. I don't know how to run the business myself, but can I trust him? He said he'd been talking to you yesterday and realised he needed to confess, maybe he has a conscience.'

'That's not quite how it happened,' said Beatrice, sighing. She explained how she'd discovered what John was up to and that it had taken several attempts to get him to tell the truth. How he'd been reluctant to tell Marina about it.

She handed over the contract Oscar Prothero had wanted John to sign. 'You need to look at this, or have your solicitor look at it. If he had signed then, in my opinion, you could have lost the whole business.'

'But I never agreed to it. Surely it wouldn't have been binding.'

'I think you would have had a very hard time proving that. By asking John to take care of the business after Simon's death you effectively authorised him to make decisions like this. It wouldn't be cheap or quick to challenge through the courts either. Also, by the time you realised, it would probably have been too late to save the business.'

'You think I should sack him?'

'I just think you need to have your eyes open, if you carry on working with him. You should take some professional advice.'

'I'll think about it.' Marina sighed. 'This is so horrible. Simon and he were best friends. How could he do this to Simon? To the business? To me? I was at his wedding. We're Godparents to his eldest son. Why?'

'I think money was at least part of his motivation.'

'Part? Why else would he want to hurt us like this?'

'Did Simon ever say anything to you about an incident with John and a girl they both knew?'

'I'm not sure what you mean. You don't think Simon was having an affair? I don't believe it.'

'I'm talking about their past. When they were both young. You don't need to know the details, but John told me yesterday about how Simon had taken his girlfriend away from him. It was a holiday romance, but it had an impact on John.'

'Are you talking about when they went to Wales? That's the only holiday I know of when they went away together. They were eighteen. How can he still be upset about it? Do you really think that's why he was prepared to steal from the business?'

'I don't know.'

'How strange.'

'What?'

'It's funny, you mentioning that holiday. John and I were talking about it a few weeks ago. We were looking though some old photos: he was feeling nostalgic. There was a striking one of him and John on the beach. He said they were on holiday when it was taken.'

'Did he say anything more about it?'

'No. He looked at it for a while, but we moved on and got talking about other things.'

'Do you know where in Wales they went?'

'I know they went to Rhyl to the beach, but they stayed in another town. What was it called? Sorry, I can't remember. Does it matter?'

'Probably not,' said Beatrice.

'I think his mother used to have a copy of the same photo in her living room. She might know where it was taken.'

Chapter 35

'Thanks for coming to meet me,' said Beatrice, after opening her front door to Susan.

'That's ok. Have you put the kettle on?'

'Yes. It's boiled once already. Come on through.' They passed through the living room into the dining room, where the table was covered in piles of paper.

'What's all this?' asked Susan.

'Don't worry, we'll get to it.' Beatrice breathed deeply, trying to relax. 'I want to straighten out a lot of things in my mind, but I'm struggling, to be honest. That's why I asked you to come.'

Susan tipped her head to one side. 'Am I here officially? Or a friendly ear?'

'Both, I hope. I've found out some things since we last spoke and I think I'm going to need police resources to finally get to the bottom of what happened to Simon Bayfield.'

'I'll listen.'

Beatrice made drinks and they sat at the dining room table, where she could show Susan what she had found. She talked through her search of Simon's office and how the records had led her to some interesting discoveries. She also filled Susan in on her conversations with John and Stella and what she suspected from her analysis of the petty cash records. Susan's abandoned coffee cooled.

'God, what a mess,' said Susan, once she'd taken it all in. 'That's a lot for his wife to sort through.'

'I think it's worse.'

'How do you mean?'

Beatrice stood up and picked up the cold coffee. 'I think there really is a chance Simon was murdered.' She walked to the kitchen, filled the kettle and switched it on.

'You think someone took his pills from him?'

'It's not as straightforward as that.' Beatrice shook her head. 'Simon always had a bottle with him and would have noticed if it was empty.'

'Someone swapped them then?'

'I think so. Swapped them for something else that looked the same, but wouldn't help him at all.'

'So you think this person waited for him to have an attack and knew that if it was serious enough he'd take the replacements and he'd die. It was just bad luck he'd had the attack right before you were due to meet him?'

'I don't think so.' She poured Susan a fresh coffee then handed it to her. 'What if it wasn't just left to chance?'

'What do you mean?'

'Well, think about it.' Beatrice sat back down. 'If you were a murderer and were going to swap the pills for, I don't know, sugar tablets – or something else that looks the same – how could you make sure those were the ones taken when he opened the bottle? Bearing in mind that what we know about Simon means he'd always have more than two left.'

Susan frowned. 'I don't understand.'

'Sorry. Let me explain properly. Ok. Simon had angina.'

Susan nodded her agreement.

'The medicine he was given is glyceryl trinitrate in tablet form. They are small, white, round tablets. If he feels an attack coming on he takes out a tablet, puts it under his tongue and lets it dissolve. Right?' Beatrice mimed the action to emphasis the point.

'Yes. With you so far.'

'If the first tablet doesn't work, then he can take a second one five minutes later. But, if that doesn't work, he is supposed to phone an ambulance straight away. Because more pills wouldn't help. Simon knew all this. So did Marina, John Jakes and anyone else who was close to him.'

'Right.'

'Now, imagine a bottle full of tablets. If only a couple were swapped, and Simon had an attack, the chances of him using the dodgy, useless pills are really low.'

'I agree. But at some point he'd get the pills that didn't work.'

'The chances are that from a load of them, with only two useless ones, he'd probably pull out a good pill. But even if the first pill was a fake one, the chances are that the second one would be real and would work. What it needed was for him to have a seriously bad attack and take two useless pills in a row. And the chance that the last two pills in the bottle are both useless ones are really, really low. The only way it works is if all the pills are replaced.'

'Ok,' said Susan. 'I understand.'

'But there weren't any left when I found him.'

'Are you saying that it couldn't be done then, that it wasn't murder?'

'I still don't know if he was killed deliberately, but I do think it is possible.'

'How?'

'What if the murderer changed all the pills in the bottle and then, once Simon was dead, took the rest of them away, so they couldn't be identified as false ones? But they left the pill bottle to make people think he had taken his medication?'

Susan frowned in concentration. 'I see what you mean, but they would have had to have known when he was going to have an attack, so they could be there afterwards to remove the useless ones. How could they do that?'

'If they knew how to induce an attack?'

'What? Is that even possible?'

'I think so. Angina can be brought on by stress or anxiety. Suppose someone knew him well enough to really wind him up? Knew exactly how to make him angry and stressed.'

'Wow. So, you're saying someone was there the morning he died?'

'If someone did kill him, that's how I think it was done. Someone replaced his tablets and did something to bring on an attack.'

'And watched him die?'

'Before removing any trace of the replacements,' said Beatrice.

'But who could do that? Who could stand there and watch someone suffer? What kind of person?'

'They would have needed a very strong motive. Only someone who really hated him, for some personal reason, could have stood by whilst he died.'

'It's horrible,' said Susan. 'Look, you've certainly made me think. I believe you're right about how it could be possible, but it seems unlikely to me. Why would anyone want to kill him?'

'I'm not sure yet, but there are several possibilities.'

'Is this anything to do with the business? Are you going to share your ideas?'

'Not yet. But there's some information I need.' She handed Susan a piece of paper with a list of questions.

'That's quite a lot of work you've given me there, covering a lot of ground. It doesn't help me know what you're thinking.'

'I know. Sorry. But I need the answers to those questions and I can't get them myself.'

'And what are you going to be doing.'

'There's some information I can get. Once we have everything I think we'll know what happened and why.'

'I'll do what I can with this,' Susan waved the paper. 'But no promises. Fisher won't be happy if he catches me and I'm not sure the Inspector would be either. This isn't a missing person: you're implying something much more serious.' She stood up and made her way to the door, before turning back. 'Be careful, Beatrice, because on the slim chance that you're right and someone did kill Simon, they're not going to be happy if they find out you're on to them and you've already had one lucky escape.'

Chapter 36

Beatrice pulled into the lay-by behind the mobile burger van. It was the same one she'd seen there before. She ordered a drink and burger and stood watching the cook as he put it together.

'How often are you here?' she asked.

'Monday to Friday,' the man replied.

'Are you always here on a Monday?'

'Normally.'

'Were you here two weeks ago?'

'Why? What do you want to know for? Are you the police or something?'

Beatrice suspected he'd be more worried about her being HMRC, but that wasn't her job anymore. 'No. I'm a private investigator.' She passed a card up to him.

He placed her food and drink near the edge of the counter and wiped his hands on his apron. 'That's four pounds fifty,' he said before taking the card. Beatrice passed the money over. 'A private investigator, eh? Like in those American cop shows.'

'Not quite, but that sort of idea. Do you mind if I ask you some questions? I'm interested in someone who may have been here two weeks ago. I thought you might have seen them.'

'Go on then. So what do they look like, this person you're checking up on?'

'I'd rather you just told me what you can remember about the day, if that's ok? I wouldn't want to put ideas in your head about whether they were here or not.'

'Fair enough. Well, I haven't missed a Monday in ages but I'm thinking about jacking them in, they're too quiet. I'd need to find somewhere else to park up though. Well, let's see.' He reached under his shelf and pulled out a small, scruffy, dog-eared notebook. He rifled through the pages. 'Oh yeah, I remember that day. It was alright actually, better than a normal Monday. See there was this minibus going by then it suddenly stops – caused a lot of hooting that did. Then the silly bugger reverses back up road into the layby. Out piles this load of lads. Big they were. Not sure how they all fitted into the minibus to tell the truth. Anyway, I thought they were caught short, you know? Needed to use the bushes. Turns out they saw my van and realised they were hungry. The whole lot of 'em had bacon sandwiches and drinks. Made it an ok day for me that. Worth coming out after all.'

'Did they say where they were going?'

'Yeah. Skegness for a day out. A rugby team trip.'

'I don't suppose you remember the name of the team?'

'They didn't say, and it was just a plain white minibus.'

'They ate and left?'

'Yeah. That's right. Scary looking bunch, but they were alright, just some lads out for a bit of fun. Didn't cause any trouble. They ate up quick and were off.'

'What time of day was it?'

'About ten or maybe a little later.'

'Can you remember anything else about that morning?'

'There was hardly anyone stopping that day. I do remember though when those lads had gone there was a car parked at the other end of the layby. He leaned out of the hatch and pointed to his left.'

'What made you notice it?'

'It was a car wasn't it. Not exactly invisible.'

'I mean, if you're in the van you have to lean out to see it, don't you.'

'Oh yeah, I see what you mean. Well, I got out of the van to stretch me legs and the rugby lads had dropped a bit of paper on the floor, so I thought I'd better tidy it up since it was from my burgers.'

'What sort of car was it?'

'A small one. You know one of those silly little things. Bet it was a woman. You wouldn't catch a man driving a car like that.'

'Why not?'

'Who wants a purple car? Too small as well.'

'You didn't see who parked it then?'

'No. Sorry, love. I didn't see it leave either.'

'If you do remember anything else would you mind giving me a call?'

'Yeah sure.'

'Thanks.' Beatrice walked back to car deep in thought. The evidence was mounting, but it was all circumstantial. How could she prove what she thought had happened to Simon?

'Hello again Mrs Bayfield. I'm sorry to disturb you, but I have some questions if you don't mind.'

'I suppose you'd better come in.' Simon's mother sniffed and left Beatrice to close the door behind her.

They sat in the dark living room, in the same seats as her first visit. Mrs Bayfield looked unchanged apart from seeming even more tired as she slumped slightly in her chair.

'I assume you are still investigating. I haven't heard from you these last few days.'

'No, I'm sorry. I've been very busy.'

'Have you learned anything about my son's death?'

'A little. The autopsy confirmed Simon died because he had an angina attack that turned into a heart attack. It also showed that he didn't take any of his angina pills before the attack.'

'Do they think it was too quick?'

'An empty medicine bottle was found on the floor with its lid off. It looked as though he had time.'

'But if the bottle was empty? That doesn't make sense. He wasn't a fool. He'd never carry an empty container around with him. He always had his pills. He must have taken them.'

'The pathologist was definite. He hadn't had any.'

'What happened?'

'That's what I'm trying to find out, Mrs Bayfield. I almost have an answer. But I need more information.'

'Very well. You'd better ask your questions then.'

'Thank you.' Beatrice took a slow breath to focus her mind. 'The first time I came here, you said Simon had been to visit you the Friday before he died, and you'd spent some of the time reminiscing.'

'That's correct.'

'Can you remember exactly what you talked about?'

'Why do you ask?'

'I think that the reason that Simon called me to meet may have had something to do with his past.'

'Like what?'

'I don't know.' Beatrice wasn't telling the whole truth. She thought she knew what had happened and why, but she had to be sure. 'That's why I'd like you to tell me what you talked about.'

'Let me think.' The old woman closed her eyes and sat unmoving. Beatrice remained still, so as not to disturb her thoughts. Mrs Bayfield began to speak, with her eyes still closed. 'We talked a little about his childhood.' A faint smile appeared on her face. 'The holidays we used to have by the sea. He loved being by the sea. We couldn't afford to go often, once every couple of years, if we were very careful with money. He always loved it. But I've told you that already. I remember he spent some time looking at pictures in the album. Especially the ones from when he and John had their holiday.' She opened her eyes, taking a moment to refocus on Beatrice.

When she'd been thinking about Simon and their holidays, Mrs Bayfield had a gentle smile on her face. Coming back into the reality of his death, her face fell and she looked older and more fragile than ever. Beatrice paused a few moments to give her time to collect herself.

'He deserved a holiday, he'd had a tough year. He caught the mumps you know: it hit him hard. He was in such pain. No wonder he did poorly in his exams, he was too ill to work. Not that he needed A levels anyway. Simon was always going to be a success. I knew that.'

Beatrice connected the mumps with Marina mentioning Simon couldn't have children. She'd heard about the disease's affect on fertility in men. She felt sorry for Marina. 'May I see the album he was looking at?' she asked.

'I don't see any reason why not.'

'Shall I fetch it?'

'Yes. It's over there. In the right-hand drawer of the sideboard. The red one.'

Beatrice retrieved the album and handed it to Mrs Bayfield, standing behind her chair to watch as the older woman slowly turned the pages.

'Here we are.' She pointed to a page of photos of two teenage boys. 'He and John had just finished their A levels. They'd saved up for two years for a holiday. A last blow-out before they started working, Simon called it.'

'What did he mean by that?'

'He promised me, once he started working full time, he'd save all of his money and buy us a home of our own. He promised he'd become rich and look after me. We'd never want for anything again. He kept his word, you know. He worked every hour he could. He learnt on the job, built up his skills and then, when he was ready, started up his own business. He was a very clever boy.' Mrs Bayfield wiped her eyes with a cotton handkerchief.

'I'm sorry this is so upsetting for you.' Beatrice placed her hand lightly on the woman's bony shoulder. Her touch was quickly shrugged off.

'What else do you need to know?'

Beatrice sat back down on the sofa. 'Where did Simon and John go for their holiday?'

'Near Rhyl, in Wales. Such a long way, especially in the coach, but Simon said he wanted to find out what the sea was like over on the West.'

'Do you remember when they went?'

'Not exactly. But it will probably say on the back of the photographs. I usually wrote the dates on them.'

'Would you mind if I look?'

'I don't want the pictures in the album disturbed. They've been in it a long time. I doubt they'll go back properly if they're taken out. Why don't you check the one on the sideboard? You were looking at it last time you were here. It was taken on the same holiday.'

'Thank you.'

Beatrice collected the photograph and brought it back to her seat so that Mrs Bayfield could see what she was doing. It was Simon and John on a beach. At the edge of the photo she could make out a brightly coloured hut. She carefully lifted the metal fixings and pulled off the back and lining paper. Sure enough a date was printed on the back in careful handwriting. Alongside the date were the words "St Asaph's holiday".

Beatrice took a picture of the inscription using her mobile phone and carefully reassembled the frame.

'Shall I put it back for you?' Beatrice spoke softly, she'd noticed the longing in the old woman's eyes.

'No, I'll do it.' She reached out and Beatrice handed her the photograph.

'I'll let myself out. Thank you for seeing me.'

Mrs Bayfield nodded without looking at Beatrice. Her gaze was fixed on the image of her dead son. Beatrice quietly left the house, pulling the front door carefully closed behind her. Once on the street she pulled out her phone.

'Susan, it's me,' she said. 'Can you come to my house as soon as you're free? Bring whatever you've managed to find out from my list. I think I know who killed Simon and why.'

Chapter 37

'Listen, Beatrice,' said Susan. 'Even if you're right, which I am perfectly willing to believe you might be, we have no proof. We can't even say for certain Simon was murdered, that it was anything other than a result of his health problems.'

Susan had arrived with answers to some of the questions Beatrice had given her. They were what she had expected and fitted with what she thought had happened.

'Do you believe that?' asked Beatrice.

'I don't think I do anymore. You've almost got me convinced.'

'Almost?'

Susan smiled. 'Ok, it's a pretty good case to explain what we know, but that's not going to hold up in court is it?'

'What can we do? I've gathered as much evidence as I can, but it's all circumstantial. The checks you did back up the motive aspect, but I agree that there's nothing certain. Even if she admitted to going to see him, she could just say he was fine when she left him, and that he ran out of his tablets.'

'What we need is a confession. One that we can use as evidence and can't be retracted later.'

'How? I don't think the good cop and really horrible cop routine will work on her.'

'I hope you're thinking of Fisher as the horrible cop in that scenario.'

'Of course. Who else?' Beatrice grinned.

'But it's not exactly a secret that you've been investigating is it? Perhaps if we set up surveillance we can get some hard evidence?'

'Like what though? Do we have enough to get a search warrant?'

'No. I don't think so.'

'So it comes back to a confession.' Beatrice sat back in her seat and looked at Susan, wondering how much the younger woman was prepared to back her up. 'Well, I've got an idea, if you're up for it.'

'Why does it sound like you're not really all that keen?'

'Because I know if I go to Fisher he'll just ignore me, tell me I should keep my nose out. Which means I'll have to go around him to the Inspector. I'll need your support. You'd have to say you think I'm right.'

'You'd better explain.'

It didn't take Beatrice long to detail her plan, but it did take longer for her to convince Susan. Eventually they agreed they should talk to Detective Inspector Mayweather and try to persuade her to let them try.

'Surely, she'd listen to you?' said Beatrice. 'Take you seriously?'

'I think so. If we put it to her in the right way.'

'What's the problem?' she asked. 'You seem unsure still.'

'The problem is once Fisher finds out, I'm in trouble. I still have to work with the guy, you know.'

'We both know there's no point approaching him. He wouldn't listen. I could take it to the Inspector myself, keep you out of it so he can't blame you. But I don't think I could convince her on my own.'

'It could be worth a try, but on the other hand, if it pays off and we do get a confession it would do my career some good. The Inspector could make a real difference if I had her support.'

'I'll play it any way you want, Susan. But you've got to decide for yourself.'

Susan nodded, determined. 'Ok. Let's do it.'

'Together?'

'Yep. I'll ring her and see if she's around today. If she is, we'll go straight away. I hope you're as good at convincing her as you have been at getting me to believe you.'

Chapter 38

The bright, sunny day was at odds with the task Beatrice was about to perform. She took a steadying breath, knocked on the office door and opened it.

'Hi,' said Kerry. 'Come in.'

'Thanks.' Beatrice closed the door firmly and sat in the chair between it and the girl. 'Is John in?'

'No, and his office door is locked, which is unusual.'

Beatrice feigned surprise. 'Do you know where he is?'

Kerry shook her head. 'On the phone you said there was something I could help you with?'

'Yes. I've been trying to figure some things out, but I'm hoping you can fill in the gaps.'

'I'll try.'

'The morning Simon died,' Beatrice asked. 'Where were you?'

Kerry's brow furrowed. 'Here, at the office.'

'Was John here?'

'I don't think so.'

'You drive a purple KA, don't you?' asked Beatrice.

'What's that got to do with anything?'

'I saw one in the car park. I assume it's yours?'

'Yes.' Kerry folded her arms.

'A car just like it was spotted in a lay-by near Simon's house on the morning he died.'

Kerry smiled. 'It can't have been mine: I was here. If that's all, I really need to be getting on with my work.'

'Did you know Emily Jones? Before you worked here, I mean?'

'A little.'

'You never said, when we talked about her.'

'I didn't think it was important.' She laughed lightly. 'Is it?'

'It could be.'

'I don't see how.'

'How did Simon find out about the money going missing from petty cash?'

'That's old news.'

'But you must know.'

'It would have been when he was doing weekly checks on the figures.'

'But he didn't start doing those until after Emily had been fired for stealing.'

'Didn't he?' Kerry frowned. 'I guess he stopped trusting people after she'd stolen from him. How do you know?'

'Emily told me.'

Kerry became still. 'You've spoken to Emily?'

'Yes. I've spoken to lots of people. Like the man who owns the burger van in the lay-by. He saw your car.'

Kerry shook her head.

'I think you lied when you said you were here that morning. I think you went to see Simon. You certainly called him: your mobile number showed up on his phone records. You called the landline he'd installed in the office.'

'So? I told you I was here.'

'Why did you use your mobile and not the office phone?'

'I must have done it without thinking.'

Beatrice had to admire how smoothly she came up with the excuse. 'I don't believe you. Do you know the police can use relay towers to triangulate the location of your mobile?' The police hadn't been able to confirm where the call had been made, but Beatrice thought she saw a flicker of fear in Kerry's eyes, which quickly disappeared. 'Well?'

Kerry shook her head slowly.

'Why did you call Simon that morning?'

'I don't remember. It must have been to do with the business.'

'You want me to believe you were here in the office, whilst your car was near Simon's house and you used your personal phone instead of the business one? It's easy to check, you know. The owner of the burger van saw your car. Chances are other people saw it. There's traffic camera footage too. The police will be able to put you at the scene.'

'The police! Ha! What do they know? Sergeant Fisher is an idiot. He couldn't investigate anything. He couldn't get out of here quickly enough.'

'I think you're underestimating him, after all, people aren't always what they appear to be, are they? You should know that.'

'I could have just parked there to go for a walk.'

'You did go for a walk. Across the fields, the back way to Simon's office. Most people wouldn't know it was there, but you did. You left mud on the carpet. The sprinklers must have been on, soaking the path. The police can check that too: check your shoes. Why don't you tell me what happened?' She watched Kerry, amazed at her calm. She must have realised that Beatrice was accusing her of murder, however obliquely it was phrased. What was she thinking? Did she have a ready-made excuse or was she frantically trying to invent one?

'I've just remembered. I popped out that morning, for food. I enjoy a burger.' Kerry looked triumphant. 'And, I suddenly realised I needed to speak to him about work and I used my mobile, so I didn't forget.'

'A few moments ago, you were certain you'd been here.'

'Shame isn't it? That I didn't remember, at first.'

'And the mud?'

'I don't know what you're talking about.'

Kerry was lying, but there was still no proof Simon had been killed, and it felt as though she was no nearer a confession.

'You kept him well fed with chocolates, didn't you? Simon, I mean. Or I should say, you tried. Do you know, I couldn't figure it out to start with?'

'What?'

'Why you wanted him to eat things he was trying to avoid.'

'He was my boss. He wanted chocolate, so I got it for him.'

'Except he didn't want it. You could see he was getting healthier, despite your efforts to sabotage his diet plans. You were worried it would undermine your scheme. Did you know he didn't eat the chocolate you gave him? He locked it away in his office drawer at home.'

'I saw the wrappers.' It slipped out before she could stop it.

Beatrice felt she was starting to get under Kerry's skin. 'Did he really leave the wrappers in his desk,' she asked. 'Or did you collect them from the bin over the weeks and put them there once you knew he was dead?'

'You're crazy. Why would I do that?'

'Because you wanted to reinforce the idea he was unhealthy, so it would back up the suggestion he died of natural causes. You didn't want anyone asking questions, did you?'

'I don't know what you're talking about.'

'He took the chocolate out of the wrappers, so you'd think he'd eaten them. I don't understand why he was worried about upsetting you. Perhaps he just didn't want the hassle. He couldn't have his wife finding the chocolate though. She'd assume he wasn't sticking to his diet. It was a lot of trouble for him to go to, trying to do the best for his health and keep you both happy. I don't know why he didn't see through you. Everyone tells me what a great businessman he was. How he didn't put up with fools.'

'There's no law against giving your boss chocolate, is there? It's up to him if he ate it or not. And you can't prove I did anything else. He wasn't poisoned. I never touched him.'

Beatrice knew she'd have to be more direct. 'Shall I tell you what I think happened the day Simon died?'

Kerry shrugged.

'You parked your car in the lay-by on the far side of the field behind Simon's house, then you phoned him to make sure he was alone. He probably told you he was planning to be there for the rest of the day. You walked along the footpath, across the field to his office, getting mud on your shoes. Did you tell him you were coming, or was he surprised when you turned up? What did you say to him when you got there? Something to make him angry?'

Kerry stared at Beatrice and didn't answer. She smiled, eyes narrowed, head tilted and sat back in her chair. Beatrice would have to push harder: it was the only way to find out the truth.

'When you saw him, did you tell him it was you who had stolen the money and had deliberately set up Emily. Got him to fire her unfairly?'

'But...' Kerry checked herself and returned to silence.

'You needed her out of the way, didn't you? Did you tell him you were still stealing his money? Is that what made him mad?'

Kerry didn't answer.

'Did you seriously think I wouldn't see through your silly scheme with the petty cash?'

'But you asked all those questions about the accounts.'

'I asked those questions to test your understanding of accounts, Kerry, not mine. You clearly knew what you were doing, but you didn't explain too much, did you? Tried to lead me away from looking in detail. I might not know as much as you about putting accounts together, but I do know a lot about taking them apart. You didn't stop stealing once Emily was fired, you just got better at hiding it. The evidence is there. I think Simon was already suspicious of you: you probably said or did something to make him question your honesty. I think that's why he wanted to hire me. He had the petty cash records at home. Why would he, unless they needed to be checked?'

'You can't think I killed him for a bit of money. No one would believe that.' Kerry folded her arms. 'It's pathetic,' she spat.

'Some people might have killed for that amount money, but not you.' Beatrice shook her head. 'It was part of your plan to get rid of Emily. To get him to fire her and later make him regret it. I think you probably used your confession as a preliminary.'

'To what exactly?' Kerry's hands were now twisting together in her lap.

'Did you talk about the protestors next? Did you tell him you had been passing Stella Bright confidential information? Like the surveyor's report, showing the new site wasn't suitable for linking to the National Grid? Or did you try the truth for once, Kerry? Do you even know what the truth is?'

'I don't know what you're talking about.' Her voice waivered.

'I think you were leading up to the bigger truth you wanted to tell him. I think you didn't want him to die without knowing why.'

Kerry laughed nervously. 'What on earth are you talking about?'

Beatrice leaned forward. 'I think to really wind him up, to get him properly angry - angry enough to bring on his angina - you told him he was your father.'

Kerry gasped and seemed to stop breathing. Her hands gripped the arms of the chair, her knuckles white. 'You can't know that. No one knows.' Her voice was a whisper.

'I followed the clues. I did my job.' Beatrice sat back. 'Tell me, how did he react when you told him you were his daughter? He didn't believe you, did he?'

Kerry sat motionless, her eyes fixed on Beatrice. The silence stretched until she finally spoke. 'You've no evidence of anything. Just a far-fetched story. The police have had complaints about you already. They're not going to believe a busybody, poking her nose in where it's not wanted.' Kerry smiled brightly and smoothed her hair down with a shaking hand. 'Well, this has been a very interesting talk. It's time you left.'

Beatrice was taken aback by the girl's recovery. Could nothing get through to her? How did she not see what she had done? 'Kerry you killed him. Doesn't it mean anything to you? Don't you care that you took his life?'

Kerry spoke as if she hadn't heard. 'What are you going to do now? Go to the police? I don't think it will be much use. You seem to be forgetting one person was definitely at the house that morning. One person who claims she found him dead. Perhaps the police need to be asking more questions about you.' Her voice became stronger, more confident. 'You say he wanted to hire you, but no-one else knew anything about it. Not even his wife or closest friend. You could be making it up. Why did you go there? What had he done to you? Why did you want him dead?'

The expression on Kerry's face was one of satisfaction and she was nodding lightly at her own cleverness. Beatrice was astonished at how she could twist and turn. Nothing seemed to touch her. Had she managed to convince herself that Beatrice was guilty, or did she know she was manipulating the truth? She worried for Kerry's sanity, but she still hadn't got a confession. There was nothing the police could use. Feeling ashamed at what she was about to do, Beatrice told herself it was necessary. Kerry couldn't be allowed to walk free from the consequences of what she'd done. She cleared her throat.

'What I've told you so far isn't all I have, Kerry.'

'What else is there?' Kerry examined her fingernails in studied nonchalance.

'There's your mother.'

Kerry's head snapped up. 'What about my mother?'

'There's things about herself that she hasn't told you.'

Kerry stood up and gripped the edge of the desk. 'What do you mean? Tell me!'

Beatrice uncrossed her legs, ready to leap up if Kerry became violent. 'Simon Bayfield wasn't the only man your mother slept with around the time you were conceived.'

'Bitch! Don't you dare say such things about my mother. You're a liar!'

'You should ask her next time you see her. If she wants to see you, that is.'

'Why wouldn't she want to see me? What have you told her?' She laughed wildly. 'If you think telling her that I killed him will alter her view of me, then you've really got it all wrong.'

'I know your mother put you up to killing Simon.'

'What?' Kerry gasped.

'She told me when I went to see her early this morning, but it was just confirmation of what I already suspected.'

'You think you're so clever, don't you?' Kerry eyed up the door. 'But you'll never be able to pin his death on me. The police don't even know it was murder.'

'I've convinced them otherwise.'

'I never laid a finger on him. You can't prove I did.'

'I can prove you and your mother plotted his death together, that she used you to get her revenge on him, for what she felt was the humiliation of him rejecting her.'

'No!' Kerry was almost shouting now. 'I did it because he left us when he knew she was pregnant. He abandoned us.'

'She lied to you, Kerry. She never told Simon she was pregnant. She was too proud. He'd discarded her and she refused to tell him she needed help.'

'How do you know?'

'Your mother. I told you, I spoke to her in the Hospice. I recorded the conversation for the police. She explained how you planned it together, but said you were the one behind it: it was your idea, not hers. You're the one who wanted revenge.'

'But that's not true. She said… It's what she wanted me to do. She wanted to know he was dead before her.'

'Your mother used you, Kerry. She used you to murder a man because he rejected her over twenty years ago.'

'No.' Kerry's voice was barely a whisper. 'She wouldn't do that. She loves me. He abandoned us.' She shook her head trying to make sense of what she was hearing.

Beatrice stood up. 'The thing is Kerry, Simon couldn't have children. He was infertile. Your mother slept with more than one man during the time you were conceived. Once you were a few weeks old she must have realised Simon wasn't your father, just by looking at you: your blue eyes and dark curls. But she was determined to make him pay for casting her aside.'

'What are you trying to say? What do you mean, she knew he wasn't my father?'

'You don't look like him at all do you?'

'So what?'

'But you do look like your actual father. The person who was with Simon when he met your mother. Who also slept with her.'

The realisation hit home and Kerry's eyes widened. 'John?'

Beatrice nodded. 'If you wanted to kill your father, you killed the wrong man. And your mother knew it.'

Kerry remained standing in silence, her face slack with shock as she tried to make sense of what she'd been told. Beatrice opened the office door. Inspector Mayweather, DS Fisher, DC Wilde and a uniformed WPC crowded into the room. DS Fisher nodded at

Beatrice as he brushed past. He arrested Kerry, cautioned her, then led her away, accompanied by the WPC who held on to Kerry's arm. Beatrice remained with the Inspector and Susan.

'Thank you for your help, Ms Styles,' said Inspector Mayweather.

'You're welcome. I think. What an awful life it must have been for her. Her mother is a monstrous woman.'

'Lots of people have dreadful lives, but they don't all go around murdering people because of it,' said the Inspector.

'No. But some do.'

'I'd better go. DC Wilde will help you to remove the recording device and sign it into evidence. Can you follow us to the station and make your statement? It will be better to get it done today.'

'I presume you'll get her seen by a doctor?'

'It will take time, but we'll arrange for an assessment of her mental health before questioning her. Social Services will appoint her a responsible adult, in case she's not considered mentally competent.'

'Did you get a statement from her mother?'

'Yes, we did. She repeated what she said in your recording. She's still saying it was Kerry's idea. The nurse told our officers she's not likely to survive more than a few days now.'

'And what will that do to Kerry, I wonder?' said Beatrice.

'I really don't know.' The Inspector nodded curtly and left, closing the door behind her.

Beatrice rummaged under her top and pulled out the wires and the recording device. She handed it to Susan, who switched it off carefully.

'Are you ok, Beatrice?'

'No, not really.' Tears fell freely down her face. 'I miss my mum and dad.'

'Come down here,' said Susan, pulling on her shoulder. Beatrice allowed herself to be pulled down and felt Susan's arms reach around her neck and hug her tightly.

Chapter 39

'How did it go?' James, wearing a shorts and t-shirt, opened the door to Beatrice.

'As well as can be expected.' She flopped down onto the sofa.

'Are you ok?'

'I will be thanks.' She smiled at him in appreciation. 'What's that I can smell?'

'I thought, since you were probably going to have a rough day, I'd make you dinner.' He frowned. 'You do like curry, don't you?'

'I love curry. That's really kind of you, I'm not hungry right now though.'

'That's ok, I've not long put it on. I'm cooking it on a low temperature, so it will be ages before it's ready. You'll be hungry by then.' They sat in silence for a moment. 'Do you want to talk about it?'

'Maybe later, but not right now.'

He stood up. 'I'm popping into the cellar to do some weight training. Will you be ok for a bit?'

'Yes. You carry on. I might have a nap, I feel so tired.' He left the room and Beatrice closed her eyes.

She didn't know how long she'd been asleep, but when she woke her neck was stiff. Other than that, she felt a lot better. She stood up, stretching, rubbed her neck and stood in the bay window looking out at the street, watching what she now thought of as her cat, slink underneath a parked car. She saw a reflection flash in the glass and sensed movement behind her, she turned and instinctively raised her left arm. A searing pain shot through her forearm as a metal pole bounced off. She cried out in agony. Mike, the boy Cassie had followed to Sheffield, stood in front of her, breathing heavily. His face was contorted: ugly with anger.

'I told you if you set the police on me I'd get you,' he hissed.

'You're in enough trouble already. You'd better leave.' She felt her pulse race as she cradled her throbbing arm. She looked towards the door, but he was blocking the way.

He smirked. 'What are you going to do now? There's no way out?' He tapped the metal weapon against his free hand. 'I'm going to enjoy this.' He raised the pole high, ready to strike.

Beatrice didn't have time to think.

As the pole swung down, even though she knew it was going to hurt, she raised her left arm again to block it, she stepped forward towards him.

Calling out in anger and fear she pushed against his chest using all her strength.

Mike flew backwards across the room, falling.

His head hit the wall with a loud crack and his body slid to the ground. His hand released its grip on the pole and it rolled across the floor.

There was a stillness and a roaring in Beatrice's ears. She stood motionless, insensible. Gradually sound came back and she became aware of her ragged breathing and her aching arm. The door to the cellar banged open. James appeared in the doorway to the living room.

'I heard a noise,' he started. He paused, then looked down at the boy on the floor and the pole, then to Beatrice's face. As he walked across the room, he kicked the weapon out of reach. He stood in front of Beatrice and wrapped his arms around her. He held her, until the shaking of her body began to subside.

When the police and paramedics had finally gone, James and Beatrice were left alone. James poured them a glass of wine each, and was about to join Beatrice on the sofa when there was a knock on the door.

'If that's the police again, tell them to go away,' Beatrice groaned.

After a quick conversation at the door, which Beatrice paid no attention to, James came back, holding out an envelope to her.

'It was your neighbour, the elderly chap. He said this came for you earlier and they needed someone to sign for it. I think he wanted to know what the police were doing here too, but I managed to send him away.'

'Oh. I'm not expecting anything.' She took the letter and opened it, grimacing as her stiff fingers tried to work. James politely didn't mention the light shaking of her hands.

Beatrice read the letter then sat staring into space.

James took her hand. 'Hey, what is it?' he asked gently. She handed him the letter. He read it and saw the cheque attached, for ten thousand pounds.

'I don't understand,' he said.

'Dad died about two years ago now, and shortly afterwards mum went missing. It's from her solicitor. He says the cheque is from her estate and as me and Rosie are her only surviving relatives, he's giving us some of her money.'

'I guess it must be hard for you thinking about her, after the day you've had?'

She shook her head. 'I always think about her. It's not that.'

'What is it then?'

'It's because I know you can't wind up a person's estate after such a short period of time. It takes at least seven years to declare a missing person dead.'

'Then why has he said that's where it's from?'

'I don't know. But I do know he is either doing something illegal, or he has been given permission to give me some of my mum's money.' Beatrice turned to look at James. 'And there is only one person who can do that.'

'Your mum?'

She nodded. 'Which means she's alive, and he knows exactly where she is.'

They sat side by side on the sofa. Beatrice reached for James' hand and squeezed it gently. 'Thank you,' she said. 'For being kind and helping me today.'

'That's what friends are for, isn't it?'

She rested her head on his shoulder and absent-mindedly stroked the back of his hands with her fingers, enjoying the warmth of his skin and comforted by his presence.

With his free hand James placed his wine glass on the coffee table. Beatrice looked on puzzled as he took her glass from her and placed alongside his. Turning back to face her, he ran a finger down the side of her face.

'Has anyone told you recently what an amazing woman you are?' he said.

'I don't think anyone's ever told me.' Beatrice was confused. What was happening? James placed his hand on her knee and leant forward. Was he going to kiss her?

'I thought you were gay!' Beatrice couldn't help but exclaim.

James chuckled. 'Why on earth did you think that?'

Rosie's name began to form on her lips, but she hesitated. She'd deal with her sister later.

'It doesn't matter,' she said, gazing into his eyes. He moved towards her again, then paused, his face mere centimetres from hers. She could feel his breath on her skin.

Thoughts of everything but him left her mind. She reached up, placing her hand on the back of his neck, tilted her head and pulled him towards her.

October

Hello Beatrice,

How are you, out there in the world? You haven't been to see me in such a long time. Have you forgotten all about me? I haven't forgotten you.

I talked to my doctor today. He told me I will probably never get out of here. It's unlikely I'll ever be considered fit for release. He thought I'd be angry. But I'm not. I can honestly say I was relieved when he told me. In here it's easy. Every day is the same. I know what's going to happen and I know what's expected of me. There is a certain relief in thinking this is my life now.

I hope you don't mind me writing to you. When you came to visit you seemed so anxious to know why. As if you still found it hard to believe it was me that killed him. The sessions with Dr Fielding have really helped. I feel I owe it to you to try to help you understand. Some people might find it odd, considering that without you getting involved, and finding out what really happened, the police would have been none the wiser. Perhaps you think I resent you for that? Hate you even. But I don't. Truly I don't. I did for a while, but I can honestly say now, I don't.

I can see now that my life belonged to her. She wanted me to do it before she died, so she'd know her revenge had been carried out: at least in part because she had to take revenge on me too. She blamed me for existing, for ruining her life because she had to look after me. I think she knew her hold over me would weaken once she wasn't around to reinforce it. She must have hated me too.

Do you know, there were times when I could forget what I was there for? I enjoyed being useful and good at my job. I would get wrapped up in the work, and would forget I was supposed to be figuring out a way to kill him. But she was there in the background: always asking questions. What was I going to do? When would I get on with it? Didn't I want to show her how much I loved her?

I've finally realised she didn't care if I was caught. She would have been happy if I'd walked up to him with a gun and shot him. She wouldn't have cared if I spent the rest of my life in prison. She just wanted him dead. And all because he rejected her. She was 'too common' as he put it.

I can't forget that day. It had all been getting too much for me. The pressure to kill him before Mother died. I wanted it over and done with. You were right, I went to see him, to provoke him to bring on angina attack. I told him how I hated him, that it was me who had been stealing and how he had fired Emily and called her a criminal. He sat there like the great blob he was, red in the face, struggling for breath.

Then I told him who my mother was. How I knew what he did to her, how he treated her and then abandoned us. I told him I was going to get my revenge by telling his wife. That did the trick. He jumped up to stop me and that's when it happened. He sank to the floor and began to crawl back to his desk, to his pills. I moved the phone out of his reach and pretended to fetch them, giving him a bottle of vitamins I'd prepared instead. It took a while finding a brand which resembled his medicine, but I managed it.

I stood there and watched him die. The man I thought was my father. But now I know better. Thank you for telling me about John. I've written to him too.

Never Forget, Never Forgive

I know it's not likely, but if you want to, and you're ever around here, I'd like to see you again. Just to talk. You see, you were the one who put me in here and I'd like to thank you properly for it.

Kerry

About The Author

Denise Smith, a prolific reader and lover of books, lived in Lincolnshire for thirteen years, which is where the idea for this story was developed. Now living in Devon, she is still a frequent visitor to Lincolnshire, allowing her to keep her old home fresh in her mind as she writes the next book in the series.

For more information about Denise or her latest books go to:

www.foursirenspress.co.uk/authors/denise-smith

Denise Smith

Keep Up to Date

If you have enjoyed this book, please support the author by leaving a positive review on Amazon.

To find out when Denise's next book will be published please sign up to our newsletter at:

www.foursirenspress.co.uk/authors/denise-smith

Denise Smith

Acknowledgements

There have been a number of people who have been supportive in the writing of this book. There are too many to mention them all individually, but thank you all everyone who has ever been kind enough to take an interest in my writing.

Particular thanks are due to my fellow Four Sirens writers, Sharon Francis and Sue Hughes, who have poured over my manuscript and offered a great deal of helpful critique and advice, over much coffee and cake.

I would also like to thank my husband, Jim, and daughter, Emma, who have been encouraging of my writing for many years, and were brave enough to read some of my early, very rough, attempts, which have finally led to my first book. I would never have got this far without you both.

Printed in Great Britain
by Amazon

79025906R00161